BLOODY MARTINI

BOOKS BY WILLIAM KOTZWINKLE

THE FELONIOUS MONK MYSTERIES

Felonious Monk
Bloody Martini

STANDALONE NOVELS

Elephant Bangs Train (short stories)
Hermes 3000
The Fan Man
Nightbook
Swimmer in the Secret Sea
Doctor Rat
Fata Morgana
Herr Nightingale and the Satin Woman
Jack in the Box
Christmas at Fontaine's
Queen of Swords
Jewel of the Moon (short stories)
The Midnight Examiner
The Exile
Hot Jazz Trio (short stories)
The Game of Thirty
The Bear Went over the Mountain
The Amphora Project

WILLIAM KOTZWINKLE

BLOODY MARTINI

**BLACK
STONE**
PUBLISHING

Copyright © 2023 by William Kotzwinkle

Published in 2023 by Blackstone Publishing

Cover and book design by Kathryn Galloway English

The characters and events in this book are fictitious.
Any similarity to real persons, living or dead, is coincidental
and not intended by the author.

Printed in the United States of America

First edition: 2023
ISBN 978-1-0940-0926-1
Fiction / Crime

Version 1

CIP data for this book is available
from the Library of Congress

Blackstone Publishing
31 Mistletoe Rd.
Ashland, OR 97520

www.BlackstonePublishing.com

BLOODY MARTINI

2 1/2 ounces vodka
2 tablespoons tomato juice
1 dash lime juice

Add tomato juice, vodka, lime juice, and 2
       cups ice cubes to a cocktail shaker.
Shake vigorously until well chilled.
Pour into chilled cocktail glass.
And never turn your back to the door.

1

The Mexican sun was fierce. My robe and straw sombrero cast a shadow that looked like a malevolent entity of the desert with pointed head and wide, floppy wings. Given my violent past, it seemed a good likeness.

Only two young girls were sharing the mountain with me, and they were steering clear of my shadow. I caught sight of them now and then as they tugged at the roots of a plant, bending their slender bodies to the task, their thin arms strong. The wax of the plant would bring their mother money enough for flour and rice and a handful of beans. They didn't know that through my abbot, I sent money to their mother and to the other mothers of the village so they might buy something for themselves—a dress, a mirror, some new sandals. The local drug lord did the same, so both God and the Devil were working the same street.

I shook out a plant, relieving it of little stones and weeds, then put it into my sack. Through the exhausting heat, I could feel the power of that hillside, which housed rattlesnakes and lizards whose bite is like hot lava in the veins. A Gila monster can smell an egg buried six inches under desert sand, and I knew they were around me, feeling my footsteps in their bellies. It was an atmosphere that tuned the spirit. Venomous reptiles give you a picture of the world as it really is, and you are a fool not to know that. The young girls on this hillside held that picture in their mind. They might be children, but they weren't fools. They knew that men and poisonous reptiles had something in common and that confrontation was always a mistake. They stayed away from me as they stayed away from all men. You can sell a bag of cocaine only once, but you can sell a girl many times a day.

Whenever I glanced their way, I could see they were ready to make a run for it. What a childhood . . . and what would they be as young women? I couldn't see their future. As for my own, monasteries around the world are the refuge of hunted men. So far as I knew, no one was hunting me at the moment. I'd inherited a significant amount of money, and money can draw an impenetrable veil over one's actions. It had been drawn over mine, so I picked my plants—plants that gave wax for candles, healed scar tissue, and were used by local villagers to treat venereal disease. Undoubtedly, it had other uses, for everything that grew around here had its secret chemistry, in league with the sun and the rocky soil and therefore magically inclined. I was a monk in the Sonoran Desert because I enjoyed having that faint, dry scent of mystery around me, and there was as much of it here as within the dark walls of the monastery.

And then the girls were running away, having sensed a vibration in the ground that I'd missed. But I felt it now, the approach of tires that were causing a rumble in the earth. I watched an expensive pickup truck nose into view, FORD in big block letters across the nose, glamorous running lamps on, aluminum running boards gleaming in the sunlight. It was a brand-new Raptor with some nice, aggressive tires that made it a real rock crawler. Above the windshield was a rack of spotlights that gave it the look of a giant spider hunting for prey. Because I'd worked in my father's auto-repair shop as a kid, I was a Benedictine with cars in my bloodstream and could appreciate the blue accent package on the body, as well as the sound of its high-output twin turbo engine. But even with all this road romance in front of me, I was only momentarily distracted. The truck was out of its natural habitat. Hunting in these hills was poor—unless, of course, you were hunting little girls.

Then I remembered that the government had decided to help the candelilla pickers, which meant that some university-trained team of scientists would interfere with centuries-old techniques that worked. Maybe this truck was a government vehicle. So I glanced at the license plates, also remembering that cartel money lined government pockets, bought government protection, and ran drugs in government vehicles. But the plates weren't government, just the usual kind announcing that Chihuahua, Mexico, was the *Land of Encounters.*

It was an encounter the girls didn't want. But they weren't fast enough, and the truck slammed to a stop beside them. Two men jumped out and grabbed the girls. Laughing, they held their light bodies in the air as the girls kicked and screamed curses at them. The young men wore shiny body-fitting shirts, expensive skinny jeans, and aviator sunglasses. Their dark hair was neatly trimmed. They wore gold neck chains.

I called down to them. "Caballeros, what are you doing?"

They turned, seemingly indifferent to my presence. The two girls were still squirming at the ends of their arms. I couldn't see the expression behind the sunglasses, but I saw a cheesy smile forming on the lips of the one who'd been driving. "Father, forgive us for disturbing your prayers."

"I wasn't praying; I was picking herbs." I walked slowly toward them. Several times in the past, the sight of my monk's robe had reminded local criminals of their ties to the church, to the priests who had guided them through childhood and blessed their families. It might not work today, but it was worth a try; I didn't want to hurt them. I'd hurt enough people in my life.

My robe was tied with a rope; a small metal crucifix dangled from it. With any sort of luck, they might decide God had sent me. I'd appeared out of nowhere, and they were superstitious like a lot of people raised in the Catholic faith of Mexico.

The girls stopped their squirming, became vigilant, waiting their chance to break free if my distraction gave them an opening. I continued slowly toward the men. The driver spoke again. "We're from the Child Rescue. A relative of these girls contacted us. Some kind of abuse is going on in their home."

He talked very smoothly. He'd given this little speech before.

"I'm sorry, señor, but they're under my care." I was closer now.

"Father, I think you must have gotten too much sun. You should avoid dehydration. Better still, you should avoid me."

So that's the way it was going to be.

They were armed, semiautomatics in their belts. This one even had a hand grenade clipped to his belt. It looked like an old Soviet-era model, and I figured it was strictly for show; it added to his swagger. Though I had at least fifty pounds on him, he wasn't the slightest bit concerned when I stepped even closer. In his eyes, I was a neutered male. He couldn't know that I was calculating how best to take him and his partner out with one quick move—not an impossibility. In my time as a clean-cut college boy, I'd been a varsity wrestler. At two hundred pounds, I'd won all my matches. In my time as a not-so-clean barroom bouncer, I'd killed a man with a single punch. And in my last leave of absence from the monastery, I'd won two professional martial arts bouts in Las Vegas. It's a long story and I won't go into it here, but let's say I felt the odds were in my favor as long as these traffickers didn't get the guns out of their belts.

As it happens, I didn't have to do anything. One of the girls got a finger into the pin of the grenade. She pulled instinctively, but nothing happened. The abductor holding her had been laughing, but he wasn't laughing now. He frantically grabbed her wrist to pull her off the grenade. Not a good move, because her wrist twisted under his grip, and with that twist the pin came free. A grenade is a simple mechanism really; when you pull the pin it releases a tiny spring under the safety lever, lifting the lever up with enough force to send it flying. And it flew now, into the air, and dropped on the desert floor with a little *ka-chink*. There was a terrible promise in that sound, and both abductors heard it. They immediately dropped the girls. Both girls dove under the truck, and I threw myself after them. Four seconds elapsed, during which the grenade's internal fuse was burning and the trafficker was fumbling to get it off his belt. I was shielding the girls with my body when it went off, sending fragments of metal in all directions. The blast deafened me momentarily, but then I heard brief cries of mortal agony. I crawled out slowly and saw the would-be traffickers on the ground, one with his guts hanging out and the other staring sightless at the sky. His aviator sunglasses had been blown away and his forehead was torn open to the bone, brain matter shimmering like jelly in the sunlight. The one with his guts hanging out and part of his ass blown off reached up to me for help, but he was beyond anything I could do. He toppled slowly backward, twitched a few times, and died, his blood staining the sand. The girls scrambled out from under the truck and took off like rabbits. The truck itself had been caught in the blast, the passenger side windows shattered and the doors studded with grenade fragments.

I looked down at the two bodies. The shirts were drenched with blood. It had been idiotic to carry a grenade around. Where would they have had occasion to use it? Maybe it had been a boyhood dream, to be armed with a grenade. Wrong dream. Macho posturing had blown them out of this world.

I found a shovel in the back of the Raptor and dug in the sandy soil. The young men weren't large. They fit in a shallow hole. Maybe their own childhood had lacked sufficient nourishment. I threw their guns in after them, then gathered the biggest rocks I could find, piling them onto the bodies until they were covered with a foot of rock. Then I put my shoulder into one of the hillside boulders and rolled it on top of the hole for a complete seal. The coyotes and vultures wouldn't be able to get through it, but ants and scavenger beetles would take care of things from below and eventually there would be only two well-dressed skeletons in that hole. The girls would say nothing to anyone, but the villagers would certainly notice that the landscape had been altered and would avoid it as an ill-omened spot. Below their Catholicism, the religion of their Aztec ancestors still functioned, and they might think supernatural entities had been at work, perhaps the hill spirits who capture people "who are not living well." The child sex traffickers had certainly not been living well.

I put their wallets, expensive wristwatches, and gold chains into one of my herb sacks. I'd taken the starter fob from the driver's pocket, and the Raptor came to life. I listened appreciatively to the smooth voice of the engine. Seventy-five thousand dollars buys a lot of truck. I punched the throttle, slammed it into drive, and ripped down the side of the mountain, crushing every rock along the way. It had a military-grade aluminum-alloy body and a ten-speed transmission, and we could've put it to good use at the monastery. But the abbot wouldn't approve; this I knew. He tolerated some of my bad habits, like doing two hundred push-ups every morning and owning a cell phone, which he held for me. I told him it was necessary for my investments, of which the monastery was one of the principal beneficiaries. But a hot truck belonging to a pair of dead kidnappers would not fit the spirit of the monastery. So I drove it to the local drug lord.

2

Our local drug lord was known as the Camel because he transported shipments of merchandise across the desert. The police and the army were on his payroll, as were high government officials, but even with this protection, his compound resembled a forward firebase in a war zone. The first thing I encountered was a slide-arm barrier gate with sand-filled bunkers on either side. I brought the Raptor to a stop and lowered the shattered passenger window, which went down with a crackling sound of shredded glass. I knew the checkpoint guys wouldn't approach me on the driver's side; they'd been taught that a driver can easily pull a firearm and blow you away.

A guard with an assault rifle stepped out of the bunker. He was looking at the pockmarked paint job and the spidery glass of the back passenger window. He waved another guard out and they both looked at it, exchanging comments. It had clearly been through combat of some kind. Did it present an imminent threat to them? Then one of them recognized me. I was frequently in the village buying supplies. And unless a rival cartel was hiring monks to do their dirty business, I was a low-threat visitor. He approached the vehicle. If he was ex-military, then he might know what he was doing, might possess the stomach for a hand-to-hand fight. But most of these cartel guys were just punks with guns—dangerous of course, deadly certainly, because anybody can wave an assault rifle around and kill a lot of people. But on their own, they were nothing. I could have kicked the crap out of any three of them at once. As the thought floated through my mind, I realized that the grenade of anger I carry around inside me was armed once again and ready to blow despite all my prayer and meditation.

I called through the open window. "I've got a gift for your boss."

"What kind of gift?"

"This." I reached my arm out the window and patted the roof of the Raptor.

Despite the damage, the truck spoke his language. Perhaps the damage even increased its attraction. A real man, a macho, belonged in a truck like this. A monk was not the proper owner, this he grasped. "Where does it come from?"

"From heaven."

He smiled and nodded toward the bunker. The slide bar was retracted on heavy-duty rollers. Tire shredders embedded in the pavement were lowered. He waved me through and I drove toward the next barrier, a wall of high-density polyethylene designed to withstand bomb blasts. It had been laid in sections and topped with razor wire. At each corner was a portable guard tower, staffed by men with submachine guns. A gate in the wall swung open and I drove through. The Camel's mansion was ahead of me. A guard pointed to where I should park on the gravel driveway. I stopped the Raptor and climbed out. One of the guards was on his walkie-talkie, calling in to the Camel's mansion. He listened momentarily, then pointed toward the front door. "Through there."

The mansion was built in the territorial style, with walls of peach-colored adobe, reinforced by round polished beams that protruded from the walls. But unlike the modest territorial houses of earlier times, this one was huge—more like a territorial fort. The door was made of vintage oak boards set with heavy black iron hinges. I grasped a round iron door handle and pulled it open. A guard on the inside indicated I should move slowly past a metal detector framing the doorway. It found only the little Christ on my crucifix, and he was satisfied with that. Air-conditioning blew over me as I walked into the mansion. Another guard signaled me to follow him, and I was taken through to the Camel's office. Outside the door, a guard sat on a heavy bench of dark wood. He got up and patted me down, then opened the door. Antique wrought iron lamps gave the room the look of old Spain. The windows faced the drive, and the Camel was looking down at the seventy-five-thousand-dollar vehicle. He owned real estate, radio stations, a chain of drugstores, supermarkets, apartment buildings, offices, and a soccer team. He owned fleets of trucks, a yacht, and several submarines. But he liked the look of that SUV, even with its damaged doors. He turned toward me. "What happened to it?"

I dropped the key fob on his desk. "It belonged to men who steal little girls." I tossed their wallets onto the desk.

"Where are they now?"

"In Tlālōcān." I used the Aztec word for the world of dead spirits beneath the earth.

His Christian name was Porfirio López, and the child traffickers were almost certainly not his. The talk around the village was that he despised the sex-trafficking business. He looked at the identification papers in the wallets. A legitimate set of IDs would be useful in his business. "These men will live again in another form. And thank you for their truck. It, too, will gain a new identity." Spanish has a natural eloquence built into its sentence structure, but his gaze remained that of a mongoose assessing its prey. "Why, Brother Thomas, do you favor me with such a gift?"

"The girls were betrayed by someone in the village. That person saw the truck enter the village and climb into the hills. When they see you in possession of it, their legs will turn to water." To stroke his enormous ego, I added, "You have that effect on people."

Liking that, he nodded his confirmation, then asked, "How did these men meet their death?"

"If I told you, you would doubt me."

"Try me."

"They were exploded."

"People are exploded all the time in my business."

"Well, today they were exploded by a ten-year-old girl using a hand grenade."

"That is unusual. This was while they were attempting to carry her off?"

"It was."

"And where were you?"

"Watching from afar."

"I'd like to meet this girl who can use a grenade."

"She keeps to herself."

"She has nothing to fear from me. I don't approve of grabbing children." He came away from the window and stood in front of me. "You're wasted in that monastery. You could work for me. We'll make war on scum like the ones you ran into today."

"I respectfully decline."

He picked up the key fob and turned to one of his bodyguards. "Drive him to the monastery in the vehicle he briefly possessed."

I walked back through his mansion. European masterpieces hung on his walls. He smuggled deadly drugs into America, but he didn't rape children. Give credit where it's due.

I walked out of the mansion and down into the courtyard. His bodyguard and I got into the Raptor. "Nice," he said, as he started it up. He drove us out of the compound and along the gravel road that wound through the hills. At various spots, I noticed snipers in camo uniforms. Heavy lies the head that wears the crown.

He let me off in front of the monastery. I took my herb sacks and went inside, where I learned that a phone call had come for me from someone whose message as he was being murdered was, *Take care of Bridget. My heart is in your hands.*

3

The interior corridors of the monastery were dimly lit and cool. Thick walls kept the heat of the sun from penetrating too deeply, and there were no windows. The smell of candle wax always hung in the air. Candles had burned here for two centuries. The monastery had been built by men who understood the interplay between stone and the flame of a candle. The flickering shadows on the walls seemed alive, their shapes enhanced by the alignment of the stones and the depths of the mortar holding them in place.

On the way to the abbot's office, I passed other monks, though no one spoke. Silence was the rule. After observing it for a while, you realized how little actually needs to be said. Perhaps it was in such silence that the old monks had received their architectural inspiration.

I entered the abbot's office. He was seated behind a desk made from an old wooden door by some earlier generation of monks. It was venerable and so was the abbot, a large, powerful man with scars on his hands and face from working in the wax business as a boy—the wax plant is processed using sulfuric acid, and its bubbling can be unruly. He was also a skilled horseman, having worked on ranches for much of his life. I had once seen him throw a knife with perfect accuracy, hardly looking as he sent it into a distant post. Realizing what he'd done, he gave me a sheepish look but didn't comment on how he had acquired this skill. Villagers said he'd killed men, but they wouldn't say when or how. He knew some of my past, in which men had certainly been killed. His only wish for me was that I could find peace, something I found impossible. I carried anger around with me the way people carry silver fillings in their teeth.

The abbot looked up, his expression serious. He was the only one of us who had to speak each day, for he spoke to the outside world, where people expected to hear a voice on the other end of the line. He pushed the cell phone toward me. "It's all on there. A man under siege who cried out to you for help."

I looked at the phone's history, saw a familiar name. "I've known him since childhood."

"And I know you, Thomas. You're already on your way to him. But those are gunshots in the background."

"I know his wife. Also since childhood. He wants me to protect her from his killers."

"I understand that. But you left here once before. By your own account, it didn't turn out well." His eyes were mild as they held mine, but within their depths I saw the knife fighter. He wore scars that had not been produced by a splash of acid. They were the marks of blades that had sliced neatly through his flesh. His knuckles were those of a fighter, permanently enlarged.

He said, "There will always be a battle somewhere." He looked into my eyes, seeing me as clearly as I saw him. We knew what we were. I had overheard villagers saying they'd seen him fighting in a cantina when he was young and that he walked up the wall and across the ceiling. They exaggerated, the way storytellers will, but I've seen astonishing displays of energy when barrooms erupt. It was in a barroom that too much energy had shot through my arm and then my fist and then into a young man who folded and died at my feet.

The abbot said, "If you go, there will be blood. I can see it." He dealt with the souls of men each day—men in conflict, turmoil, pain. He watched over us, knowing that our agreement with the world had failed and that in its place we'd made another agreement, with the saints in heaven or with something less well-defined; something invisible but helpful. I thought of it as grace, and I didn't want to lose it. But I said, "I have to answer this call for help."

And because he knew I could see into him, he said, "Yes, I would have to answer it too."

He gave me the phone and his blessing, and I made arrangements for a morning flight to my hometown in America, where I'd grown up in a family dedicated to organized crime. I'd spent years trying to distance myself from its influence, but those wiseguys of my childhood had set up permanent residence in my soul. And they were saying, *You're a player, Tommy, always were and always will be.*

4

The flight had been long, with the usual airport delays. And I felt as though I'd been sucked through a vacuum cleaner. I told the cab driver to take me to a sleazy motel.

"Plenty of those," he said.

I took out the phone the abbot had returned to me, and listened to the only message in my inbox—that of an old friend saying, *Take care of Bridget. My heart is in your hands.* Followed by the gunshot that ended his life.

Finn Sweeney, whose upper-class background made him a target in those Coalville barrooms where he liked to drink. The best-looking girls in Coalville came from the other side of the tracks, and their bars were the rough ones. He'd gone in wearing expensive clothes and a watch that cost more than any of the men at that bar earned in a month. Perhaps if he'd kept his mouth shut, it might've been all right, but as he got plastered his black Irish humor would come out, cutting, perceptive, and usually directed at some hulking drunk twice his size. Many were the nights I'd had to step outside and deal with someone who wanted to knock Finn's teeth down his throat.

I wondered if he'd befriended me because I was big enough to fight his battles for him. While I was away in a monastery, Finn stopped arguing in bars and used his trust fund to buy a Coalville TV station and fight local corruption. Now he could argue with the whole town.

"This sleazy enough for you?" asked the cab driver.

The Luna Motel hadn't seen paint for fifty years. The sidewalk was cracked. A few rooms had bent metal folding chairs in front of them. "Perfect."

"It's none of my business, but bad people stay here."

"There are bad people everywhere."

"They're concentrated in this place."

It was certainly humble. Instead of a chocolate on my pillow, I found a strand of hair. I called my cousin Dominic in Las Vegas and asked him if he knew that Finn Sweeney had been murdered.

"I heard. Tough break. He was a nice guy."

"He called me right before they whacked him. He asked me to take care of Bridget. You remember her?"

"I had wet dreams about her."

"We all did."

"Long legs and blond hair. We see it, we want it. From six blocks away."

"She's gone missing."

"You sure you know what you're doing?"

"Finn was my best friend."

"And now he's dead. Forget it."

"He reached out to me at the end. I can't let it go."

"Then Duke Devlin is the guy you want to talk to."

Duke Devlin, a blood-freezing Irish wiseguy from my childhood who'd worked as an enforcer for my grandfather, Primo Martini.

I was orphaned early, and Primo had raised me. Since he was a mob boss of the old school, I had unusual life lessons. Dominic said, "Bob Elfwine of Wrestling Universe still wants you to fight for him."

"I'll keep it in mind." The money was good, but I had enough money, and professional wrestling is brutal. Those who think it isn't have never been slammed to the mat by a huge man supercharged with steroids.

Duke arrived at the motel driving a 640-horsepower Cadillac CTS-V in metallic black. When I was twelve, he was into motor sports and had taken me for a ride on the interstate in a modified five-liter Mustang. I remember my head snapping back when he gunned it, and the engine sounded like a *Tyrannosaurus rex* eating something smaller than itself. My hunger for speed was born in the mouth of that monster.

I got up off my bent chair, and we shook hands. He wore a perfectly tailored tan silk suit that hung without a wrinkle on his muscular form. "You're bigger, kid. You filled out. They feed you pasta in the monastery?"

"Rice and beans."

"Close enough. You look like you could fuck a horse." Duke's eyes were dark green, and they said he was glad to see me, but the old suspicion was there, mirroring a life of criminal enterprise. It wasn't that he was suspicious of me particularly, it was just the look of a man from the shadows. He glanced around the motel parking lot. "You inherited big dough. What the fuck are you doing here?"

"Keeping a low profile."

He was a heavyweight like me and known as a battler. His black hair was streaked with gray, but he'd kept in shape. I pulled over another bent chair and we sat down under the motel overhang and reminisced about my grandfather. "That was a man," said Duke, his voice becoming suddenly formal, almost a perfect copy of Grandfather Primo. "You were fortunate to be under his care. It's why I'm here talking to you tonight. Otherwise, I wouldn't give a fuck. I'm not on call."

This was as it should be. To ease things along, I asked him, "Are you still into racing?"

"I sponsor a Russian woman. She used to smuggle cars in and out of Moscow."

"I'd like to meet her sometime."

"You're celibate, right?"

"At the moment."

"She'll like that. Like going to a zoo." He glanced at his watch. "The little hand is moving." His eyes drifted back to me. "Why am I here?"

I told him about Finn Sweeney's phone call, the cry for help, the gunshots.

"Stay the fuck out of it. That was a hired hit."

"Tell me."

"A shot in the back, the body is left where it sends a message."

"What was the message?"

"*You come after us, we kill you in your front yard.* Sweeney was always a loudmouth. Only now he had a TV station."

"Has his family made any noises?"

"They're fucking numb. They know they're next if they don't stay clammed up."

"Who did Finn try to bring down?"

"A lot of people. Take your pick."

"Who would you pick?"

"Our illustrious governor. He pushed through legislation to get a casino licensed here and Finn went after him, on air in a long string of broadcasts, about the bad effects casinos have on the moral fiber of a community."

"He always liked to argue."

"Well, he argued with the wrong guy."

I gave Duke my phone, and he listened to the message from Finn. He shook his head and said, "A call from hell. And you want to go there?"

"I figure I owe him."

"You owe shit, my friend."

Primo had once given me his assessment of Duke Devlin: *I need that fucking Irishman on my crew. Cut him off at the legs and he'll come at you on his stumps.*

But Duke would never be a boss, underboss, or crew chief. The most he could aspire to was *associate*, which suited him fine. He wasn't a made man, but he was a feared man and had been entrusted with many jobs that Primo wouldn't have given to anyone else.

"To fight corruption around here you need a dark heart. Otherwise, you get played. Finn Sweeney didn't have a dark heart." Duke took out a cigarette, lit it with what looked like a fourteen-karat-gold lighter. Finally, he said, "He was a spoiled child of fortune."

He took a long, slow look around the parking lot, as if gauging possible threats. Just a habit. A way of life for Duke Devlin. Then he said, "This state runs on corruption. Bribes, kickbacks, influence peddling, money laundering. And you . . ." He pointed the end of his cigarette at me. "You're like the baby Jesus."

He gazed at me for a long while, the criminal look playing there until I got the message. "Duke, I'm forgetting my manners. You showed me many kindnesses when I was a boy."

"That's right, kid. I did."

"So can I give you a small gift for old times' sake? Say, five grand?"

The offer bounced off him. "I can ask around, but then I'm in somebody else's action. And they won't like it, which puts me at risk."

I could almost hear the voice of Grandfather Primo in my head, his formal style coming back to me as I said, "You're a man of experience, Duke. No monetary value can be put on that experience, but ten grand is a figure that comes to mind."

"No checks."

"I'll have the cash for you tomorrow."

"Your gift is appreciated." He flipped his cigarette into the parking lot. "That little Irish loudmouth must have meant a lot to you."

"And Bridget."

"As I recall, you danced attendance on her." Owing to his having been educated by Jesuits, Duke occasionally came out with this kind of ornate language. "You're going to need a car. You want me to steal one for you?" When I protested, he gave his dark laugh, the one that said he was kidding. "We'll go see your uncle Silvio. He's the car guy."

We got into his Cadillac. He said, "It'll do two hundred miles an hour."

"And we need that kind of speed."

"We do." He drove us to the south side of town—the poor side, where all the Martinis had their beginning and where Uncle Silvio still had his towing service. His house was nothing to speak of, but he had six gleaming tow trucks in the backyard, which took up half a block. All the trucks bore the Martini name and were decorated with painted martini glasses containing swizzle sticks and olives. When we entered the garage, he was seated behind a grimy desk, wearing a baseball cap with a martini glass printed on it.

Duke announced me. "His Holiness is in town."

"Tommy," said Uncle Silvio, getting up from behind his desk and throwing his arms around me. He was all lean muscle from a lifetime of lifting tow chains. His eyes were merry—a result of always coming out ahead in anything involving money, trucks, and scrap metal. "You coming back to work for me?"

"I'd love to, Uncle Silvio, but I'm not going to be in town for long."

His powerful hands gripped my shoulders. "We'll go out on a job together. Remind you what real men do." A little reminder from Uncle Silvio that your exalted opinion of yourself was scorned by those who climbed under automobiles for a living. Though they have the pleasure of battling steel beasts into submission, their day is not complete unless they insert their grease gun into your ego. I was used to it. But I felt how different it was from the atmosphere of the monastery, where men struggled against self-importance in stony silence. The monastery was a humorless place, and Uncle Silvio's garage was a place of joy. The pleasure of raucous male company is like no other.

"So what are you in town for?"

"I want to find out what happened to Finn Sweeney."

"What happened is, he got himself killed. What's that got to do with you?"

I let him listen to the phone call. He handed it back to me, his eyes no longer merry. "Let me tell you something. You ready to hear?"

"I'm ready."

"I get calls in the middle of the night, *please come and tow my car*. And if it's out of my range, I don't care if the guy's in a pothole that's swallowing him alive—I turn him down. And this is out of your range. Turn it down."

A man who tows cars and trucks for a living meets a lot of people, and they come from every level. He was a mine of information. It was part of that solidity you felt in his presence. I asked, "What do you know about Finn's death?"

"He died and he's dead." Which meant Uncle Silvio didn't want me to get involved.

His office was lined with shelves of model cars and trucks lovingly put together by him when he was a kid. Their bright, shiny shapes were a playful contrast to the seriousness on his face. "You understand? You look like you're not listening."

"I had a long flight."

"Town has changed since you left. There are new elements here." There were framed photos of him beside overturned eighteen-wheelers and other spectacular wrecks. There was a framed newspaper article about how he'd risked his life to get a woman out of a car that had rolled down an embankment and hung a hundred feet over a flooded river. There was a photo of me as a kid in a soapbox racer, holding up a trophy.

"What kind of new elements?"

"Very dangerous elements. You look out your window in the middle of the night and a kid is walking up the street wearing a backpack. And I ask myself, is he on the way to hike the Appalachian Trail?" He held up two fingers. "He's got only two things in that backpack: tools to break into a house, and the stuff he's already robbed from the last house."

He pointed toward his trucks. "I never used to carry a gun when I went on a job. Now I get a call at two in the morning, there's a car with a dead battery behind Home Depot. You think I'm going on that call without a gun?"

"But you go?"

"I go, and there's three cars parked there. With out-of-state plates. They just happen to be in back of Home Depot, and they're not looking for drywall in the middle of the night. I give them the finger and go home." He sat back down behind his desk. "They come in from Philly, Jersey, New York. And you can hire them to do a job for you. They get it done, and they leave town. They have no ties here, there's no trace of them, and you'll never find them. So apart from everything else, you're wasting your time."

"You heard the phone call. Finn asked me to take care of his wife."

"We're talking about Bridget Breen, right?"

"Now she's Bridget Sweeney."

"To me, she's Bridget Breen, the hellcat from South Side. She doesn't need you to take care of her."

"Finn thought so."

"Under pressure he thought of you. It's not binding."

"He was my friend. I don't have many of them."

"That's because you went around beating people up."

"They asked for it."

"And they're still here. Guys from Coalville hold grudges for fifty years. You'll have enough on your hands without pledging yourself to a dead man. And Bridget Breen has a hunk of coal for a heart."

Duke intervened. "Tommy had a hard-on for her. You remember."

"Sure, I gave him a car so he could take her out." He looked back at me, scorn in his merry eyes. "How did that go?"

"Not well."

"And it's not going to go any better now."

Duke added, "But he still needs a car."

Silvio got up from his desk, went to a wall where dozens of keys and fobs were hanging, each with a label. He checked the labels, then pulled two of them down. He swung a key fob in front of my face. "Ten-year-old Acura MDX. A refined Japanese ride." He swung the other one. "A 1968 Dodge Charger, American star quality and fear in one package. Take your pick."

"I'll take the Charger."

He handed me the keys. "Come on, it's in the alley." We walked through the garage where an employee with a welding tool was performing some modification on a truck. Silvio customized all his trucks, making them more efficient, more powerful, and more glamorous. His trucks won prizes at tow truck shows around the country.

We went out the back door of the garage, into the alleyway. The south side of town, like all the neighborhoods of Coalville, was honeycombed with alleyways between houses. Horses had been kept there once. The stables had been converted into garages. Most of them were dilapidated, and Silvio's was no different. The shabbier, the better. He didn't want to announce there was something valuable inside. He opened a padlock, and there was the Charger, a pioneer muscle car, in red. "Like a beast in its lair," said Silvio.

Duke looked it over appreciatively. "You take it out much?"

"Not enough." But the hood had to come up, the modifications examined, and then a walk around to the rear, and I was right back in my childhood. An exorcist would say Satan had set the perfect trap. Duke and Uncle Silvio talked and I listened, but it was more like following a map back to my real self. I understood this language of the alleyway, of souped-up engines and modified bodies, and I understood the men who spoke that language. For them, life was not a text you read or a prayer you said. It was taking hold of the world with your hands, overcoming its resistance, shaping it to your will. And they knew, in the deepest possible way, that they were in touch with the roots of reality. And everything else was bullshit. My soul was spinning as I stood there in the dilapidated garage. There was wisdom in its greasy old boards if you had the eyes to see it.

Duke said, "I've got to run. I'll swing by the motel tomorrow morning."

Silvio and I stayed with the Charger. Silvio said, "He's working for you?"

"I need help."

"You need your head examined." He closed the hood of the Charger. "How much are you paying him?"

"Ten Gs."

"Vittorio's money, I suppose." He was referring to the legacy his brother had left me—a fancy home I'd already sold, and several million dollars along with stock worth several million more, all of it gotten in the usual Martini way.

"I'm his heir. I didn't want to be, but I am."

"I don't begrudge you the dough. I just want you to use it wisely. Tracking down Bridget Breen isn't wise. I meant it when I said things have changed in this town." He ran his hand over the brilliantly polished hood of the Charger. "Your grandfather was a hard man, but in his way, he was a civilized man. He followed rules." He looked up at me. "Now we've got a gang from Chechnya, pimps from Russia, Haitian car thieves, Mexican cartel guys, and the old rules mean nothing to them. Something's missing from their brain. I go out on a police call, I get to the car and there's a dead guy behind the wheel, and his dick is jammed between his teeth. You want more?"

"Not at the moment." I got behind the wheel of the Charger. To match the car's character, Uncle Silvio had hung fuzzy dice from the rearview mirror. I turned the key. The beast rumbled out of its slumber. I let it warm up, then put it in gear and backed out of the garage. Silvio spoke to me through the open window. "For your ten Gs, make sure Duke gives you something useful. Don't let him play you along."

"I can handle Duke."

"The Devlins are all slippery. Since they were kids." With that, he waved me on my way. I drove down the alley. When I was a kid, I drove down it in the soapbox racer Silvio had made for me. It had flames painted on its nose, and interior metal plates to give it weight on a downhill slope. He'd kept tweaking it until I was ready for competition, and then we took it to Akron, Ohio, and I came in first in the All-American Soapbox Derby.

At the foot of the alleyway, I swung into a second alley, which took me past Saint John's Church, church of my childhood. I would have liked to pay a visit, but I knew it would be locked. Churches aren't left open these days, because everything in them would be stolen, from statues to holy water. So I drove on by and headed for Bridge Street, the main drag out of town where we used to do our racing. When I reached it, I slammed the gas pedal to the floor, and the Charger jumped like a supernatural animal. All those modifications by Uncle Silvio came into play, feeding the beast what it wanted. I ran to the top of Bridge Street and swung onto the interstate. In six seconds, the Charger was screaming well over a hundred and showed no sign of strain, not a vibration anywhere, just smooth movement as I kept my foot to the floor and hit 125, still without a protest from anywhere in the Charger's anatomy. Any good mechanic can build speed into a vehicle, but it takes a master mechanic like Silvio to harness that speed and balance it to perfection. Otherwise, the beast will be uncontrollable and have you fishtailing all over the road. At 150, I called it a day and came down from that wonderful high that only a monster car can give you.

At the next exit, I pulled off the interstate and drove back toward my sleazy motel, the Charger rumbling under me. I was feeling the old code. You had to be ready to die—at the wheel, or in a barroom brawl. And in one of those brawls, a young man had died, and I had killed him.

5

The inscription carved in the stone was part of the code of Coalville. The fight is never over. I'd killed Mike Muldoon, and his family would soon know I was in town, and his brothers would come after me, their right hands filled with justice.

I left the cemetery and drove to MacBride's Bar, where the fight had taken place. I'd been the bouncer and Mike Muldoon had been a local tough guy, the kind who goes out every night to get drunk and push somebody's face in.

I'd been scheduled to compete in the summer Olympics in London, and I was favored to win gold in wrestling. And then Mike Muldoon smacked a guy in the face with a beer-soaked bar rag. The guy picked up a barstool and tried to hit Mike with it. I was paid to stop this kind of circus, and I got between them. "Take it outside, gentlemen."

Mike's eyes had been wild. I glanced at Bridget Breen and wanted to impress her. Muldoon came at me with a heavy overhand right, but in return he got something he never dreamed possible: a punch so hard it stopped his heart. He couldn't have spelled it, but *commotio cordis* killed him, a lethal disruption of the heart rhythm, resulting from the kinetic energy of a projectile—my fist. A doctor had explained it to me in those gloomy days when I was trying to figure out how such a thing could have happened. My grandfather spread a bunch of money around to make the charges go away. He'd paid off the Muldoon family, he'd paid for Mike's tombstone, and I was shipped off to a monastery in Mexico. And that was the end of my Olympic dream.

Now, years later, my heart was pounding. It wasn't going to kill me, but it was unsettling. I'd come here to look the past in the eye, and it was looking back at me—Mike's eyes wide with the kind of amazement that comes only once in a lifetime, when you realize you've pushed it too far and that you're on the way to an early grave.

Somebody stepped in beside me at the bar and I turned, anger rushing to the surface from that place inside me where it's always smoldering. But the face was a friendly one.

"Tommy, I heard you were in town." Vincent Nowitzki, known in my youth as Knucklehead, owing to a brief boxing career in which he lost every bout. But he'd built a reputation as a scrapper, and politics gave him a scrap he could win. And he won the position of city magistrate, proving that if you knew how to knock on doors, it didn't matter that you'd spent your early years getting knocked out in the ring. Now Knucklehead Nowitzki was Magistrate Nowitzki, sitting in judgment on his fellow man. And he was sitting beside me on a barstool, and my heart resumed its regular rhythm. I wasn't about to call him Knucklehead, so he was Vince and I was Tommy, and he seemed glad to see me. "Are you back for good?"

"Just a visit."

"I heard you went into a monastery. You bone any nuns?"

"It wasn't part of our daily observance."

"The Sisters of Silence are still here in town. You remember their place? With the stone wall around it?"

I told him I remembered it fondly. He nodded and we both looked into the mirror, thinking about those silent, mysterious women behind the stone wall. "These days," Knucklehead continued, "they work with girls who've been abused."

"You seem to have given some attention to this."

"I think about it in the middle of the night. I have to wear a thing on my nose to keep me breathing correctly. Otherwise, I wake up choking."

"What's wrong with your nose?"

"Broken too many times." He touched its irregular shape, which flared out on both sides; the bridge was jammed up into his forehead, giving him the look of a pugnacious pilot from an alien spaceship.

We talked about guys we'd known, and finally about Finn Sweeney. Knucklehead raised his beer glass. "Taken from us too soon."

"Somebody shot him in the back. Any ideas?"

He turned toward me, his eyes wary. "Rich Irish guys should stay in bed and enjoy life." He finished his drink and stood. "Tommy, I've got to run. I ordered a pizza to take over to the county jail."

"You make deliveries to prisoners?"

"It's a guy I know. His wife left him, and he took all his clothes off and ran around the block. I put him away for a few nights to rethink his position." Knucklehead held out his hand. "It's good to have you back. We'll talk again."

6

The action in Coalville took place at Parade Square. The action tonight was a young man beside me on a park bench, putting the flame of a butane lighter under a fentanyl patch. I'd seen it done in Mexico City. Those who are right in the head do not attempt this. He leaned over the bandage and inhaled. Immediately he began gasping for breath. I yanked him upright and ground my knuckles into his breastbone. His lips were already blue. "Stay awake, bright eyes."

A kid who looked to be about twelve grabbed the fentanyl patch from between the young man's fingers and took off with it. I dialed 911 and continued massaging the doper's chest until the ambulance arrived, the first responders asking, "What did he take?"

"Vaped a patch."

They injected him.

"Naloxone," said a voice in the gathering crowd. "Gets you breathing again." When someone in a park knows the name of a medication used to block the effects of opioids, you know what kind of park you're in.

After a few minutes, the doper's lips were no longer blue. The responders rolled him onto a stretcher. Staring up at them, he mumbled, "That was some bad shit."

"You almost checked out, pal," said one of the responders. "Next time, you won't make it."

"Bad shit," he repeated, as if the makers of the patch had failed in their quality control.

The responders carried him to the ambulance. I sat down on the bench. A young woman sat beside me. "How did you know what to do?"

"I've seen it done before."

"Awesome." Her running shoes had red and white laces. She forgot about me and went back to looking at her phone. From the flickering images, I concluded that it had something to do with maximizing eyebrows. She turned toward me. "You interested? In eyebrows?"

"I don't think too much about them."

"Shape is everything." She spoke with authority.

"If you say so."

"Guys notice them unconsciously."

Feeling that it was incumbent on me to notice and comment, I said, looking at hers, "Sculpted to perfection."

"Everybody else is painting them on. That do anything for you?"

"I've been out of the country."

"Where?"

"Mexico."

"Your eyebrows are nice and thick. It's an ethnic thing."

Whatever she thought about my eyebrows was fine by me. Since we'd gotten this far, I asked, "Did you ever know a guy named Finn Sweeney?"

"He got shot, right?"

"In the back."

"You a cop?"

"No."

"A plainclothes guy?"

"My close relatives are gangsters."

"For real?"

"Very fucking real."

"Awesome." She went back to her phone but then looked up and said, "He used to come around here with a microphone, asking questions. He tried to pick me up a few times."

"And?"

"I told him to fuck off. Not my type." She gave me a clinical look. "You're more my type."

"Because of my eyebrows?"

"It's the whole ethnic thing. Listen . . ." She stood up. "My boyfriend's coming; I've got to go."

Her boyfriend was a prison weightlifter. His eyes had that prison shine of constant hunger and low tolerance for other people's existence, which now included me. The demon of anger inside me stirred again, blind and mindless, prepared to launch a preemptive strike on the boyfriend. My anger medicine would have chilled the demon out, but having weaned myself off it, I handled the moment as if I were a normal human being. I got up from the bench and walked on.

The kid who'd pinched the fentanyl patch approached me. He was still working on his swagger, but he was getting there. "Fix you up with some pussy?"

Ordinarily, I don't believe in child labor, but I handed him a fifty-dollar bill. "I'm looking for a tall blonde named Bridget."

"She work the square?"

"She's married to the guy from the TV station. He came around here asking questions."

"I remember the dude. Got himself wasted on a permanent basis."

"How old are you?"

"Twelve." He gave me a defiant look.

"What's your name?"

"Zigzag." He swiveled back and forth on his heels, possibly demonstrating a capacity for avoiding pursuit. Intelligence bubbled out of him. If he didn't get himself wasted on a permanent basis, he was going to go far. I gave him another fifty and a complete description of Bridget.

"I'll get back to you," he said, and took off.

I went back to the motel.

7

As the cabdriver had said, there were bad people at the motel. Through the ratty shade on my window, I watched them come and go. The room they entered and left was the resupply point for a drug business. I closed the shade and sat in a wobbly chair. I began my Lectio Divina, reading from my evening prayerbook: *Help me to see and understand the path that you have opened for me.*

Someone started hammering on my door. I ignored it but it continued, accompanied by shouting. "Open the door, Crystal."

I closed my prayer book and called through the door, "Wrong room."

There was a pause and then he said, "Where the fuck's Crystal?"

"How the fuck should I know?" I was jet-lagged, and perhaps I didn't show the proper patience with a man searching for his true love. My inquisitor resumed hammering on the door.

"Crystal, you bitch, come the fuck out *now*!"

I saw no point in discussing Crystal's whereabouts. I returned to my Lectio Divina. Then I heard a sound from under the bed. It sent a shiver up my spine. I knelt and shined the light of my phone under the bed. "Crystal?"

Two mirror eyes shone back at me. Then an orange tomcat raced past me and headed toward the door. I noticed a large pair of orange balls. A tomcat on the prowl. I approached it cautiously. It looked at me with menace in its eyes. I wasn't about to spend the night with a tomcat in my room, so I opened the door. The cat shot out, leaving a fleeting image of orange balls in an uproar. The guy standing at my door reacted badly, pulling out a large handgun and spinning around. He seemed uncertain who or what to fire at, so I clocked him in the back of the neck just to be on the safe side. He went down hard, hitting the metal folding chair, the sound of which brought an associate rushing to the scene, so I clocked him too.

A woman came out of the next room and looked at the two guys lying on the sidewalk. She was in the tightest shorts I'd ever seen. I asked her if she was Crystal.

"Yeah," she said, and looked down at the two unconscious men. "Were they pulling some shit?"

"One of them was trying to get into my room."

"That's Reno. He's dyslexic. He gets numbers mixed up."

We looked down at Reno and his partner. They were still tangled up in the folding chair. I hadn't unpacked my bag. I went back into the room and retrieved my bag.

"You're leaving?" She seemed saddened by my departure.

"When they wake up, they'll start shooting."

"That's no reason to run off," she said.

I felt it was quite reasonable, and I threw my bag into the back seat of the Charger. She came toward me. Her shorts were orange, a fairly close match to the tomcat's balls. I said, "There was a cat in my room."

"That's Pumpkin. He follows the maid around."

"Well, Reno almost shot him."

"He'd never do that."

"He was taken by surprise." I opened the door of the Charger. Reno and his associate were beginning to stir. I got behind the wheel, and Crystal leaned against the door and tapped on the window with a long false fingernail. I lowered it. "I'll handle Reno," she said. "We can have a party. They've got a shitload of coke."

"I'm a Benedictine monk."

"Ain't that some kind of cognac?"

"Made with herbs and spices."

Reno was gripping the folding chair to aid his ascent. I switched on the ignition and backed slowly away, but Crystal remained friendly, keeping pace with the car. "You know what room I'm in. Come and see me. I read palms."

Reno was helping his partner to his feet. As I turned the car around, I caught sight of mirror eyes and orange balls—Pumpkin on the move. And so was I, out of the motel lot and back onto the road. I drove along it for a while, then crossed a bridge and turned again so that I was traveling with the river that ran through that part of town. When I came to a sign that said *Vacancy*, I pulled off into the Riverview Trailer Park.

The manager of the trailer park greeted me from behind a desk that looked as if it had been pulled from the river. "I have a single-wide with a view of the river. Four fifty a month. Nobody gives a shit what you do so long as you don't fire off a weapon. Do you plan on firing off a weapon?"

"Not at the moment."

"Then you've passed our rigorous vetting process."

The manager had a large birthmark on top of his head, as if a wine bottle had been broken there and the wine seeped into his skull. Between his lips was a lit cigarette, from which smoke curled up past large bushy eyebrows flecked with gray. The gray parts protruded outward in wirelike curls. The whites of his eyes had a yellow tint, suggesting a liver taxed by alcohol. He pointed to a building across from his office, on which was written in large letters GAME ROOM / LAUNDRY. He gave no explanation, but I heard washing machines and the electric zapping of *Space Invaders*.

He placed his cigarette in an ashtray, inside which was written *God Bless Our Mortgaged Home*. I gave him cash, and he wrote a receipt. "Staying long?"

"I'm not sure."

"Your rent can be applied to the purchase of your trailer."

"I'll hold off on that for a while."

"Fine. Trailer's not going anywhere." He gave me the key, then took the cigarette from his ashtray and applied its glowing tip to a fresh cigarette. "Enjoy your new home."

I left him smoking and parked the Charger beside my trailer. The inside of the trailer was clean enough, though slightly worn. The ceiling was a faded yellow, decorated with water stains. Since the bed wasn't wet, I assumed the leak had been fixed. As promised, I had a view of the rust-colored river, on which the moon was shining. The path to the water was lit by solar-powered lamps, not all of which were working. At the river's edge, I saw the handlebars of a bicycle rising out of the water like a two-headed baby Loch Ness Monster checking out the world.

The river wasn't a stately, slow-moving giant and would be far down on anyone's list of impressive waterways. When I was a kid, we were told never to swim in it. To reinforce the message, we were told the water was so polluted, the fish had horns and three eyes. I didn't see any horns tonight, only the handlebars of that submerged bicycle. Floating past it were popsicle sticks, condoms, plastic bottles, and other assorted bits of trash. I felt at home.

8

Finn's father came to the phone and asked coldly, "What do you want?"

"Finn called me right before he was killed."

"Explain."

"He left a message for me. He asked me to take care of Bridget."

"Did he say where she was?"

"He didn't."

"Then how can you take care of her?"

"I thought maybe we could put our heads together and both of us protect her."

He let this hang in the air, mulling over what might be involved. I helped him along. "I can work the underbelly of this town."

Finally he said, "I'll give you that."

"Then also give me some of your time."

Again he paused. Through my entire relationship with his son, he'd insulted my family, called me a criminal, even threatened me with a restraining order. But he wasn't born yesterday. He knew the Martini family cast a wide net, possibly down into the darkness in which his daughter-in-law had disappeared.

The Tudor mansion was ahead, its steeply pitched gable roofs, elaborate chimneys, and small diamond-shaped windows suggesting that I might meet William Shakespeare inside. Instead, I met Benjamin Augustus Sweeney. He was waiting in the main hallway. An impressive staircase led to a balcony above. Hanging beside it was a chandelier, twenty feet over our heads.

Without bothering to shake hands, he said, "Under normal circumstances, I would never have you in this house again."

"Under normal circumstances, I'd be in a monastery in Mexico. But your son called me with his dying breath."

We walked toward a wing of the house I remembered well, though I hadn't often been let into it, for it held the great living room reserved for Ben Sweeney and his cronies. They were the gray eminence at work behind the scenes in Coalville. Sweeney was old money, and old Irish money, which meant his forebears had been among the tough sons of bitches who shaped this town at its beginning. His veneer might be sophisticated, but inside he was a player, and a mean one. My grandfather had opposed him in the battle for local power, and he hated me for it.

We passed a dining room with a long, dark table and some uncomfortable-looking chairs. We passed a study lined with bookshelves, and a music room with a grand piano. We went through a carved archway into the living room. It held a large stone fireplace. Milord had not called for it to be lit today, so we sat facing each other. Since he wasn't about to open the conversation, I said, "I'm sorry for your loss."

He looked at me with his cold fish eyes. His tweed jacket was tailored to his lean physique, and every inch of him was meant to express his exalted status. The easy chair I sat in was leather, smelling of some scented oil to preserve it, but it had been there for decades and was webbed with fine cracks. The cracks were to tell you that you were in an atmosphere of generations. The Sweeneys had partnered in one of the local coal mines but had sold their interest at the first sign of King Coal's demise. Industrial chemicals had kept them going, and now they had huge real estate holdings. His eyes played over me, contemptuous as ever and spiced with naked hatred. "Play Finn's message. I assume you haven't erased it."

"I wasn't going to erase Finn's last words on Earth."

He listened, asked me to play it again, listened still more deeply to his son's voice from the edge of the grave. *Take care of Bridget. My heart is in your hands.* He looked at me. "And you came all the way from Mexico to act on this request?"

"We spent a lot of time together."

"Yes, you did. You fascinated him. I think it's called gangsteritis."

"I call it friendship. Fewer syllables."

We sat in silence, neither looking at the other. I waited. If he didn't tell me anything about Bridget in the next two minutes, I'd leave. I studied the balcony at the far end of the living room, constructed of the same dark wood that trimmed the windows throughout the house. It was a comfortable house and, in its somber way, a charming one. As a kid, I'd found it slightly intimidating, but now I could appreciate its old-world feel, with the different wall heights and the jumble of rooms at odd angles to one another. The Sweeney who built it must have been a romantic fellow. He had probably come to America from a house without windows, made of mud and straw. His lucky four-leaf clover had paid off—he'd struck it rich, and a few generations later, here we were in a country manor house with walls of fine brick around us, and casement windows letting in the summer light.

There was a framed photo of Finn on the mantelpiece; it wasn't a corny color photo, but a black-and-white study of him that might have been done by an old-time Hollywood photographer. The light around Finn's form had a silvery shimmer, and the shadows he cast on a sheer background were deep. You could see the star quality in him as he gazed beyond the camera toward some unseen partner—a woman, or maybe just his fate.

"When you killed that Muldoon fellow, I thought I was rid of you."

"Has anybody contacted you asking ransom for your daughter-in-law?"

"No one."

"Call me when they do."

"I'll call the police."

"They'll give you what they can. I'll give you Bridget."

He gazed at me, trying to read me as he never had when I was his son's best friend. Back then he'd throw open the door to Finn's room, point to me, and say, "*Out.*" And I went. I didn't want to make it hard for Finn, who liked his privileges, his Corvette, his guaranteed future. He and his father had been a pair of icicles when they were in each other's company. My grandfather was a murderer, but he could occasionally show affection. "I'd like to see the room Finn and I hung out in."

He stood and we walked together down the hallway to Finn's wing. *Be sure you play the Danse Macabre at my funeral*, he used to joke, intimating that he wouldn't make old bones. I used to think it was a romantic pose. I didn't think so any longer.

"That's the room you want," said Ben, "and you know the way."

It was Finn's bedroom, still cluttered with the computer gear he'd mastered. He'd built gaming machines as well as other electronic devices, including a miniature camera inside a tie pin. We wore it to parties, catching our friends in embarrassing moments. It was stupid kid's stuff, but we enjoyed it.

There were magazines, years old, and souvenirs from trips Finn had taken around the country, among them a Route 66 road sign. And an electric guitar he'd built himself. I was hoping this room would tell me something I didn't know, and put me on the trail of his killer. But there were only memories.

I heard Ben's voice behind me. "You got him killed."

"Mind telling me how?"

"When he met you, he changed. That's when he grew secretive." He gestured toward Finn's worktable. "Making that spying stuff."

"He was good with technology. It had nothing to do with me."

"The FBI was spying on your grandfather."

"They probably were. So what?"

"It was not our way of life." His eyes were blazing with that mad Irish fury I remembered from street fights. "My boy was brought up as a gentleman. You were raised by Italian scum who bled this town dry."

I turned toward the hallway. "I'm going to find Bridget."

"He never should have married her."

This turned me back. I wanted to know more, and he obliged me. "She wasn't from his world. Our world." He gestured, indicating the mansion, the lush gardens outside. "It put Finn off balance." He gazed at me for a long moment. "She should have married you."

"She wouldn't have me."

"No, she wanted what Finn could give her."

I said, "I see her differently."

"Of course, and that's why she should have married you."

Not only did he hate me, he really didn't care about Bridget. There were tears in his eyes, the fire of his fury mixing with his grief. "My son called you as he was dying. Your corruption of him was complete. He called you instead of me. Now you'd better leave. There's a gun in this house, and I'm tempted to use it."

As a gray eminence, Benjamin Augustus Sweeney could kill me in his own house and get away with it. But as I looked into those mad Irish eyes, I had the feeling he might find another way. I left him in his Tudor mansion. When it was built, it had been a place of dreams. Now it was just a peculiar building in the woods.

9

"Tommy Martini, big as a boxcar." Bridget's mother was living in a house built around 1900—a drafty place, furnished with a woman's taste: no big leather couches, no recliners, no huge TV screen. Instead, there were lots of little tables with knickknacks, silver frames with photographs of Bridget Breen, Bridget and Finn, the pope, and the late Mr. Breen. There was plenty of female fuss in the air, including a collection of miniature china bells lined up in an open cabinet made for such things. Everything in the room was arranged thoughtfully and had been selected with terrible taste. All of it made me feel claustrophobic.

But Veronica Breen was a good-looking woman, her blond hair streaked, her makeup cleverly applied, and her clothing well chosen—at least from the point of view of yours truly, no expert in women's fashions. But I was an expert in spotting a drunk, and Veronica was loaded at high noon. Her embrace lasted too long, as if she was counting on me to keep her standing. She wasn't anticipating a fall, but having found a support, she let herself go, and the unsteadiness came through. "I'm so glad you're here," she whispered in my ear with an intimacy that made me nervous. When we broke the embrace, I saw past her makeup to bloodshot eyes. But she pulled herself together. "Let me play mother. Tea and cookies? You always liked my cookies, remember?"

"Chocolate chip."

"The very thing for young gentlemen." Benjamin Augustus Sweeney might not think I was a gentleman, but this charming woman did, and she hurried off. I was remembering how welcoming she'd always been to Bridget's friends. She liked young people—pretended to understand us, and maybe she did.

Now she brought me tea and cookies, and we sat down on opposite sides of a little table in the living room.

"Since the night Finn was killed, there hasn't been a peep from my girl," she said in answer to my first question. From fear or too much booze, the edge of an Irish accent sneaked into her voice. "Holy Mary, I hope they haven't killed her too."

"I'm sure she's alive." At least, she was there in the room with us, in her photographs, a blond beauty I had to believe still walked the earth, her long legs adding to the joy of mankind.

Veronica had put more than sugar in her own tea, because after the first few sips, her mood shifted suddenly. "We had such good times, didn't we? Lord, it was fun." Her concern was gone on the wings of whatever she'd poured for herself in the kitchen.

"Do you have any out-of-town relatives, Veronica? Someplace Bridget might hide out?"

"You know us, Tommy. We stick close to home."

And now there were tears in her eyes—the easy tears of a drunk, some of them for herself. Her daughter's marriage to the richest kid in town had come violently apart. Veronica's own marriage had ended early, her husband a flaming Irish drunk who, like Finn, was the life of any party. At Christmas, it was cookies from Veronica and the strongest eggnog known to man, concocted by Rory Breen. By the time I went to college, his liver had gone south and he followed into an early grave. But his photograph was on every table, where Veronica could always call him back because the Irish know how to tear at their own hearts. She saw me studying his face.

"I love the foolish bastard still. This was a happy house, wasn't it?"

"Very happy." And to stay happy, she was plastered in the middle of the day.

Her sentimental smile faded. "Finn was just like Rory. That's why Bridget fell for him, don't you think?"

"I don't know. Her heart was hidden from me."

"Ah, that's right, you loved her." She studied me with bloodshot eyes. "You still love her."

"Probably."

"It's written all over your face. But I hear you're a monk, so that's that." Her gaze narrowed. "Unless you're just hiding your arse to stay out of trouble."

"I wouldn't be the first."

"But you came back for Bridget. I cherish you for that." Her gaze drifted to a photograph of Bridget in her majorette costume. "That's when you two had something going."

"She liked me, Veronica, but I didn't turn her on."

"Sure you did, but she got involved with that nutjob, Brian Fury."

"I didn't know that," I said, trying to keep dismay out of my voice. "Wasn't he much too old for her?"

"Of course he was. But she was always attracted to big shots, and at that age she confused cruelty with power. That's why she let him do things to her that a woman his own age wouldn't tolerate." Her emotions were taking a wild turn; the blood in her eyes turned to fire. "He hurt my girl, and I mean he *hurt* her."

She reached for her teacup, drained it, smacked the cup down. "I would've cut his arms off," she said, her mouth distorted by rage. There was real menace in her voice, the maker of the chocolate chip cookies gone now and, in her place, a vengeful being I never would have imagined lived inside the pretty widow. "Bridget's throat was bruised, and after I interrogated her she admitted he'd choked her. And he did other things I won't discuss. And now he's the district attorney, a big muckety-muck. Can you believe that?"

"I can. He tried to put me in jail."

"And that's why you became a monk?"

"It is."

"Hiding your arse, like I said."

I didn't protest.

"We kept it from her father, because if Rory knew what Brian did to Bridget, he would've killed him."

She looked down at the tea tray, then up at me, and in her eyes was something I used to see in Primo's eyes: the reptilian coldness necessary for carrying out an evil plan. But with Primo it was a constant. With Veronica it faded, slithering back down under whatever rock in the soul was its home. She sighed and stood. "I'm going to make a fresh cup for myself. How about you?"

"I'll guard the cookies."

She went back to the kitchen, and I looked at an old photograph of a middle-aged miner with a carbide lamp on his head, his face black with coal dust except for two white rings under his eyes, where he'd wiped the dust away. The photograph had been taken with a cheap camera, somewhere in the early 1900s. Veronica's great-great-grandfather Breen, gazing out as if from the dark hole he labored in, a creature of darkness. Was that where the anger in the family began?

Bridget's wedding photo was a brighter picture. She and Finn were a handsome couple, shining children of Coalville, but she was from a line of men who wore the carbide lamp. And Finn's family owned the lamp, the mine, and the miner.

"And he goes and gets himself murdered," said Veronica, coming up behind me.

"I don't think that was his plan."

"He had all the money in the world, and he had my lovely daughter. He could've sat back and enjoyed life. But no, he had to show off."

"Is that what he did?"

"Sweet Jesus, Tommy, use your loaf. Things don't change around here just because you point a TV camera at them. Those boys hit back." She set fresh cups down and gave me a pitying look, as if I'd forgotten how Coalville worked.

I didn't have to ask which boys. "You don't think he had a chance to improve the town?"

"Not a chance in hell. Drink your tea. Finn used to send for it.

He said the shite you get in a store is the sweepings from some floor in India."

"When you and Bridget talked about Finn, did she ever say she was afraid for him?"

"We talked about clothes. It was fluff." She pointed to a picture of Bridget in an evening gown. "It took us weeks to find that." She turned to me, tears in her eyes again. "Bring her back to me, Tommy."

"I will."

"The poor girl is frightened out of her mind; I can feel it." The anger sprang back into her voice. "Finn Sweeney telling us right from wrong—it's a joke." She picked up a cookie, held it delicately, her pinky extended. "If Granny wants to play the slots, let her."

"I'm with you there."

"A casino never hurt anyone. I love Atlantic City." She stood, picked up the photo of her late husband. "Rory and I used to go." She held the frame to her breast, closed her eyes, and turned gracefully as if dancing. She was really plastered now. She put the photo down, adjusted it carefully. "I'm so lonely without him." She looked at me, yearning in her eyes, for him in the photograph or for me, I couldn't tell. She'd always flirted with Bridget's friends, but it had been playful. I couldn't tell what she was up to today. I said, "It's time I headed out."

She tried to keep the conversation going. "Ever see the house Finn and Bridget built? Like a villa on the Riviera. Not that I've been to the Riviera."

"I'll drive by and take a look at it." I started toward the door.

"You were always sweet on her."

"There's no denying that."

"It's never too late." She was next to me now, giving me a motherly pat on the cheek.

I gave her my cell phone number. "Call me the minute you hear something."

"Take some cookies." She made up a little bag, handed them to me. "And come back, Tommy, for old times' sake."

There was desperation her voice. She would cling to me like a barnacle if I didn't get away. As it was, she followed me to the car. "This is pretty hot," she said, admiring the Charger. "You could be sixteen in a car like this."

"I'm sixteen without it. Never grow up, that's my motto."

"Come back and take me for a ride. Promise?"

"I promise." I was trying to get in, but she was holding my sleeve. She let go when I started the engine, so I didn't have to drag her down the road.

10

Station WVIM, from which Finn had lodged his attacks on the valley below, was housed in something that looked like a concrete bunker, and instead of the receptionist saying *How can I help you?*, she said, "You're Tommy Martini. I was a year behind you in school. I'm Queenie O'Malley."

"Queenie, sure, I remember."

"No, you don't, but that's okay." She held out her hand. "You're bigger than ever."

"I tried to stop growing, but it didn't work."

"Do you want a tour?"

"I want to find who killed Finn."

"So do I." Queenie O'Malley was the kind of Irish beauty the valley was famous for. She wore her dark hair in a slick pixie cut that went perfectly with her pale round face. Her big green eyes had two tones of eyeshadow to make them bigger, and her eyelashes were long and luminous, and I was swimming in them, wondering how I could have overlooked her in high school. "Let me introduce you to our station manager." She led me toward another knockout, a woman around thirty-five with a stack of file folders under her arm. She was in a two-piece business suit, and the authority she emanated was that of *woman-in-charge, and who are you?*

"Miranda, this is Tommy Martini, a friend of Finn's and one of my high school heroes."

I could see that Miranda wanted to be elsewhere. Her boss had been murdered and a message had been sent to the living: *Back off.* But she held out her hand. "My high school was in another state, so I missed your heroics."

"I miss them too."

"No college career?"

"Two years, and then I went into the wind."

"The wind to where?"

"Mexico, actually."

"And what's in Mexico?"

"A monastery."

"You're a monk?"

"I like a quiet life."

"Then what are you doing in a TV station? Come to think of it, what am *I* doing in one?" She looked at Queenie. "I've had an offer from a station in Florida."

"Manager?"

"Assistant. The money isn't great, but it's a long way from Coalville. Or I could do a naked newscast in Russia. That's even farther."

Queenie turned back to me. "We're all running a little scared since Finn's murder."

I said, "I got a call from him. The last one he ever made."

"What did he say?"

"He asked me to take care of his wife."

"The hero returns," said Miranda. Though fearing for her life, she was at heart a reporter. "Can we get an interview with you?"

I thought about Duke Devlin, who wouldn't give you two words in a dark alley. But I wasn't Duke Devlin, and Primo had told me in one of his life lectures, *Let the pricks know you're after them. It fucks with their nerve.* "Sure. Anytime you like."

"We'll tape you now and put you into the talking-heads show at eight o'clock." She looked at Queenie. "Tell me no and I won't do it."

"It's asking for trouble," said Queenie, "but it's what Finn would've done."

Miranda looked at me. "What do you think?"

"I like trouble."

"He likes trouble." She took my arm. "Come along, high school hero."

She led me to a studio with two couches angled toward each other and a low table in front of them. "Fuss will hook you up with a microphone."

Fuss was Jeffrey Goldfuss, a nerd whose world was a bank of computers, a digital sound board, and other devices for which I had no explanation. He hooked a mic to my shirt and went back to his lair. A light came on over the two couches, then a second, and a third one.

Miranda and I sat. The camera started moving by itself, coming closer to us, and I realized Fuss was controlling it from inside his sound booth. Miranda said, "We're waiting for Gabrielle."

"And Gabrielle is . . . ?"

"*Gabbing with Gabby*—it's her show." I thought Fuss might feel overwhelmed working with women, but then another male appeared, carrying a tray of cosmetics, brushes, sprays. He introduced himself as Kip, the makeup man. He was Black, had lean, muscular arms, and was astonishingly good-looking. With all the beauty Finn had assembled to run his station, it could have passed as a modeling agency.

He looked me over quickly. "The lights are distorting your skin tone and bringing out flaws."

"I was sent unfinished into the world."

"All you need is a nice blanket of coverage." He dipped into his makeup box. "And some contouring."

As he worked, I checked out his tattoos. In the vines that curled down from his right shoulder, I found a tiger peering out. Alongside it were three Japanese characters, identifying Kip as a practitioner of Shotokan karate.

He worked me over with his foundation powders and whatever else he required to subdue the effect of the strong lights. He stepped back, studied me again. "Ready for prime time." Then he packed his box and withdrew, leaving me on the couch with Miranda.

"Kip is sweet, isn't he?" she said. But I'd managed to see the long callus on the knife edge of his right hand, and it was like a car bumper. Unless I was much mistaken, he could break a brick with that hand.

"Yes, very sweet." And if you tried gay-bashing him, you'd be in for a surprise.

I looked at Fuss on the other side of the studio glass. He was gazing at Miranda the way a fish looks at the walls of its bowl, as something familiar but incomprehensible. I didn't understand her myself, except to see that she was genuinely frightened of being murdered.

"I've got a level on the guest," said Fuss over the intercom. His voice had a mechanical edge, as if he had just enough speech for limited exchanges.

Gabbing-with-Gabby appeared. She too was Black, and again it was model agency time, for she was stately and aloof, nine miles above me in self-confidence. Miranda told her a bit of my story. Gabby's smile was sympathetic. "When we talk, let your feeling come through."

She'd already taken my measure—a wild man from a monastery, who might be good for ratings. She pointed to the couches and said in a voice like velvet, "Shall we dance?"

Theme music for the show came on, then died away as she said, "I'm talking with Tommy Martini, a good friend of the man who ran this station—a man who was my friend too. We're all in shock over his death, perhaps none more than Tommy Martini, who received a call from Finn Sweeney just before he was murdered. Am I right about that?"

It was hot under the studio lights, and I wondered how the fuck I'd gotten there. That kind of reflection, when you make it, always comes too late. "I'm going to find the people who killed Finn. And I'm going to destroy them." The mindless intensity of my anger demon came out as I turned to the camera lens and said, "I'm coming for you."

Gabbing-with-Gabby chatted on as if I hadn't just threatened to kill someone, then turned away from me and faced the camera. "If anyone has any information regarding the death of Finn Sweeney, they should call the number on their screen. There will be somebody here twenty-four hours a day to take your call." After ten minutes more of question-and-answer, she closed it down and Miranda came toward me from the sound booth. "The camera likes you. Ever think of a career in broadcasting?"

"It's at the top of my list."

When I returned to the reception area, Queenie was at her desk, working with a computer stylus, tracing something on her screen, and suddenly I knew who she was. She was the girl who had drawn cartoons for our school magazine. She'd done one of the football team.

I nodded toward the stylus in her hand. "You still draw."

Her face brightened. "You *do* remember me."

"It wasn't easy. You've changed your look."

"Kip did it for me. You like?"

"Absolutely. What about dinner?"

She held out her other hand. On it was an engagement ring. "You're too late."

"Just my luck."

"I thought you were a monk."

"I don't know what I am."

"You're Tommy Martini, captain of the football team."

"Ancient history."

"Not for me." She got up slowly from her chair—soft and round, and I don't mean the chair. "I keep a scrapbook," she said. "There are two whole Tommy Martini pages."

Sparks were jumping between us. She asked, "Why didn't you come back sooner?"

"I was praying."

"Well, I was getting engaged, so that's that."

"I want to see you again."

"Business hours only."

"Who's the guy? Do I know him?"

"Richard Mittleman. He's in business with his dad. Mittleman Produce."

"One of their trucks went off the road when I was helping my uncle

Silvio. We pulled the truck out of a mud bank. The driver gave us a crate of oranges."

"It might've been Richard."

"Why are you marrying him?"

"For his oranges." She gave me a poke with her stylus. "You'd better go."

II

When I got to my Charger, Kip was climbing into his own set of wheels, metallic red, top down——a Mazda Miata. He glanced over at my red Charger. "Sister ships."

"Is there a decent bar around here?"

In minutes, we were standing at a smooth white marble bar that made you want to rub it while you drank. Reflected in the bar mirror was a bright array of bottles promising advanced alcohol dreams. Booze is a poor substitute for anger medication. *You're liable to kill someone*, my doctor had said when he prescribed Eufexor, but since I'd already killed a number of people, I didn't see the need to deprive myself of the banked fire of rage in my guts. It had been there since childhood, probably because I'd been raised by a mobster. *I'm always angry*, Grandfather Primo had said. *It saves time.*

I asked Kip how he'd gotten into the beauty business.

"Ten months, fifteen hundred hours, and twenty thousand bucks. Are you interested in hair-relaxing theory?"

"My hair's relaxed, but I'm not."

"I can see that. So drink up."

We drank up and ordered another. He said, "I listened to your interview. You're a monk."

"It takes all kinds."

"But you're out on leave? The monks don't mind?"

"They've got their own problems." I pointed to the tiger tattoo. "Karate?"

"I've had a few lessons." He'd had more than a few, but you learn modesty in the martial arts. His eyes met mine in the mirror. "What about you?"

"I did some wrestling. Mostly I just tear people apart."

We concentrated on our beer for a while. Then I asked him how well he'd known Finn.

"When he bought WVIM, I thought he was just a jerk with too much money. But one day, we got a call at the station from a kid who said his dog had been stolen. Finn did some digging and found out there was a dogfight outside town every Saturday night."

I was remembering the dog that had hung out with us in Finn's bedroom when we were kids ourselves. He was a bullmastiff named Pigwiggen, and I liked wrestling with him. And I remember Finn looking into Pigwiggen's stubborn, loyal, brutish face and saying, *That's the purest love on Earth.*

"The cops looked the other way about the dogfighting ring, but with the station making things hot for them, they busted the operators, and Finn put the kid and the dog on the air. It made great TV, that chewed-up mutt with one ear half gone and a bandage on his nose. The kid with an arm around him, of course. The station lit up with callers, and Finn suddenly had all kinds of causes to fight for. But I wondered if all his causes came back to the kid with the dog. Like that's what he was really fighting for all along."

"How well do you know Bridget?"

"I do her hair."

"I'm looking for information here."

"We talk about bad dye jobs."

"Nothing else?"

"If somebody shot my husband, I'd be in a wig and dark glasses on a plane to Paris. But Bridget is a hometown girl."

"So she might be hiding out with a friend?"

"She wasn't very girly-girly, if you know what I mean."

I was remembering Bridget as head majorette at halftime. White uniform trimmed with sequins, cut high on the thighs. My teammates and I would be coming back out from the locker room, and the majorettes would be finishing their routine, with Bridget leading—always the center of attention, in a barroom or on a ball field.

A young couple entered the bar and the guy said, "I think somebody just stole the red Charger that was parked outside."

Kip and I headed for the door. "My car," he said. The top was down and we hopped in.

The Charger's distinctive taillights—long horizontal red streaks— were still visible on the narrow two-lane road. I saw the large shaved, round head of the car thief, the hunched shoulders of a passenger swayed with the car. Feeling us on his tail, the thief floored the Charger. The rear end fishtailed, and I knew he wasn't used to vintage muscle cars. He stole new cars with computers controlling the engine and transmission, along with the braking and steering angles. The Charger was a primitive beast that made heavy demands on you when you called on its power, and he'd just experienced the shock of the beast jumping sideways on him.

Kip closed on him, and the driver executed a wild turn down an even smaller country lane. He immediately spun out the other way and barely brought the Charger back under control. Kip pulled up alongside it and we got a good look at the driver—a very big man with his mouth hanging open in wonder.

"It's Prince Gran-Gran," said Kip. "He used to sew on zippers in a pants factory in Haiti. He came here and found stealing cars was easier."

Prince Gran-Gran lost it completely, spinning out onto the shoulder and then into a drainage ditch. The rear wheels spun in mud up to the axles, whining in frustration but getting no traction.

The big man knew he was screwed. The Charger was tilted on its side, and he had to push against the door with both hands, which prevented him from pulling his piece. I helped him the rest of the way out, yanking him by his shirt. He flailed wildly with both fists, but I drew him tight against me to spoil his leverage and butted him in head. He buckled, and I settled for a hammer fist to the top of his naked dome. Two fists to the temples would have been sweet, but it might've killed him. As it was, he went facedown into the drainage ditch, but he quickly rose up like a mud-covered buffalo and drove me across the road with his head against my chest. If he'd had horns, he would have caved in my rib cage. I lost my balance, and he landed on top of me.

Like many big men, Prince Gran-Gran relied on weight instead of technique, and I rolled him before he knew up from down. His eyes opened wide in surprise at being turned so easily, and suddenly I saw a guy from a pants factory who was far from home. He'd come across the Caribbean to get hammered in a ditch, and I was a monk in the order of Benedict; it wasn't in me to waste the guy, so I just grabbed his piece and tossed it into the nearby field.

His companion was crawling out of the Charger, gun drawn. Kip was on the roof, holding a baseball bat. No fancy karate kicks, just one swing through the strike zone. The other car thief's head went sideways; he twisted slowly around, then sank into the mud. Kip hadn't swung for the fences, and the guy's eyes were open as he stared up at me, trying to figure out why he was on the ground. I separated him from his weapon, handed it to Kip.

We waited until he and Prince Gran-Gran crawled out of the mud, looking as if they'd spent a hard day in the cane fields. Prince Gran-Gran asked, "Why you butt me in the head?"

"You tried to steal my car."

"Just for fun." He smiled. He had a resilient nature.

"Well, just for fun, you're going to push it out of the mud."

Kip held the gun on them as I got behind the wheel and they got behind the Charger. Now we were just four guys trying to get a car out of the mud. There were instructions, curses in Creole, renewed efforts, and then a cheer as it broke free. I looked at Prince Gran-Gran. "You walk home, zipper man."

"Long way. How 'bout a lift?"

"Not going to happen."

He looked respectfully at the Charger, whose power had proved too much for him. "Devil car. Keep it."

"Thanks, and if you steal it one more time, I'll have to kill you."

"Sure. Hundred percent."

12

When you visit a mob boss, you bring flowers because his wife is going to open the door. I handed Misty Branca the biggest bouquet I'd been able to find, and said, "When I was a kid, I used to dream about you."

"And look at you now, all grown-up." She was a dyed-blond beauty, pushing sixty without a wrinkle, her bronzed skin tightened by expensive creams or even more expensive surgery. Her smile was warm, but her eyes were those of all the women of my childhood—gangster wives with gazes as cold as the diamonds they wore. They'd fascinated me then, and she fascinated me now, letting me bask in her beauty, but I sensed wariness. She didn't know how I stood with her husband, and neither did I.

"Are you back to stay, Tommy?"

"I'm just in town for a visit."

"I won't keep you. But we should catch up later, okay?" She pointed me toward a hallway. I checked out the family photos hanging there: kids and grandkids, and Phil's father, an old-time bookie smiling at the camera, a cigarette stuck behind one ear. Misty came up softly behind me. "He's in his study. He'll be glad to see you. Little Joe is with him," she warned.

The door to the study was open, but I tapped anyway and Little Joe opened it. He was enormous, and not from steroid use. He was one of those human beings predisposed to carrying huge amounts of muscle mass. His hands were like manhole covers. His suit was single breasted in the style of all bodyguards, for easy cross-drawing of a handgun. He gave me a nod but didn't pat me down—a sign of respect for my position in the family.

Phil Branca got up from his desk. As I was his cousin and the grandson of his old boss, he greeted me with an embrace and a kiss on both cheeks. He stepped back, gazing at me with his dead moon eyes. "You leave your halo with Misty?"

"They haven't issued me one yet."

He looked more like a monk than I did, with a bald dome and a close-cropped wreath of hair that didn't rise much above his ears. Primo's mantle had been passed to the member of his crew murderous enough to merit it. And that was Phil. "You look good, Tommy. All muscle and no fat. Primo would be pleased."

Phil himself was a fine physical specimen, shorter than I was but a strong side of beef anyway you sliced it. He'd started as a bodyguard, but he had brains, so Primo had elevated him quickly and after a lifetime of service had given him the crown. "Have a seat. You want something? Coffee? Tea? A cannoli?"

"I'm fine, Phil." I took a seat across from him. Little Joe remained standing behind me. I tried to ignore his hovering, ominous form as I spoke to Phil. "Congratulations on taking over the reins."

"Headaches and heartburn. But there are compensations."

Gangster etiquette was expected here, so I reached into my pocket. "Please accept this small gift in recognition of your new leadership." I slid a Cartier watch toward him. Roman numerals on a white dial, alligator band. It had cost me four grand.

He took off his thick presidential Rolex and slipped on the Cartier. He looked at it on his wrist, then looked back at me. "You know what I don't like?"

"Something about the watch?"

"The watch is fine." He'd expressed his affection, taken my tribute, and now we were down to business. "In this family, we don't go on TV. But I tune in and there you are, mouthing off about righting the wrongs of the world." He paused, looking at the watch, twisting it this way and that. "You were raised by a crook, but you act like a saint. Which is it?"

"I was following Primo's advice."

"He talks to you from hell?"

"I remember his instructions. *Smoke out your enemies.*"

"Tommy, any time a mob-connected individual goes on TV, it usually results in somebody going to jail. So you will not go on TV. Is that clear?"

"It won't happen again."

"I'm gratified to hear that." Then, to keep me off balance in true mob boss fashion, he switched moods. "I can testify to Primo's love for you. He made me go to all your football games."

"I knew you were there."

"Every one of us was there. We wouldn't have missed it, right, Joe?"

Joe grunted from behind me—a deep guttural sound, as if a dinosaur were taking a difficult crap.

Phil swiveled back and forth in his leather desk chair. Then he centered himself on me again. "How do you know *I* didn't kill your pal?"

"Because it was done on his own property."

Little Joe grunted an acknowledgment of this. Primo's rule regarding a killing: It's never done in a man's own house, or while he's enjoying a barbecue in the backyard. *Even a rat deserves some respect.* I wondered how much I could ask of Phil, then took a shot. "His wife's gone missing."

"Not my problem." Our gazes locked. "What, it's yours?"

"Just before Finn was whacked, he asked me to take care of her."

"I never listen to deathbed requests. And I've had lots of them. You want to work for me?"

"I'm honored, Phil. But Primo told me to stay out of the life."

"You wouldn't have to hurt anybody. At least not too much."

"I try to avoid violence."

"You cracked a Haitian in the head with a baseball bat."

"Actually, that was done by a gay hairdresser."

"Maybe I should hire him instead." He looked at his new watch again, nodding his satisfaction. Then he looked back up at me. "When you were growing up here, it was different. Cops, crooks, civilians—we watched out for each other. There was harmony. We hijacked trucks, the cops got their cut, and the civilians got a turkey at Christmas. You understand what I'm saying?"

I nodded my assent, and he continued. "But now it's changed. These fucking Albanians—"

"Russians," corrected Little Joe.

"Russians, Albanians. They'll be up our asses dry if we let them. Then your pal Sweeney starts making trouble for me."

"What kind of trouble?"

"He was trying to shoot down the casino. Which is stupid because it's going to bring a lot of money into the community. Some of my card games will suffer, but I accept that." He made a gesture indicating his own selflessness. "With the casino, people around here will get hired. Maids, valets, whatever. You get the picture."

The picture I got was Phil getting his cut from the casino, somehow, somewhere, like a slot machine payoff—three cherries in a row, and little bells ringing.

He made another gesture. "And people who say it brings a bad element, people like your dead friend, are better off dead. And since you've got somebody's ear at the TV station, tell them to lay off the casino story."

"They're already running scared."

"Then make them run a little faster. Tell them to do a story about the mine fires. I can smell that fucking coal gas in my basement. You know I have mine insurance?"

"I didn't know that."

"If there's a cave-in under the neighborhood and all our dishes fall on the floor and break, my insurance company pays."

He signaled Little Joe with a flick of his finger, and Joe opened the door for me. He squeezed the back of my neck with the lever action of locking pliers. "Nice to see you, kid."

Misty was waiting for me in the kitchen. She saw that no blood had been spilled, so she could relax. "Come on, talk to me."

I sat across from her and told her how beautiful she looked. She laughed away the compliment and said, "You loved the ladies when you were this high." Her palm was level with her knees. "Are you going to look up any of your old flames while you're in town?"

"I might."

"I bet their little hearts will go pitter-pat."

I took a bite of cannoli. The sweet cream burst across my taste buds. "Delicious."

"I make them myself. The secret is white wine in the dough. Who's the old flame? Maybe I know her."

"Bridget Breen. But first I have to find her."

"That shouldn't be hard."

"Turns out it is. She's gone into hiding."

At which point Misty shut down. Her eyes were rock hard again. I finished my cannoli and said it was time to go.

She walked me to the door. "Thank you for the flowers. You always were a gentleman."

I kissed her cheek. "Don't tell Phil I used to dream about you."

"You don't dream about me anymore?"

"I don't want to hasten my end."

"So forget about Bridget Breen." She made me take a bag of cannolis with me when I left.

13

Red and blue misery lights began rotating behind me. The siren was mounted low on the front bumper of the cop car, and a short 110-decibel burst felt like an electric eel crawling up my ass.

I parked beside a boarded-up department store. Graffiti took the place of a window display. Scrawled in red letters three feet high was the name RUBY. A snake was coiled around the letters, and in its mouth was a red apple. The cop car pulled in behind me. I was waiting with my license and registration, but the cop didn't need identification. Standing at the driver's-side window, uniform nicely pressed, belt heavy with gear, he said, "Follow my car, Martini."

So he knew Silvio's Charger, who was driving it, and where to find it. The evil eye of local law enforcement had scanned me into its system.

I followed him to the courthouse, an old granite structure resembling a castle. Its round towers had gun emplacements carved out of them, just to give the look of power. I already felt it—a somber presence that wants to unnerve you before you even get to its doors. We climbed a wide flight of stone stairs and passed between stone pillars gray with age.

"Through there," said the uniform. The glass door was the only modern touch to the face of the building. It opened automatically, and I was met by a security guard who ran a metal detector over me and finished by patting me down.

We were in a large rotunda, with high old ceilings and a framed photograph of the governor. He had silvery hair and calculating eyes, which, according to Duke, had looked with disfavor on Finn Sweeney.

I followed the cop over a marble floor. At its center was a decorative compass of black marble. It had pointed at me, and I had come.

"Stairs or elevator?" asked the cop, as if I were disabled.

We took the wide stairs, with an elaborately carved banister beside us. Primo had always had somebody on the inside here, somebody in his pay who could tell him the mood of the castle and deliver a message or a fix. But that time was gone.

Two white globes were on each side of the upper staircase, no light in them at the moment, their round shapes like faces of the dead. Ahead of me were offices with high old doors, their glass frosted at the beginning of the previous century. We came to one on which was lettered in commanding black: DISTRICT ATTORNEY BRIAN FURY. The cop pushed it open, and we stepped through.

Fury was wearing a summer sport coat of pale blue. His white shirt collar was open, his tie hanging loose over his broad chest. He was upper-world Irish and he'd enjoyed all the blessings the valley could bestow on one of its privileged sons. His father was a judge, which had made him untouchable in his teens—a time during which he'd been known as a sadistic prick.

He nodded toward his secretary. "No calls."

"You've got it," she said, chirpy as a cheerleader, and she wasn't cheering for me.

We went back out through the frosted door and walked to the far end of the hallway, past other frosted doors. All the political games of Coalville were played here, and Fury knew how they were played. Primo had known, too, but he was in the ninth circle of hell unless the afterlife had provided him with a brilliant lawyer.

"We go down here," said Fury, indicating a back staircase—less grand, leading to the basement of the castle. The bulbs of the staircase were caged and cast grim institutional light on the steps. It was not a dungeon but a close relative, and at the bottom of the staircase was a mean-looking warren of maintenance rooms.

The room we entered had only one wooden chair, pushed up against the granite wall. Steam pipes ran along the ceiling, where a single bare lightbulb hung. Fury closed the door behind us, its hinges groaning. Then he slipped the tongue of the latch bolt into place, followed by the clunkier action of a dead bolt. The door was heavy and would muffle sounds from within. He removed his sport coat and hung it on the doorknob. He was tall, his hair closely trimmed, his cologne an expensive concoction dabbed on earlier in the day—just a few discreet touches to underscore his charming presence.

"No one will bother us here," he said, smiling. "Have a seat. It's a comfortable chair. It has testimonials to its comfort."

As children, our paths had rarely crossed. We were separated by class and age, but I'd always known who he was and had avoided him since his reputation for cruelty had been firmly established. Example: I'm age five, prowling the alleyways because you never know what you might find. And I'd found Fury, ten years older than me and accompanied by several of his pals. At that age, older kids are titans, unpredictable and generally thought to be malevolent. A garter snake was wriggling between his fingers. At his feet was a circle of stone with a fire at its center. He tossed the garter snake into the flames and laughed as it squirmed to escape. My comic-book mind believed he was performing an evil spell. I waited until he and his pals left, and then I walked to the circle of stones. The snake had been burned black and was like a stiff, twisted pretzel. Feeling the evil spell still hovering in the alleyway, I hurried away. Now, gazing into his eyes, I knew that the spell had been designed to last through the years. And I was in it still.

He took out a tin of little sweets and popped one, probably in place of the cigarette he really wanted. Rolling the sweet around in his mouth, he said, "I've dreamed of this day, Martini, as you no doubt realize."

Primo had schooled me for this kind of encounter. His teaching was simple. *Say nothing.*

"The elves and the leprechauns have returned you to me, allowing me to say, welcome back, asshole."

I watched him closely, measuring the degree of his sadistic madness.

The light of the single bulb shone on his patrician face, its only flaw the button nose that gave him his boyish look. I wondered if his sadism was to make up for it. He said, "Eight years ago, I had you for killing Mike Muldoon, and I was told it was time to bring the Martini family down. The orders came from on high. *Get Primo's kid on murder two. Put him away for ten years minimum. Show those jumped-up guineas they're not above the law.*"

The sweet candy, a little red thing with a faint odor of cinnamon, slipped across his teeth. The sweet reached the far corner and melted into his smile. "Those were the words put in my ear by a very important person, someone crucial to my advancement. I was told that yours was the kind of case the newspapers love, the kind that builds careers. But you beat the rap. And my advancement was put on hold. In certain circles, I'm still thought of as the guy Primo Martini fucked over. It has left me with a bad feeling. You might say I've been emotionally wounded."

The sweet reappeared, slightly smaller now, and began its slide back across his teeth. I was staring at it when he hammered me on the jaw. My head twisted sideways, and he slammed me against the wall.

"Don't hold back, Martini; it's just us. What happens in this room will never leave it."

My anger doctor had said, *Pinpoint the exact reason why you feel angry.* I knew the fucking reason. But there was a camera hidden in this room somewhere. The footage would be edited to show me striking the district attorney without provocation and the judge would be a guy he played golf with. With a tremendous effort, I kept my arms at my side.

"Well, then, fuck it," he said, "I might as well have some fun."

His next punch drove the back of my head into the granite wall. I blacked out for a moment and wound up on the floor. The bare bulb swung over us, lighting one side of his face and then the other, embellishing his psychopathic grin.

"I'm enjoying this, Martini. What about you?"

Blood had gone from my gut to my muscles, signaling flight or fight. I couldn't do either. His face was right over mine. "When you walked on a criminal homicide charge, I lost traction in my career. Carefully laid plans . . . were . . . disrupted." He punctuated his pauses with kicks to my kidneys. It felt like a cattle prod, as if shock waves were shooting through my body. If he kept it up, I'd be pissing blood through a catheter.

He reached down, put his fingers into my hair, and twisted my head up toward him. "I've prayed for this since the day your greasy grandfather sprang you." He punched me in the face and threw me back to the floor. "He got to somebody. And word went around town that Brian Fury was outplayed by a Mafia hood."

I was hoping there was only one more kick in him. He was a busy man, after all.

"But now Primo's dead," he continued, "and I'm still young and beautiful."

Would he hit me with the chair? But if he killed me, his fun would be over.

"You see, Martini, I don't reign alone. I perform at the pleasure of those who have gone before me and are perfected. One of them is Ben Sweeney. A big man in Coalville. I got a phone call from him yesterday. He told me to give you his best regards. So here they are." His shoe buried itself right through to my liver, and I heard Ben Sweeney's voice in my head: *There's a gun in this house and I'm tempted to use it.* Having fought down that temptation, he'd found a different way to punish me for being his son's friend.

Fury straddled me, looking down, and I saw the rich kid who burned snakes alive for the fun of it. He was still that kid. Nothing had developed in him but his sadism.

He prodded my chin with the toe of his shoe. "I saw that grandstand performance you gave on TV. So did those people I mentioned earlier. The ones who live on high. They called me in. They said, *Here's that fucking greaseball you let get away.*" He lifted my chin so that we were looking at each other. "My future is in their hands, Martini. All my joy, my mental health, and the smoothness of my arteries. I don't know how it will play out. I like to think I will soar into national prominence.

If not, I'll work off my disappointment by beating the shit out of you on a regular basis."

If he kicked me one more time, I was going to kill him in the basement and then run to Mexico. I could lose myself in Veracruz, somewhere along its four hundred miles of coastline.

The toe of his shoe lifted my chin again. "I heard you went into a monastery. What a crock of shit."

He gazed at me, trying to figure me out. I'd taken a beating and hadn't struck back, which had denied him complete satisfaction. And my monastic connection puzzled him. As if to counter it, he said, "I support a number of Catholic charities."

He spit the remains of his red candy in my face. Then he put on his sport coat, unlocked the door, and closed it behind him. Maybe he came down here often. He seemed completely comfortable with the space. Just the right amount of kicking room.

I sat for a while in the chair he had offered earlier. Then I turned off the light, like a model citizen, with one punch of my fist. The light-bulb swung, sputtering into darkness, and I left it swinging there and went up the steps to the hallway. I proceeded to the white globes at the head of the staircase. They were still unlit, old ghosts wondering where their energy had gone. For the moment, mine had been kicked out of me. I navigated the white marble stairs with some difficulty, but I finally reached the main floor and stood in the center of the black marble compass. My ribs were hurting, but I could see all four points of the compass clearly. I had a large bump on the back of my head, but I was more or less myself. I checked out the governor's photograph on the wall. His benevolent look said, *My friends, I want to bring you a world-class casino.*

And then I was breathing freely, though painfully, outside in the parking lot. There were some cop cars, some cheap government vehicles, and those of the big wheels in the courthouse—a BMW, an Audi, a Mercedes, and a vintage Plymouth hardtop, circa 1961. I wondered who the collector was. Then I saw the license plate: DABF.

District Attorney Brian Fury.

I got into my Charger and drove by the dead and dying businesses once again. A junkie was conversing with himself in a lively manner. A knot of teenagers on the corner were high-fiving each other. One of them was a foot and a half taller than the rest. A kid that size knows how to bounce a basketball. I could see the golden dream around him. His basketball would bounce him out of this town, off the street of the dead.

14

I was applying ice to my jaw when Knucklehead called. "Meet me at the old Adeline mine in an hour."

It was closed when I got there, but the guy who ran the operation was a friend of Knucklehead's. "We get schoolkids coming here with their teachers," said Stashu. "Don't ask me why."

For a few bucks, a vintage mine car will take you down. Its four doors had once opened to a full shift of miners on their way to a day's work in the dark. It was lowered by a cable, and its wheels ran on narrow-gauge rails that disappeared into the steep slope of the mine. I was peering into it when Knucklehead arrived. He looked at my swollen jaw and forehead but said nothing.

"Going down, gents," said Stashu. Knucklehead and I sat side by side as the daylight receded and the depths of the mine opened before us. Just beyond the mouth of the shaft was an antique warning sign announcing what a miner should do if injured. It was in six languages. English headed the list, then German and Italian. In answer to my question, Stashu said the other three were Polish, Hungarian, and Czech.

The cable kept the car from flying wildly down the steep slope, and the dank air of the shaft greeted us like the breath of an underground giant. As we descended, Knucklehead reminisced about us playing as kids in a mineshaft in our part of town. When the owners sold out, they'd done a half-assed job of sealing the mine, and we easily pried off some rotten boards. The adventure was in seeing how far we could get before the mine gas asphyxiated us. "Completely nuts," said Knucklehead.

"But fun."

"We were twisted."

"We're not twisted now?"

"I'm a city magistrate, my boy. My oath of office forbids it."

The car rumbled slowly down the shaft. After ten minutes we leveled off. The transition was marked by the mannequin of a child stationed at a pair of swinging doors. A descriptive sign told us his real-life counterpart had worked the swinging doors to let fresh air into the mine. Knucklehead said, "This is why I stopped jerking off and went to college."

Stashu braked the cable car and equipped us with hard-hat lamps. "You can walk through the doors. I'll be down that spur." He pointed to a small passageway that had been blasted through the rock. Then he put on his headlamp and walked off, carrying a small pick and bucket. Knucklehead explained that there were still odd pieces of coal to be had, and Stashu sold them to tourists as souvenirs. When Stashu's lamp disappeared into the darkness, Knucklehead and I pushed through the swinging doors. "What are we doing here?"

"Having a private talk."

Our headlamps illuminated the rails ahead and the damp, glistening walls on both sides of us. Anything spoken down here was not going to be heard above. Then I saw two eyes glowing ahead of us in the dark. They belonged to a stuffed donkey. The display sign informed us that from never seeing the sun, donkeys went blind in the mines. Knucklehead stopped beside the donkey and said to me, "Sorry you got a beating today. I didn't know he'd take it that far."

"He's pissed about Primo getting me off for killing Mike Muldoon."

"He's a psychopath. Everybody knows it, but what can you do? His father's a judge."

I ran my hand over the donkey's coarse hair. It was matted with mine dust. I was sensing Knucklehead's reluctance to talk about Brian Fury, but being three hundred feet underground was going to make it easier for him to open up to me. His lamp played slowly over the glass eyes of the donkey as he said, "I had relatives die down here. What about you?"

"The Martinis weren't miners." To escape this ride into the earth, some enterprising Martini in 1920 or thereabouts had realized there was easier money to be made working in a different underworld, of whore-houses and gambling dens, exchanging dank air for perfume and poker.

Knucklehead had already committed himself to bringing me into the loop, so I waited until he said, "Fury has shut down the investigation into Finn's death."

"Why?"

"Orders from the governor."

"How does that work?"

"It's complicated."

"Uncomplicate it for me. I feel like this donkey."

Knucklehead patted the back of the donkey, and mine dust floated up into the beam of my headlamp. "The governor said something like, *This guy with the TV station* . . . and a certain expression crossed his face, and the ball started rolling downhill and along the way an interested party said, *It stops here.* At that point, Finn was a marked man."

"But why?"

"With all due respect, the governor is a bigger crook than your late grandfather. I've been to some of his fundraisers. After he shook my hand, I checked that I still had my wallet and watch. When the new casino opens, he stands to make a great deal of money, but the legislation okaying it could still be overturned if there's enough public outcry. Finn was leading that outcry."

When he saw me pondering this, he added, "Those at the top don't fuck around. If you annoy them, they kill you. It's much easier than battling it out in a public forum."

He took a few more steps into the darkness. "It's not just this gambling legislation that's rotten. The town is rotten. The state is rotten. I'm rotten." He tapped on one of the beams supporting the ceiling. "This has been down here a hundred years. Wrestled into place by a Polack named Nowitzki." The light from his headlamp played over the beam. "He was a better man than I'll ever be. I have his lunch pail, a battered tin box with a little handle. To carry a bologna sandwich and a flask of rotgut."

Knucklehead ran his hand reverently over the aged timbers and sighed. "I come down here to remember what it is to be a decent human being. Only a memory, you understand."

"Why don't you quit?"

"A question I ask myself every day."

"And?"

"I've had to kiss ass and chew glass, but I'm the youngest magistrate in the state. I'm going somewhere in politics. And when we get back up to the bright light of day and breathe the air of corruption, I'll feel just fine. It's only down here that I falter. Let's go a little deeper. Let's get close to the gas. For old times' sake."

We continued walking. I already had a headache from the beating, so I couldn't tell if the fumes were getting to me. But the smell of the gas was stronger. We came to a pillar of coal and stone on which a fading sign still hung. MAIN SUPPORT. DO NOT ROB.

"Robbing the pillars," said Knucklehead. "Ever hear that expression?"

I was getting dizzy. I leaned my head against the pillar. Knucklehead said, "They calculated how many of these pillars were necessary to keep the roof from caving in." He pointed to a signature on the sign. "Mining engineer. Long gone."

I felt I was going to puke. "I'm starting to cave. Let's get out of here."

He ignored me. "Finn was robbing the pillars." The bright beam of his lantern drilled into my tearing eyes. "He thought he was the good guy, but if he'd had his way the town would have collapsed."

We walked back up the shaft toward the swinging doors and pushed through them. The child mannequin was still standing there, gazing up the mineshaft, waiting for the ghost crew. Knucklehead put two fingers to the corners of his mouth and whistled. It was the same piercing whistle I'd heard him use when we were kids, and his dog would come barreling out of the woods or bushes, hound ears flapping. Now it was Stashu coming out of the darkness toward us, carrying a bucket of coal. We got back into the mine car and started the slow ride back. I gazed at the rock walls and the scars left by blasting powder and jack-hammers. I could take no pride in seeing how men had worked for a day's wages in hell. The Martinis had been just as strong, just as tough, but they mined desire, that richest of all veins.

Back on the surface, I took huge gulps of fresh air. Knucklehead looked at me and said, "You're not as tough as you used to be."

"I've had a hard day."

"When I got knocked out for the eighteenth time, I knew boxing was no longer a viable career choice."

"Are you trying to tell me something?"

"I wouldn't dream of it." He looked around the darkened neighborhood. The lights of the Adeline mine went dark. Stashu was going home.

I looked at Knucklehead's misshapen nose, which made him look even more like a character from another planet. "Thanks for the tour."

"Let's do it again sometime. After your next bout with Brian Fury."

"I'll win the next one."

"That's what I used to say. And I'd wind up on the canvas with little birds singing around my head."

15

"Bridget is at a cathouse in Bellefontaine," said Duke, beside me in his Cadillac. "She's drugged out of her mind by some Russian nutjobs. They shot her so full of quaaludes, she thinks she's on the fucking moon."

"They'll sell her on."

"Sure, she's too recognizable around here. She'll wind up in Saudi Arabia. But we'll get her out before that happens. It'd be good to have a third man to improve our position. You know somebody we can trust who's good with his hands?"

"What about Little Joe?"

"Little Joe is easily irritated, and I don't want dead Russians left lying around when we leave."

"When I see them holding Bridget, I'm going to be very irritated." But I pulled out my phone and left a message for Kip. A minute later, he rang back. I said, "Bridget's being held by some Russian pimps, and I need help, but it could get hairy."

"Hair is what I do," said Kip. "We'll get her, and I'll touch up her roots."

He gave me the address where he was and said he'd be waiting. I hung up and turned to Duke. "You know where the New Wave Hair Salon is?"

"He's getting his hair cut?"

"He gives them. It's a beauty salon."

"Our third man is a barber?"

"It's one of his skills."

New Wave Hair Salon displayed photoshopped beauty images in the window. Inside were ladies sitting in gleaming chairs, their figures wrapped in dark-colored luminescent gowns to catch hair clippings. They weren't dreaming of mayhem. The contrast between their mood and mine was sobering. Here was the normal world, and I was in a distorted reality, anger twisting my will toward destruction. The monastery seemed far behind me now. I asked Duke for a cigarette. The blue jet from his lighter might just as well have been coming from my eyeballs.

Kip came out, his hair now in many colors of the rainbow. He had earrings in both ears. His jeans were fashionably torn at the knees. His walk was slightly grand, as if he were a diva coming down a runway.

Duke was staring. "You've got to be shitting me."

"Shotokan karate, very fast."

"He looks like a Barbie doll."

"Only superficially."

"Where did you find him?"

"He does makeup at the TV station."

"Christ al-fucking-mighty," muttered Duke, unlocking the doors of the Caddy. Kip slid in and I introduced him.

"Pleased to meet you," said Kip, leaning forward in his rainbow hair. He was a fighting machine tempered by chemicals from Clairol.

Duke placed a call through the speaker system in his car, and we heard a young woman answer. She sounded like she was eight years old. Apparently, she'd been expecting the call, for we heard her tell Duke that he could come by anytime.

He said, "I've got two friends with me now."

"No problem," said the girl, without expression, adding us to the immense well of boredom where she seemed to be dwelling.

"We'll be there in fifteen minutes."

"No problem," she repeated with even less effort at actual communication.

Duke rang off and looked back over his shoulder at Kip. "So you do hair?" He said this as if talking to a hand puppet leaning toward him from the back seat.

"Hair, makeup, whatever."

"But you can handle yourself if things go sideways."

"When necessary."

"It might be very fucking necessary."

"I like Bridget. She's a friend."

On the night of the Hatian car thieves, Kip had told me he'd grown up on the streets running errands for pimps, loan sharks, and small-time hoods until he saved enough money to go to beauty school. There he'd learned to cut and color hair, but from the street he'd learned loyalty, and as he said, Bridget was a friend.

We drove out of Coalville along the river of rust. We crossed railroad tracks at the edge of town, and then we were in Bellefontaine and the seedy remains of a century of mining in the Northeast—beat-up houses, pawnshops, and plenty of bars. An individual who had chosen methamphetamines for his pleasure was walking along, limbs twitching as if he'd been bitten by a snake. His face had an even layer of dirt on it, and through it shone his youth, but as if it belonged to someone else, someone forgotten.

"Just bury him," said Duke.

The young man met another meth head, and they huddled together on the street corner. They looked like a pair of alien travelers dying in a dimension their bodies couldn't handle. In a nearby vacant lot was a burned-out school bus, weeds growing up around its tires. It seemed to go with the burned-out young men. They could get in it and drive it through a crack in time, back to their own world.

Like Coalville, Bellefontaine was built above a mine in which a huge pocket of gas was building toward an explosion. So was I, fists opening and closing.

"Martini is ready for ten rounds," said Duke.

I said, "It won't last that long."

"Don't hit anybody until I make my move. We want to be deep into the place so we can get Bridget out in one piece."

"I hear you."

"But there's smoke coming from your ears."

"I'll be fine."

"So," said Duke, "let's go get laid."

When we were twelve, Knucklehead and I had ridden our bicycles to Bellefontaine in the hopes of getting laid. When we knocked on a well-known cathouse door, the madam wouldn't even open it. She'd paid off the police, but underage kids were not covered by the payment. So we'd ridden away, two brokenhearted young johns.

Now, posing as johns, Duke, Kip, and I got out of the car in front of an old house with porch railings of gray twisted wood showing through peeling paint. The clapboard was cracked, some of the cracks huge, and sagging like an old mouth.

"Love the curtains," said Kip. They were a ripped and bilious yellow, hanging unevenly.

We walked to the front porch. The door, like the porch railing, looked as if it would come apart with a single kick. I was calculating the force that would be needed when Duke growled at me, "Smile, goddamn it. We're here to get laid, not pull the building down."

A young woman acting as receptionist opened the door. She was wearing a pale green dressing gown that matched her eyes, which had the dreamy look of someone wrapped in the soft embrace of heroin. When she extended her hand to Duke, the sleeve of her gown slipped back, exposing an arm without track marks. "Just chasing the dragon," said Kip softly, meaning she was only smoking the stuff to get her through a day in the arms of strangers. Duke identified us as the three-man party she had given an invitation to over the phone.

"You pay cash or credit card?" Her accent was Russian.

"Credit card works," said Duke.

I was looking down the hallway, ready to thunder along it, throwing open doors, but Duke cooled me with a glance. He didn't want the Russians bundling Bridget out the back while I banged heads in front. Kip was putting on a better performance, looking critically at the receptionist's hair. Duke gave her a credit card I was certain had been stolen. Its owner, or the owner's wife, would be surprised to find a brothel visit on the bill when it arrived sometime later this month. "Hundred for blow job," said the receptionist. "Full service five hundred."

Duke said full service for three. She ran the card through a phone reader, then handed it to Duke. "Sign, please."

It was all very businesslike, while I was imagining Bridget lost in a drugged dream.

Duke scratched a line on the screen and hit the icon that sealed the transaction. A line I'd learned from the Benedictines ran through my mind: *Nemo enim potest personam diu ferre*—a mask is hard to wear for long. How long could we maintain ours? Again Duke whispered in my ear, "Calm the fuck down."

The receptionist checked the screen and nodded, as if deeply gratified, then pointed to a dingy living room. The frayed furniture went with the curtains. I could feel Duke casing the situation; wiseguys have a feeling for the indoor takedown and Duke had done it many times before. There's nothing like a wild Irishman for breaking up furniture. I looked down the hallway again. In Mexico, older women employed by the cartels were often in the back rooms, administering drugs and threats to the captive girls. I was imagining a retreat, Bridget in my arms.

Kip started talking to the receptionist about her hair and touched at it expertly, explaining how to improve the shape, which was a tangled mess. A man with skin the color of a poisonous white mushroom appeared in the living room doorway. He looked us over thoughtfully, his eyes lingering on Duke as the obvious leader. "Welcome, my friend."

My nerves were jumping, and Duke put his arm around my shoulder. "My son's nervous. Never been laid."

Our host nodded his approval. "You give him good start."

"He wants to be a priest," said Duke. "But I won't let him."

The pimp smiled sympathetically, then introduced himself as Popov.

"I was TV producer in Moscow," he said, as if this qualified him to run a cathouse.

He pointed toward the staircase. A young woman in her underwear descended slowly, heavily made-up, smiling woodenly. She had wolf-blue eyes and had cultivated a ghostly kind of eroticism, maybe from watching reality fashion shows. Modeling fame, rich men, fast cars, and caviar—this is what guys like Popov, former TV producer, Moscow, had dangled in front of her.

There was a second female footstep from above, and we saw a pair of long legs on the stairs, in a satin slip that did little to hide the shape of splendid thighs. The rest of her came into view, and my heart turned over. There was the dead-straight blond hair and the high cheekbones. If her short satin slip were a majorette's uniform cut off at midthigh, she would be the twin of Bridget Breen. But only a twin, not the original.

Duke saw it too. "Shit," he muttered under his breath. His informant had mistaken this girl for Bridget.

"Something wrong, my friend?" asked Popov. "Is beautiful girl. Recently virgin."

"She's fine; they're all fine," said Duke, but the fun had gone out of him. He had come to break the furniture, but now it was just girls in their underwear. But they were paid for. He turned to the one with the wolf eyes. She returned his look and asked politely, "We go upstairs?"

"Yeah," said Duke, "we go upstairs."

The flames in my abdomen went out, leaving only the ever-burning pilot light of anger. My blood pressure went down, and my lungs deflated back to normal size.

Kip was still talking hair to the receptionist. Which left me with Bridget's twin. She looked at me, a bit of mischief behind her sleepy eyes. "I am Valentina. You are big guy. But I don't charge extra for weight."

She extended her arm toward me, so slowly it might have been the tai chi move called *elegant lady's hand*. I took it in mine, and her languidness ran up my arm. There was a soft spot in her somewhere, and she was offering it to me, though it was probably just a facsimile. I followed her to the staircase, putting my hand on a banister dulled from a hundred years of use, some of it by the seat of a kid's pants. You got that ride for only a few short years and then it was gone forever. Valentina was offering me a ride that would last a few short minutes and then it, too, would be gone forever. It wasn't what I had come for, but her sexual allure seemed to be carrying me up the stairs.

In the second floor hallway, I saw a vintage gas fixture protruding from the wall, left there when electric light arrived and drove away the flickering shadows of an earlier time. There were five rooms, one for Mama and Papa Bear, and four smaller ones for the little bears. I might have been back in Primo's house, walking in my sleep, which I often did as a troubled child in a mob boss's house. Had I been trying to get away?

Valentina's hand was holding mine, her languid movements draining the dammed-up adrenaline out of me.

There was no paper on her wall, just vintage plaster, painted over so many times it had a sort of shimmer. Or was it the slip Valentina was wearing that made it look that way? She certainly lit up a room with her tall, healthy body and her yellow hair. Reaching the bed, she turned, hands on hips, and posed as if modeling the satin slip. "What you think?" she asked, opening her sleepy eyes wider.

"You remind me of someone."

"Old girlfriend?"

"I never got that far."

"But you still like her?"

"I'm searching all over for her."

She nodded sympathetically. "Love is terrible."

She was probably an expert on terrible love. The expression on her face remained sympathetic as she brought her body against mine. "I help you forget. We forget together."

The adrenaline was completely out of me now. I was relaxing into the satin sheen of a slip, and the soft flesh behind it that moved along the length of my body. It was this I'd been dreaming about on my bicycle ride to Bellefontaine long ago.

Valentina tapped my forehead admonishingly with her finger. "You hang on to her, she wreck your life."

"I think she might be in trouble."

Valentina let out a sigh that blew across my cheek. "Every girl in trouble sometime. How you think I wind up here with Popov?" She pointed toward the floor. "My husband."

"Popov is your husband?"

"Why not?"

It was a fair question. Why not Popov? Though only partially human, he seemed nice enough.

"I marry him to get the fuck out of Russia." Her sigh was almost finished. She began running her fingers through my hair. "Nice. Curly." She unbuttoned my shirt and removed it. "You lift weights?" She didn't say this admiringly; rather, her voice had an academic edge, as one who has encountered a wide sampling of male muscle tone.

I told her I lifted weights. Then I lifted her. Her arms came around my neck as my arms came under her knees. She was not light as a feather. She was long and well put together. I carried her to the bed, laid her down gently, and stepped back to get the full angle of her repose. She raised one knee, draped her elbow over it, her arm hanging loosely. Her satin slip moved up her thighs, showing black panties with red roses, from Russia with love. If I'd seen this when I was twelve years old, my life might have gone in another direction.

Seeing I was in a sort of stupor, she pointed with one finger. "Remove pants." She wiggled her finger up and down. I was reminded of a woman gesturing to her dog. I'd given up trying to understand the female sex. I'd gone on my knees to statues of the Virgin Mary, not understanding her either, but a row of candles burning in front of her gave the illusion of mystical life. Burning in front of me now was the flame of true life, calling me back, telling me to stop wasting my life in a monastery and get real.

I hung my pants on a chair whose wooden curves were scarred and whose legs rested unevenly on the floor. "I know," she said as the mismatched legs moved up and down. "Is a dump. Furniture by Popov."

"I used to live in a house like this."

"You come from dump? I too. Soviet special. I thought, go to Amerika, live in McMansion."

My chest and legs were now as bare as my soul. She wiggled her finger at my jockey shorts and I dropped them. Brother Thomas in the nude.

She raised her arms and drew off her slip, then her Russian-rose panties.

"Now come to Valentina," she whispered.

I hadn't slept with a woman in two years. The last one had tried to kill me, which might account for my abstinence, but there's only so much resistance in a man. A Siberian goddess with natural blond hair was summoning me imperiously. She knew what she had to offer, had known it for some years now, probably upsetting an entire Russian village in the process.

Her hair was spread out on the pillow like rays from the sun. I sank down beside her, and she pressed against me, delivering me from all evil. Hard kneeling on a wooden pew was behind me. I was in softer, warmer density, she and the mattress cooperating to cushion my fall from grace.

"Forgetting her now?" she said, breathing in my ear, in charge of this moment, lazily calculating the time she had for me. I was a slight variation, but not all that different from the basic male pattern. She was probably thinking about Amerika the land of promise, the dump she had come from, the thousand things peculiarly connected to her body.

As for me, I was in a cathouse in Bellefontaine, with a young married woman from Russia, on a mission laid out by a wiseguy, to find a missing widow I once loved. And Valentina was undulating under me, giving me what her husband called full service. It included love words in Russian—at least, I thought they were love words, but she could have been swearing at Putin. The broken-down bedspring sang beneath us.

When it was over, we lay side by side quietly. "Now you go back to girlfriend refreshed," said Valentina, indicating that full service had ended. I got up and put on my shirt and pants.

"I should've met you when I was twelve."

She gave me a questioning look. I said, "It's hard to explain."

She rose from the bed and helped me button my shirt. Smoothing out the collar, she looked up into my eyes. "Come back to my McMansion, okay?"

"Okay."

"Otherwise, I miss you." She brushed the sleeves of my shirt with her elegant lady's hand, her fingers hardly touching the fabric, but the energy came through, as she knew it would. Everything done in this room came from her flame.

I went out through the door and into the hallway. From the hall window I could see an SUV parked behind the house. Popov's wheels.

I traced the wallpaper with my finger as I walked toward the staircase. Primo used to wake me from my sleepwalking, keeping his voice in a whisper, understanding I was in another world. *Tommy, you're dreaming.*

I still am, Grandfather.

Downstairs, Kip had wrapped his girl in a sheet and cut her hair. He carried scissors on him the way some men carry a knife, in a holster on his belt. And the girl had undergone an amazing transformation. The tangled mess was gone, and in its place were long face-framing layers that slimmed her somewhat chunky jawline and showed off the length of her neck. The girl was smiling at herself in a mirror Kip held for her.

"Look like million dollars," said Popov, then turned to me. "How you like Valentina?"

"Great," I said, somewhat awkwardly since she was his wife, but if he was okay with it, so was I.

"Valentina only comfortable in five-inch heels," he said. I figured he should know. He seemed proud of the fact.

Kip told the receptionist which products she needed, and she signaled to Popov for paper and pen, which he immediately provided, sensing the high level of information being shared. He seemed like a caring pimp: fairly easygoing, and good-natured for a man running a cathouse at the ass-end of nowhere. He carried the hair trimmings out through the front door and over the porch railing, snapping the sheet briskly as if sprinkling enticing bits of magic on his parched lawn.

Duke came down the stairs, straightening his impeccably tailored suit jacket and tie. Popov performed a snappy little bow, sensing that this customer came from the upper echelon of something. "Everything satisfactory?"

"Very nice," said Duke, with his artificial smile. His information about Bridget had been a bust, but so what?

Then Valentina appeared at the top of the stairs in a midnight-blue dressing gown that moved against her thighs as she navigated the steps in five-inch heels. Popov pointed at her shoes while nodding toward me, and I returned the nod. She was sauntering into the room with a cigarette between her lips and looked, as he'd predicted, comfortable. I could see how Duke's informant had gotten it wrong. Bridget had married the owner of a TV station, and Valentina was stuck with Popov, but the radiance was there in both of them, shining like light through a nightgown. Duke's informant had been dazzled, and it was the dazzle he reported on—a blend of beauty and confidence that had clouded his mind.

"Your son really like Valentina," observed Popov.

"I see that," said Duke.

"Other son does very excellent work on hair," said Popov.

My eyes were on Valentina. She looked supernaturally regal in her midnight-blue gown, blowing smoke toward the ceiling as if to some ancient goddess of the steppes. Her eyes came level with mine, completely in control of my gaze, knowing I couldn't look away, because anywhere else was nowhere. There was tolerance in her eyes—not particularly for me, but for men in general. "Thinking about girlfriend," she said to the room as she gestured toward me with her elegant lady's hand. "Making comparison."

There was a soft step on the stairs. Then red furry bedroom slippers and Duke's girl, on whom he'd just spent somebody else's money, came down. Her wolf-blue eyes took us in as she stepped into the living room and sidled over to Duke.

He opened his wallet and slipped her a fifty. "Buy yourself a balloon."

Popov said, "You are now close friend."

We were all close friends. Valentina pressed her lips to my ear. "I hope you find old girlfriend. Make her good husband and see me Friday afternoons."

Duke moved toward the door, Popov moving beside him. "You and sons always welcome." If he'd been running the cathouse when I was twelve, I would've gotten in.

"We'll find Bridget," said Duke as we drove away. "It's not over yet."

We passed some cyclists on their way to Bellefontaine in tight-fitting bicycle wear and aerodynamic helmets. I could see their dedication to the sport—heads down, bodies arched according to the latest technique.

Duke rolled his window down. "Keep inside the line, jerk-offs."

There had been no bicycle lane when Knucklehead and I pedaled to Bellefontaine, and our gear had been crude, but we'd gotten there. *You've got to give a special knock*, Knucklehead had said, assuring me he knew this knock, but even before he applied his knuckles to the door the madam was pushing the lace curtain aside, her eyes going down to the heads of a pair of twelve-year-olds. *This is all I need*, she'd said to herself. And so I was dismissed along with Knucklehead, kicked down the road of time for a return trip to Bellefontaine. We hadn't found Bridget, but as Duke had said, it wasn't over yet.

16

It was Sunday morning in the trailer park. I was sitting beside the river looking at the handlebars of the submerged bicycle when a young boy sat down beside me. He pointed at the bicycle. "Think it's still any good?"

"Why? Do you want one?"

"It'd make my life easier."

"Your life is hard?"

"I have places to go and things to do."

For a moment, I was south of the border again, for his skin had the tinge of a strong sun imprinted in it, and though English came to him naturally, I heard the cadence of Mexico. So, in Spanish, I asked him his name.

"I am Santiago Flores. How come you speak Spanish?"

"I live in Mexico."

"When I was young I lived there too. Now I'm ten and live there." He pointed to one of the trailers. "What you do in Mexico?"

"I take care of a couple of horses."

"You ride them?"

"Sometimes."

"If I had a horse, I'd ride away." I could see he was a dreamer.

"You really want a bicycle?"

"Hell, yes."

"How much does this bicycle cost?"

"I'm not fussy."

"All right, you can come to work for me and you'll make enough to buy a bicycle."

"Doing what?" He eyed me suspiciously.

"Detailing my car. Inside and out. I want it waxed and polished. I want it to look like new."

"Great! You'll be my first employer." Obviously, he did have plans to go places in life. We agreed on a price, and I went to church.

———————

The cathedral swept gracefully upward, stone upon stone, created by master masons when the twentieth century was born. Phil and Misty Branca were in the pew ahead of me, Phil kneeling, head down, praying to his version of the Lord, a don above him in the hierarchy.

Monsignor Crispin gave his sermon in a persuasive voice, his pudgy hands moving gracefully, well-timed with what he said. His fluffy hair and plump cheeks gave him the look of an aging cherub. When I was a kid, he'd given me the sacrament of confirmation. We'd been told he might question us about the Catholic faith, and for weeks I'd lived in fear, but his only question had been directed to a girl, who answered it with confidence, and the rest of us had breathed a sigh of relief.

During Holy Communion, Queenie O'Malley went to the altar and came back, cleansed of her sins, in which I might possibly figure. She certainly figured in my sinful thoughts as she walked down the aisle, hands folded in prayer.

After the somber moments of Communion ended, hymns resembling pop tunes were sung to the accompaniment of amplified guitar and drum kit. Monsignor Crispin proclaimed the mass was ended and everyone turned to their nearest neighbor to shake hands. Phil Branca shook hands with his bodyguard.

Queenie O'Malley went out of the church ahead of me. I joined her on the sidewalk, and she impulsively held out her hand. When I took it, she seemed to be reading my feelings through my fingertips and getting no satisfactory answer. I was confused myself and said awkwardly, "You looked lovely after receiving Communion."

"Everyone does after Communion."

I thought of Grandfather Primo after Communion. He'd never been able to break the habit of looking toward the side doors, just in case the FBI rather than the angels were watching him.

"Missing your monastery?" asked Queenie.

"I haven't thought about it much lately."

"I once thought about being a nun. Most Catholic girls do. Usually after boy trouble."

"And now?"

"Same old boy trouble."

The question that had been in her fingertips was now in her eyes. What answer could I give her? I'd barely noticed her in high school because she hadn't yet come into her beauty. But now that she had, it was formidable, and she was laying it before me.

Still gazing up into my eyes, she said, "I had a music box when I was a kid. Two skaters went around and around while the music played. They never touched, just went around and around."

"That's us?"

"I wanted so much for the skaters to touch. Some nights I thought it would actually happen. That they'd suddenly be in each other's arms." She lowered her eyes. "That tinny music made me cry. A fragile little orchestra. Playing just for me."

I couldn't take my eyes off her. There was only one flaw in her beauty and it was the softness in her soul, a vulnerability she couldn't hide. The women like Misty Branca who had shaped me were hard as the coal that burned in their souls. Bridget had just enough of that hardness to have become head majorette in my heart, and Queenie had been a shy flower watching from the sidelines. It had made her invisible as a teenager, until her transformation into a beauty brought her into full view.

"Poor Tommy," she said with a forced smile, "going around and around."

"Give me some time."

"I'm engaged to be married in three months. Time enough?"

"It's not easy. Coming out of the monastery, I mean. Some part of me is still back there."

"What's the attraction?"

"I like silence."

"What happens when you're silent?"

"I think about what it means to live on Earth."

"You *have* changed."

"So have you."

"I learned how to dress and use makeup, that's all. Valuable knowledge for a girl living on Earth."

And here we were, outside church, looking into each other's souls while Monsignor chatted up his congregation and Phil Branca slipped him a fat little envelope, as was the custom of mobsters. Those little envelopes squared things, and Phil was squaring heaven.

He and Misty approached us, Misty smiling at Queenie, and then sensing something was going on, she kept Phil moving. Little Joe came behind them, eyes sweeping the street. I detected his piece underneath his well-cut Sunday suit. Queenie said, "Those guys are from your late grandfather's crew, right?"

"Just a pair of businessmen, so they tell me."

"My mother knew your grandfather. They belonged to some Catholic charity, and she said he was a perfect gentleman."

I knew his black heart too well to accept that view of him. But he'd had old-world manners and had cultivated a rough sort of gallantry around women, and Queenie's mother had obviously been one of those women.

Queenie asked, "Your grandfather raised you, didn't he?"

"He took me in when my father and mother died."

"How was it growing up around him?"

"Frightening."

"But here you are, all in one piece."

"Sometimes I wonder." We'd drifted away from our deeper feelings, and the pressure was gone. We could just be two people talking after mass. She held out her hand and I took it again, but we were still the two dancers on the music box, not really touching.

Duke Devlin drove up beside us and rolled down his window. "There's trouble. Get in."

I got in and he pulled away. "Killian Muldoon bought a semi-automatic yesterday. It's hot, of course, because no legitimate gun dealer would sell anything to that lunatic. It's got a hellfire trigger, by the way, which means it fires at the rate of a full automatic." Duke rolled slowly along the block, as if we were sightseeing. "There's a timeline at work here. You come to town and Killian gets himself a piece."

Ever since I'd put Killian's brother in the ground, I'd known there would be a reckoning. I'd half expected him to track me down in Mexico. Instead, I'd made it easy for him. "It gets better," continued Duke. "The other brother, Connor, who's equally nuts, bought a high-capacity shotgun. Why have just two rounds when you can have sixteen? We assume he did not buy it to shoot pheasants. Do I have your full attention?"

"I'm listening."

"The Muldoon brothers deal drugs, roll drunks, do some housebreaking, a bit of pimping, for which they're ready to serve a little time. They look at it as overhead. But if the cops nail them for any of the above and they're carrying illegal firearms, they'll do a lot of time. So this gun purchase has a single purpose, which is killing you, after which the guns will go in the river and the Muldoons will go back to being small-time hoods."

"How will they come at me?"

"Their best chance is to blow you away in your car. They don't amount to much, but with you in town they've found a higher purpose. The question is, what are we going to do about it?"

"I'm open to suggestions."

"Plan A: I arrange for them to buy heroin laced with fentanyl. They won't know that, of course, and when they sample the stuff, they'll croak. It's elegant, but it leaves too much to chance."

"What's plan B?"

"I shoot them in the head."

We continued rolling slowly in Duke's Cadillac. It could take us up to 100 miles an hour in eight seconds, but we were having a more thoughtful ride, to facilitate planning. I said, "I don't want any preemptive moves. I'm going to let it play out."

"They're small-timers, but they take away some of my business. Whacking them would send a nice message to anybody else thinking about muscling in on me. So I'm at your service on this one."

"I appreciate the offer, but I don't want to destroy the entire male line of the Muldoon family."

"They're the worst kind of Irish fuck-up known to man." Duke fell silent for a moment, as if searching for greater clarity. "They've got a corrosive substance in their brain." Then he added, "You did the world a favor when you killed their baby brother."

"I've got to let them come to me, Duke."

"They'll be coming heavy."

"I want to make amends."

"That monastery has had a bad influence on you."

"Probably."

"The Muldoon brothers fluctuate between towering rage and mindless scheming. They'll ram your amends down your throat." He wheeled the Cadillac around and headed back toward the cathedral. "The Muldoons have guns and they're looking for you. Why don't we just go and whack the fuckers?"

His eyes betrayed an eagerness he ordinarily kept hidden. But I couldn't see myself visiting three graves, all the occupants put there by me. He pulled up alongside my Charger. I got into it, and he called across to me. "The Muldoons are spur-of-the-moment types. And the moment is now, so watch your back."

He pulled away. The churchgoers around the cathedral had thinned out, and Monsignor Crispin was no longer greeting the flock. I drove away thinking about the Muldoon brothers, the living and the dead. Mike had been my age and would age no longer. Killian and Connor were older, but I remembered them all too well. They'd gone to technical high school in preparation for the manual trades, but their trade quickly became beating people up. Killian was a tall, rangy middleweight with a mean right hand and might have made something of himself as a fighter, but training was too much like work, so he just fought in barrooms, where nobody else was trained either, and his long right arm got the job done. Connor was smaller and chunkier, and when drunk, which was most the time, he was truly dangerous. I'd seen him rip a television screen off a barroom wall and bring it down onto a guy's head, then laugh maniacally while his victim lay underneath it on the floor. They were bad news with hundreds of barroom fights under their belt, but they'd never killed anybody. I'd been a clean-cut high school hero, and one summer night I'd killed their brother.

Now I drove slowly through the empty Sunday streets, knowing this town was poison. I had been glad to put it behind me, but here I was again, in the same old atmosphere of touchiness and macho pride. And there was something else—another ingredient, subtler, more sinister, having to do with a narrow kind of ambition this town created in some men: to be the big fish in a small pond. But never leaving home put a chip on their shoulder. I didn't think women around here were as susceptible to the poison, but I could be wrong. When it came to women, I usually was.

I drove into my old neighborhood. A bus was pulling to the curb to unload passengers. One of them was an older woman, lugging two stuffed shopping bags and muttering to herself as she reached the sidewalk. It was Knucklehead Nowitzki's mother. I pulled in alongside her and rolled down the window. "Hi, Mrs. Nowitzki, can I give you a lift?"

She looked up at me suspiciously. She'd always been half-cracked and an embarrassment to Knucklehead.

"It's Tommy Martini, Mrs. Nowitzki. You remember me."

At the mention of my name, her paranoia diminished, not completely but enough for her to approach the car. She peered in through the window. "I got to be careful."

"Sure, you do. Let me drive you the rest of the way."

She opened the door, shoved in her bags, and climbed in after them.

Her hair resembled an abandoned bird nest, and her eyes had the wild look I vividly recalled from my childhood. She'd been a beauty when she was young, and Knucklehead's father, a civil servant from a respectable family, had fallen for her, choosing to overlook the eccentric behavior he probably thought went with her proud beauty. When it dawned on him that she was truly batty, it was too late, because baby Knucklehead was in the oven. After he established himself firmly in this world, Knucklehead and I had played together in the shadow of his mother's madness, her mutterings a kind of musical background, much of it having to do with suspicion of her neighbors, particularly the Jewish families.

She peered at me over her shopping bags. "You used to be a little wop."

"Now I'm a big one.

"And your father was a crook."

"Grandfather."

"Same thing. All you wops are crooks."

I knew better than to dispute any of her observations. In the summer when we were kids, she would take Knucklehead and me to pick blueberries. We'd follow her anti-Semitic rant as we picked. It just seemed part of summer with Mrs. Nowitzki.

She was still staring at me, her eyes as bright and wild as ever, some force long ago having twisted her mind into its paranoid shape. But she could laugh, and I remembered her laughing when we were kids, followed by remarkably accurate observations about some pompous neighbor. She might be nuts and prejudiced, but there was little that she missed when it came to neighborhood hypocrisy. She'd been like a beautiful fortune teller, and I'd had a crush on her, a crush as crazy as she was.

She shoved a shopping bag against me by way of inquiry. "Where you been since I last seen you?"

"In Mexico."

"Spics. We got a lot of them around here now." She was an equal-opportunity bigot, I'll say that for her. Now she asked, "What were you doing in Mexico?"

"I was in a monastery."

She examined my face more closely, her shopping bags pressing against me. "I saw your first Holy Communion. You and Vincent."

Was she really remembering this? And then, like a goldfish coming to the surface, that long-ago day swam up into my mind and there we were, the two of us standing before her outside the church. "You gave each of us a dollar."

"You looked like little saints. All dressed in white."

"I ran into Vincent the other day."

"He's a big shot now. He'd like to get rid of me."

Having a madwoman for a mother might be an impediment to a city magistrate's political ambition. When I didn't contradict her, she smiled and said, "I ain't goin' anywhere."

"I can see that."

"Some people would like to run me out of the neighborhood." She gave me her mad-wise smile. "I can't think why."

I pulled over to the curb. We were in front of her house. It was one of the old ones, surrounded by high hedges I remember her carefully tending, urging them higher to form the walls they finally became. In all my days playing with Knucklehead, I'd never been in his house. She didn't let anyone in. She'd peer out through the curtains, her wild eyes gleaming. She'd be in a housedress and usually say something like *Vincent isn't home. Get the fuck off the porch.* Then Knucklehead would emerge, shrugging off her report on his whereabouts, and we'd go play in an abandoned mineshaft.

"Thanks for the lift, Tommy. You were always a nice kid. You killed somebody around here, didn't you?"

"It was unintended."

"How'd you like to kill someone for me?"

"Who did you have in mind?"

She gave a little toss of her head, indicating the house next door.

"Not today, Mrs. Nowitzki. Maybe some other time."

"Anytime is fine." She edged out of the car, dragging her shopping bags behind her. On the sidewalk, she turned and lifted a shopping bag toward a car coming toward us. It was slowing down, and I saw Killian

Muldoon at the wheel. He'd found me without much trouble, and I questioned my decision to drive around in a red vintage muscle car you could spot a mile away. Connor was in the seat beside Killian, the same maniacal grin on his face I remembered from the barroom, except that now the grin was hung on deeper creases. He was an adolescent in a man's body, and so was Killian—a pair of brawlers happy only when they were stomping somebody. If they fired on me, they were bound to get Knucklehead's mother. I shouted, "Get in the house, Mrs. Nowitzki."

"I ain't goin' anywhere," she repeated, and shook her bags toward the hood of their slowing car. It came to a stop, and I saw Killian looking puzzled as she marched toward him. "Get the fuck off my street!"

Killian was shifting his gaze between us, trying to compute. Now she was right beside his car. "You heard me—fuck off!"

He lowered his window. "I'm a friend of Knucklehead."

"You're a piece of shit."

Killian decided any further exchange would be counterproductive. Mrs. Nowitzki's madness was bolder than his own. He might be a little unhinged, but she was a door flapping in the wind, shopping bags smashing against his car windows as she shouted, "Clear out, you mick son of a bitch!"

He put the car in gear and drove past us. Connor gave me the finger, which was considerably better than sixteen rounds from his shotgun. Mrs. Nowitzki, having won her point, marched between her fortress hedges and shuffled up the stairs to her porch. I waited until she'd made it safely through her door and was peering back out at me through her shabby curtains before I waved goodbye. She snapped the curtains shut, and I drove away.

17

When I told Monsignor Crispin I wanted to talk about the death of Finn Sweeney, he received me in the cathedral parish house. But instead of the office where his routine business was handled, he saw me in his private quarters—an acknowledgment of my being a brother in the Benedictine order. There was a small study, and we faced each other in comfortable chairs. His hands were folded over his cozy little paunch, and his gray eyes were inquisitive but not unkind. He said, "I admire the Benedictines. I especially like your adherence to *conversatio morum*. An ongoing transformation of the heart, isn't that how you think of it?"

"I've had a few transformations of the heart, but they happened outside the monastery walls and involved women."

"The spirit works in wondrous ways."

"Wonder was certainly part of it."

"I knew your grandfather. Every year, he bought new equipment and uniforms for all our teams and provided a bus and driver to transport the players around. The driver carried a firearm. He said, and I quote, *Nobody is going to jack these kids*." Crispin smiled indulgently at the memory. "Your grandfather built our gymnasium and repaired our church. The only thing he didn't do was send you to our school."

"He was afraid the nuns might soften me."

"But he forced you into a monastery. Is *forced* too strong a word?"

"He thought it was necessary. You know why I had to go?"

"Because of the death of the Muldoon boy." He drummed his pudgy fingers on his little paunch. "I confirmed Mike Muldoon. As I spread the oil of chrism on his forehead, he gave me a look I won't soon forget."

"What look was that?"

"A deeply mocking look. I'd seen it on grown men but never in a boy." Crispin paused. "The sacrament bestows right judgment on the confirmed. In his case, it failed."

"It certainly failed when he took a swing at me in a bar."

"He was an active party in his fate." He opened a cabinet, took out two shot glasses and a bottle, Glenfiddich by the label, fifteen years old. "I think we might have a bit of this." He poured, we drank, and the spicy warmth of the brew was an undeniable benediction. "Finn Sweeney was much liked in this parish. A generous man and a very funny one. He often treated me to his humorous side. But behind that charm was a . . ." He tugged at his cassock as if trying to find the right word in its folds. "A paladin."

When he saw my surprise, he said, "From the Latin *palatinus*. A knight renowned for heroism. Are you the new paladin?"

"I'm going to find who killed him."

"Forgive me, but isn't that outside the prescribed duties of a Benedictine monk?"

"I may never return to those duties. Since coming out of the monastery, I've been questioning my commitment to the order."

"The life is not for everyone." He poured another round of Glenfiddich, and I asked him how well he knew Bridget.

"I confirmed her along with the rest of you. She was a beautiful child. Willful but beautiful."

"Finn left a message for me just before he was killed. *Take care of Bridget.*"

"And here you are."

"But I haven't taken care of her. I can't find her."

"We've got a great many busybodies in our church. At times, they can be quite useful. I'll consult them and get back to you."

18

TV station WVIM was on night shift. The evening program had been taped—just flip a few switches and the shows would unfold. But Queenie was staying late. "Miranda is gone. I'm holding things together until we get a new manager."

"Why not you as manager?"

"I'm too short."

"High heels are the answer."

"I'm already wearing high heels."

She was, and they looked great—pink sandal straps wrapped cunningly around her ankles, showing them off to advantage, along with her smooth calves. I said, "You can manage *my* TV station."

"Since when did you have a TV station?"

"I'll get one."

"By that time, I'll be working for Mittleman Produce."

Like an astronaut on a flyby mission, I gazed down at her pale moon face. "I acknowledge our situation is impossible. But is that any reason to give it up?"

"You had your chance."

"When was that?"

"The week before your senior prom. I was available."

"I was preoccupied."

"You were chasing Bridget Breen. You're still chasing her."

"I want to save her life."

"And I want to save mine."

So there it was, two skaters on a music box, going around. I said, "I've got a time capsule parked outside."

She went to the window, looked at the red Charger. "That's the kind of car no girl should ever get into."

"Unless she's driving." I flipped her the keys.

She caught them neatly, switched off the light on her reception desk, and went to the front door of the station. "Let's try this time capsule of yours."

I followed her across the parking lot and held the driver's-side door for her. "It's all yours." She got in, and I slid in from the other side. "I know a quiet place we can talk."

"I bet you do." She adjusted the seat to accommodate her compact body and started the Charger. Uncle Silvio had attached a suicide spinner to the steering wheel—one of those small round knobs that lets you quickly turn a car. It was baby blue, and underneath its transparent dome was a blonde in a bikini. Queenie steered as if she'd been born with a spinner in her hand, and we pulled out from the station in a fast right turn. I looked across at her, at that perky nose and determined chin and that black pixie haircut. Feeling my glance, she said, "I'm going to marry Richard Mittleman."

"You'll never run out of oranges."

"I shouldn't be in this car."

She had nice toe and heel work, keeping the Charger steady on the moonlit turns. When the men of the valley were filthy miners who rarely saw the sun, take-charge women like Queenie conquered them with willpower as fierce as their own.

I laid my head back into the Charger's neck rest, letting the beast soothe my brain, but Queenie's knees were all too visible as she moved gas and brake to the left of me, deftly tapping them to suit the mood of the moment, lines of trees passing with the Charger's headlights on them, branches gesturing to the next forest curve. "It's heavy but it's responsive," she said. "A cannon on wheels."

We were descending from the TV station toward the trashy lights of the town. At the bottom of the hill, we rolled past a bowling alley, an auto-parts store, a Krispy Kreme. "Familiar to you?" she asked.

"I recognize every inch. Of it and of you."

"You think you know me, Tommy?"

"I know enough."

"How much is that?"

"Too much for my own good." I wanted to tell her that I'd always loved her, but I knew she wouldn't swallow it. However, I did remember her drawing the football team, and that had been the problem. She'd been so concentrated, her skirt wrapped around her down to her ankles, while the majorettes were kicking up their legs on the field behind her. So take your pick, gentlemen: the crouching girl with the pad and pencil, or the long-legged majorettes, a whole line of them strutting by. "I missed you at the start, but I've caught up to you."

"I think two guys are following us," she said, her eyes going to the rearview mirror. "They pulled out after we went by Krispy Kreme. Some of your old buddies?"

I didn't have to look in the rearview mirror. "You remember Mike Muldoon?"

"How can I forget? You rang his bell."

"His brothers are looking to ring mine. Pull over and I'll get out and deal with them. Then you drive on."

"I can't do that."

"They're my problem. Not yours."

"And you're going to settle it in some stupid macho way." She was angry now, not understanding that this was not about machismo. Mike Muldoon was seeking vengeance from his coffin. *His Right Hand Is Filled With Justice*, as it says on the stone that was supposed to keep him well and buried. If so, why did they have to chisel those words above him? We Italians are cracked, but the Irish go us one better when it comes to settling a beef. With us, it's just business; with them, it's mysticism.

"Last chance, Queenie. Pull over."

But she didn't take it. "I don't want you getting in trouble."

So that was that; we were passing razor wire and storage sheds, then darkened buildings, the vestigial appendages of the city.

"They're still following us," she said.

This became vividly clear when the back window of the Charger exploded. Glass blew around us. "Hit it, Queenie."

My head snapped back as the Charger responded to the press of her sandals. "I think you have the picture now," I said, picking glass out of my hair.

"They want to kill you."

"Mike Muldoon wants to kill me. They're just his right hand."

"Don't talk crazy."

"It's on his tombstone."

"Well, it's not going to be on mine."

She whipped the suicide spinner; an assortment of buildings went by us in a blur, and we were on a road out of town. Over my shoulder, I watched the Muldoon car try to make the turn, then think better of it. They spun onto the shoulder, backed up, and were starting to turn around when I looked back at them. Another line of buildings passed in a blur, Queenie taking a series of lefts and rights until we were climbing the hill to Quarry Road—not a bad choice, because it was built like a tortured snake to slow trucks with heavy loads of gravel. And Uncle Silvio had modified the Charger for high-speed maneuvering—quicker steering box, high-performance racing suspension, and wide tires for attacking corners with extra grip. I knew that the shit box the Muldoons were in had nothing to match us. The fuzzy dice danced madly below the rearview mirror as Queenie's foot banged down on the gas pedal. The Charger surged forward, and we straightened out of the first turn.

But headlights came through the shattered rear window again. The Muldoons were back in the hunt. I looked over my shoulder and could see the maniac grin on Connor's face as he leaned out with the revolving-barrel shotgun. He let loose with it again just as Queenie whipped the suicide spinner, and Connor's blast took apart a road sign instead of us. Then he was lost behind a turn as Queenie urged the

Charger. "Come on, come on . . ." It responded with a vintage roar, and up we went.

The Muldoons came back into view, Killian grinning over the wheel. He reached out the window and fired his semiautomatic. The mirror blew off on Queenie's side. "Bastards," she muttered, pushing the gas pedal to the floor as we went into the next turn, spinning through it, the Charger bouncing wildly over the chewed-up pavement but keeping upright as the landscape jumped up and down in front of us. She shot a quick glance at the rearview mirror. "Fuck them and their dead brother."

"I'm with you on that." I was still looking back over my shoulder, taking in both brothers, one shouting to the other as Killian spun the wheel. Connor was aiming the shotgun again, but this time the ragged teeth of Quarry Road screwed up his aim, and the trunk of the Charger took the blast.

"Jesus Christ," murmured Queenie as bits of chrome landed between us on the seat. She had glass in her hair and it seemed to be covered with a net of silver. I said, "Your hair looks great that way."

"I'll be sure to tell them at the salon."

I noticed a thin gold chain around her neck, and the shamrock of tiny emeralds that bounced around at her throat. Would it bring us luck? A round from Killian's automatic seemed to be the answer to that. A shot came through the empty back window and shattered the windshield. It was now a spider's web, forcing us to squint through the glistening threads. "Hard right coming . . ."

She spun into it, her emerald shamrock sliding across her throat. She muttered, "They're doing this for their brother? What a load of macho bullshit."

She floored it again, and the emerald shamrock swung the other way, tethered by its gold chain, as we bounced up and down. I looked at Killian through the missing back window, and he was still grinning, wild with drink and certain of running us down before this night was out. He shouted at Connor, and Connor's evil elf face twisted into a frown of concentration. Uncle Silvio's other side mirror blew off in a shower of chrome and glass.

We had one advantage. I'd been on this road many times, and I knew what was coming. "Full throttle, everything you've got."

The Charger answered, and the darkness jumped forth to meet us. "Hard right!"

Queenie whipped the suicide spinner. Killian wasn't quick enough and missed the turn. His headlights dipped, then vanished as an almighty splash sounded through our shattered windows. The Muldoon brothers were sinking as fast as their car would take them, to join the rusty pumps at the bottom of the Martini Stone and Sand quarry pit, now under seventy-five feet of water.

"Over there," I said, and pointed to the abandoned office building that stood beside the quarry. Queenie parked the Charger, and we opened our bullet-riddled doors. Exhaust fumes rose up between us and the quarry. When we were kids, my cousin Dominic and I had labored here, shoving stone around, earning money the hard way for Primo and his brothers, who sometimes appeared where I stood now, smoking cigars and calling down, *Break-a you balls, guys.* They'd called it quits at the seventy-five-foot mark because water had finally overwhelmed the pumps. Like good environmentalists, they'd abandoned their machinery to rust on the bottom. Now Killian and Connor had joined that rusty tableau.

The crickets and frogs were holding back their chorus, waiting to see what was what. Waves broke against the quarry wall and slowly subsided. We walked to the pit, and Queenie stood at the edge, staring down. She crossed herself. Her hands, so steady on the wheel a moment ago, were shaking.

The image of the moon on the water had regained its steadiness—a mirror only slightly disturbed now. Killian had ripped through the warning fence at the edge of the quarry, and now the fence hung in the water. I dragged it out. The Martini sign came with it, attached by a few rusty bolts. I reworked the wire until I had enough to stretch the fence across its old opening. It had been sagging for so long that it looked convincing enough now. Somebody had outlined the Martini name with bullet holes, for target practice or for commentary. We stood in front of it, looking down at the water.

"I killed them," said Queenie.

"They killed themselves."

Neither car had burned much rubber, and what marks there were had blended with patches of tar from long ago. We walked down the road and picked up pieces of chrome and one of the side mirrors. We tossed them into the quarry, then got some pine boughs and smoothed out the dirt in front of the fence. Queenie concluded her prayers and looked up at the moon. It was, in fact, a lovely night.

We walked back to the Charger and I called Uncle Silvio. "I'm behind the office next to the Martini quarry. The Charger is totaled. Get up here with your tow truck."

"What happened?"

"Shit happened."

"I'm on the way."

19

Queenie slid back into the driver's seat. I walked around and got in the other side. Glass covered the seat between us—not exactly an invitation to get closer. But we were close anyway, our bodies still tuned to the same quivering pitch of excitement. She was picking glass out of her lap. "Do I mention the Muldoons in my next confession?"

"I looked into this once. The Church says lethal force is lawful if your life is at stake."

"Where did you do this looking?"

"I was named for Thomas Aquinas. So I read his *Summa Theologica*. It's in there."

We fell into silence again, but the invisible embrace of intimacy remained. I wished it could last. I started brushing the broken glass off the seat.

"Stop it. You'll cut your hand."

"It's shatterproof, no sharp edges." She was picking glass out of her hair. Her voice was heavy with guilt. "I knew Killian and Connor when we were kids."

I didn't want us to sink into eulogies for two dead creeps. Queenie didn't either, her voice growing suddenly harder. "They tried to kill us."

"Duke wanted to whack them. I told him not to. A mistake on my part."

She looked toward me, picking more glass out of her hair. "It wasn't a mistake. I'm glad you're not a killer."

"I'm what I am, but you're certainly no killer. They were asking for it."

Her pale face seemed paler now, but maybe it was just the moon shining through the shattered windshield. Her hands were no longer shaking. She pointed to the suicide spinner, turned it toward herself, looked at the blonde in the bikini. "She saved us."

"Not our fuzzy dice?" I tapped them with my finger.

"Them too."

We sat in silence. A bullfrog gave a tentative croak. Another one answered. Pretty soon, they all joined in, croaking voices ringing the quarry like a burial party for the dead men at the bottom. Queenie said, "I can't believe they're gone."

"They're gone and they're not coming back."

"They must've been wasted out of their minds."

"They've been out of their minds for years." I finished clearing glass off the seat between us. The way toward Queenie was open. My namesake, Thomas Aquinas, was known for eating an entire chicken without realizing it, so deeply involved was he in introspection. And introspection told me that if I moved on Queenie, it would break the closeness we already felt. She said, "Are we going to get away with it?"

"There was no one else on this road."

"What happens when their friends start wondering where they are?"

"They were a pair of lowlifes. On that level, disappearance is no cause for wonder. The assumption will be, they fucked with the wrong people. And they did."

Again we fell silent, leaving further comment to the frogs. Queenie was looking toward the old Martini office building. "Your family used to own this place."

"They still do. You never know when you might need seventy-five feet of water."

"That's how deep it is?"

"It was when I worked down there. Before the water, of course."

She considered this, calculating, as I was, the likelihood of anyone discovering a car that was seventy-five feet below the surface of an abandoned quarry. "When did you work there?"

"High school, college."

"Loading stone?"

"Strong like bull." I held up my fist, arm angled at the elbow.

She tugged the edge of her skirt down, giving it a shake to get the last of the glass off. Then she looked out through the broken windshield. "Richard and I used to park up here."

I said, "I have a hard time accepting you and Mittleman as a couple."

"You should've thought of that ten years ago."

"Ten years ago? You've been seeing him for that long?"

"Off and on."

"What, you can't make up your mind?"

"He's been very busy with the business. He gets up at three o'clock in the morning to meet the trucks."

"Good morning, grapefruits."

"Something like that."

"So if you marry him you'll have early evenings. Because of his bedtime."

"Do you mind if we don't discuss this now? I just killed two people."

"I repeat, you didn't kill them. They came barreling after us and missed the turn. It was a traffic accident. You have more glass in your hair." I reached across and picked out a tiny piece from the sharp corner of her pixie cut, the part that fell by her ear and gave her the look of a forgotten film star, one of those beauties sculpted out of studio lights. "Guys like the Muldoons don't expect a long life. It's why they're so dangerous. For them, every night is the night they kiss their ass goodbye."

A bat flew toward the car, its little wings flapping, the shadowy membranes stretched tight against its outstretched claws. And then it flitted by, stalking fliers smaller than itself, the bugs of nighttime it loved so well.

"Somebody's coming," said Queenie.

I heard it, too, the rumble of a big truck. I reached across and gave Queenie's shoulder a reassuring squeeze. "The Martinis are strong around here. This is our road and our town. So nothing bad is going to happen to you."

She put her hand on top of mine. "I always knew you'd be trouble."

"And here I am, as expected. And here's Uncle Silvio." I pushed against the shot-up door. Queenie pushed against hers and we got out. Silvio's truck lit her up with a halo of headlight beams, and I saw glass still sparkling in her hair. "You're the kind of job he likes to go to. High heels, tight skirt, and car, in that order."

The truck went through its guttural grunts as it came to a stop and the red door opened. Silvio in his best style—shirt neatly pressed, *Martini* in red above the pocket. He swung down, powerful and confident, a man with a big truck. But the sight of his beloved Charger torn apart by gunfire gave him pause, though only for a moment. "Let's get it out of here."

We hauled out the chains, and Silvio slid under the Charger and attached them to the frame. Then he walked back to the truck and threw a lever. The truck lowered its tail like an obedient beaver, and Silvio threw another lever. The hoist started pulling gently on his beloved automobile. He shook his head sadly but said nothing, concentrating on getting it fixed securely on the beaver's tail. The two vehicles coupled together, one on top of the other. Once that was settled, he came over to us. "Queenie O'Malley, right?"

She nodded.

He said, "What's a nice girl like you doing with my nephew?"

"We're old friends."

He helped her up the big step into the truck, and the smooth line of her legs was amply displayed. He looked at me. "At least you wrecked my car in a good cause."

"The Muldoons wrecked it."

"Where are they now?"

I pointed toward the quarry. "They went through the fence. I put it back together."

He walked up the road toward the fence, gave it a quick examination. "I'll come back tomorrow and pick up any pieces you left around.

But it looks good enough for now." He gazed down at the moonlit water. "Rest in peace."

Queenie was waiting for us in the cab—a short girl in a high ride. When we had ourselves seated beside her, Silvio started the wrecker rolling. He glanced at Queenie. "Comfortable?"

"I'm fine."

"Your dad and I belong to the same overpriced country club. I've gone nine holes with him a few times. He's very proud of you."

I was looking at the emerald shamrock at her throat. It had brought us through, as shamrocks sometimes do. I was still jammed up with adrenaline, but Silvio had the momentum now. He steered the wrecker out of the old office parking lot and onto the road. The truck rumbled over the broken teeth of the pavement, and the Charger swayed in its chains. I could see some of the tension going out of Queenie. She was in strong hands, and she knew it. The Martinis would spare no effort in making this evening vanish into thin air.

Silvio adjusted the rearview mirror, keeping his beloved Charger in view. "Your father plays a good game of golf."

"He should; he owns a sporting-goods shop."

"I know it well. Bowling balls, whatever you want. You go bowling?"

"Sometimes."

"I'm into bowling these days." He said it matter-of-factly, as if we weren't carrying a bullet-riddled car on our backs but were just out for a little ride through the woods. "When the pins go down, that's *amore*." He looked across her toward me. "You should try it."

"Bowling is good." I was gazing out the window, remembering riding with Cousin Dominic in a cement truck to get rid of another body. It was becoming a family tradition.

Silvio was gazing down at Queenie. "Didn't you work in your old man's shop? I seem to remember you at the checkout counter."

"In summers during high school. When you came in, I knew you were Tommy's uncle. There's a resemblance."

"We live in the same tree."

The wrecker rumbled around the curves, the Charger swaying

behind us. The chains rattled and the big pneumatic brakes pumped and groaned. Silvio worked the wheel easily, he and the pavement in close combat, the road broken from neglect but the big wheels on the wrecker winning every time. I could see Queenie checking him out, a man who might as well be in a suit of armor. But Silvio was used to this situation, of people rising from some form of blown-out car and finding him there, in control. I watched him at the wheel as I always had, with an eye to learning his secret, but he kept it well hidden. His eyes were on the road, all his concentration there, and you'd have to read his shirt for the rest. But there it was, sewn in red: *Martini*. In this town, that name carried the weight for you. Silvio simply was MAN written large. One of my idols, and here he was, pulling me out of a jam.

"My nephew is okay, don't get me wrong. He's well-mannered. A perfect gentleman in some ways."

I was wondering what ways they were, so I could practice them.

"But he never was much of a driver."

"I was driving tonight," said Queenie, with the voice she used in confession.

"No, you weren't. Because this night never happened." He looked across at her and smiled. His teeth were big and white, as if sculpted by Michelangelo. "That's the great thing about our service."

Queenie came from a line of women who had learned that the men of this valley got things done in rough but thorough ways. Her trust in Silvio was already like iron, like the iron he had arrived in.

He leaned around her as if she weren't there—something men of his generation are well known for. "Tommy, where'd you pick her up tonight?"

"At WVIM. She works there."

Silvio looked down at her, still smiling his Michelangelo smile, large and white. "Your car is at the TV station?"

She nodded. He said, "We're going back to the garage now to get Tommy's handiwork squared away. Then we'll take you back to your car. It'll be like nothing happened. You walked out of the TV station tonight and there was your car waiting for you, *capeesh?*"

"*Capeesh.*"

He tugged at the bill of his cap as if to bring back a lost thought. "Didn't you used to draw stuff for your old man's store? In the window, drawing of a guy with golf clubs, whacking one off into the clouds?"

She smiled, whether at his peculiar choice of words or from the pleasure we get when our work is remembered, I couldn't say. But it pleased her; that I could see. She said, "I used to do all the signs we put in the window."

"The power of advertising. I bought my golf clubs from your old man because of that sign. He gave me a good deal. Not perfect, but I got my own back when I beat him on the ninth hole with his own golf clubs."

Queenie laughed, some of the tightness gone from her voice. Silvio was manipulating the situation with one thing in mind, that this night goes off the air, leaving only darkness behind.

"When you ask her out next time," he said, leaning around her again, "why don't you just take the wrecker? Save me a trip."

Heavy chains rattling around us, heavy metal swaying behind us, we took the last curve off Quarry Road. Queenie swayed with the rhythm of the truck, her eyes remaining on Silvio. His hair was iron gray, peeking out from under his Martini Towing cap. There was authority around his chin, accentuated by a bit of grizzle. He was towing away the situation.

We came into the trashy lights of town. It's when you're rolling on a city street that you feel the advantage of a high cab ride, because everybody else is *down there*. I'd had this ride before with Silvio when I was younger, but Queenie was feeling it for the first time: the rough, high ride in shining chrome, huge mirrors off the windows, red lights going around above her head—an official vehicle in the game of darkness where shit happens.

"I like your truck," she said.

"And I like you, so what do we do about *him*?" He hooked a thumb toward me. I knew he was never going to let me forget I'd wrecked his Charger. We'd be hearing about it until I carried him to his grave or he carried me to mine. This is what it is to be the nephew. I loved him at this moment exactly the way I'd loved him as a kid. He rammed around town in the biggest rig he could find, and he owned five more just like it.

The shops and bars went by, and we rode above them, looking into their empty windows. A cop car came toward us, and Silvio waved, just a flick of the wrist as he'd done countless times before. Wave to the cops, nothing to it. "I carry a lot of scrap," he said to Queenie. "That's what I'm carrying tonight. I have no need to report it. I do quite a bit of business with scrap." Again he leaned across to me. "I'll take it to Frankie Bang in Jersey."

Scrap of all kinds, including some with body parts attached, had gone to Frankie Bang. I said, "I haven't seen Bang in a long time."

"I'll tell him you said hello. I'll tell him you blessed him." Silvio laughed to himself.

We pulled into the alleyway where he had his garages. He parked and got down, opened the garage door from which we had first taken the Charger. He lowered the beaver tail and then lowered the ruined car. When it was back on street level, we pushed it into the garage. "I'll put it in the crusher tomorrow." He turned to Queenie. "All gone. Never existed." He lowered the garage doors and parked his wrecker in the vacant lot beside it. Then he led us up the alleyway to the main garage. We went inside, where some of his other wreckers, like a stable of mastodons, brooded heavily. All of them were bright red, beautifully maintained, and decorated with martini glasses. "My children," he said, rapping on one of them affectionately for Queenie's benefit. "What do you think?"

"Very nice."

"Some guys collect stamps. I collect trucks." He led us into his office, and I gave him the keys to the Charger. He hung them back in their place on the wall. Then he took down an electronic key fob. "The Acura. It's a nice ride. Everything you want." He looked at Queenie. "You don't mind traveling with my nephew one more time tonight?"

"I don't mind."

"You're sure about that? I've got a pet goldfish drives better than he does."

He pointed toward his photographs of spectacularly wrecked cars.

"Tommy's will go right on that wall. A lasting memento of his driving skill." He chuckled to himself, then glanced at Queenie. "Or maybe not, what do you think?"

"Maybe not."

She was looking at a framed newspaper article about a pileup on the interstate, to which a Martini truck had been summoned. Then she looked at the trophies from beauty shows in which wreckers were judged for their high levels of customization. Silvio nodded toward a side door. His house was beside the garage. He asked Queenie if she was hungry. "We've got pasta, soda, whatever."

"Thanks, I don't have much appetite at the moment."

He looked at me. "*You* can have six protein drinks."

"I'm okay."

Silvio sat on the edge of his desk. "Now, here's how it goes. Tommy was praying somewhere, and you were working. That's the night. There is no other." He let this sink in for a moment, then switched off the office lights. Again we followed him past the brooding mastodons and out into the alleyway. "I've got cars all over town," he said to Queenie. "I'm like a dog who buries bones just to be on the safe side."

She put her arm through his. "How do I say thanks?"

"By keeping my nephew out of trouble. Set him a good example." He opened the door to another garage. A white Acura MDX was waiting. "Like I said, a good ride. Satisfies the needs of everyone involved."

I got behind the wheel and Queenie sat in the bucket seat beside me. I lowered the window. "Thank you, Uncle."

"I didn't hear that."

"And I never said it." I waited until he waved me out, following his direction into the alleyway. He made a big show of guiding me past a telephone pole. "Plenty of room. Even you can do it." When I was clear of the pole, he gave us the same indifferent wave he'd given the cops. And I drove down the alley as the night recalibrated itself.

"I want to find who killed Finn," she said. "Now more than before."

As they say in foxhunting, she'd been blooded. The death dive of the Muldoon brothers had touched her nerves, keyed her up. It seemed to go with the memory I had of her as the class cartoonist; though the image was vague, I remembered her being focused in a way the majorettes and cheerleaders never were. They'd pranced around in high boots, flaring their skirts, while she had crouched, concentrated, the way she'd been tonight. Different from Bridget, who had been watching herself in the mirror of our eyes, an entire football team ogling her.

"You were fantastic tonight," I said.

"It never happened." Her voice was as cold as her emerald shamrock.

I drove her to the TV station. We sat outside. I reached across, slipped my arm behind her. She turned slowly and looked at me, that emerald flame dancing in her eyes. This was not the girl for a fruit-and-vegetable salesman. I leaned across, our lips meeting briefly.

"That's enough for now," she said. As if it were in league with me, the Acura's bucket seat had pushed her skirt halfway up her thighs. The alluring thing about Queenie was that she'd gone from shy cartoonist to seductress. But it had been for the benefit of Richard Mittleman, whose presence I could feel between us, enriched by the many exchanges she'd had with him—plans large and small, little dreams and big ones, for marriage ever after. I had to bring her back to fast living with me. I said, "It might've been us going into the quarry. Right through the Martini sign."

"Well, it wasn't us." She was putting an end to our evening, sliding toward the door.

"How about just one more kiss? As a kind of offering."

"Offering?"

"To Saint Thomas Aquinas. For protecting us in our hour of need." I leaned toward her.

"For Saint Thomas," she said, her shamrock necklace disappearing against my chest. We held the kiss for Saint Thomas long enough for our lips to get to heaven. "What am I doing?" she said, pulling away from me. "I must be nuts." She pushed open the passenger door, and I watched her walk toward the station door. She didn't wave.

But the skaters had touched.

20

"What happened to the Charger?" asked young Santiago the next morning, when he discovered the Acura MDX parked outside my trailer.

"Totaled."

His face fell. "My beautiful polish job."

"Also totaled."

He looked dubiously at the Acura SUV, not a car to capture the imagination of a ten-year-old. But I said, in the melodious Spanish more suitable to things of the spirit, "You'll polish it with the same fervor."

"I will try."

"A bicycle remains the goal."

"That is understood." And he went to retrieve his tin of car wax.

By midafternoon, the Acura was gleaming. I drove it to the supermarket to acquire a six-pack of Guinness Extra Stout and a bag of Doritos for their high nutritive value. The young woman working the cash register paused between the Doritos and the stout. "It's Tommy Martini, isn't it?"

She was very pregnant, seemed ready to give birth before she finished scanning my six-pack. By some miracle, I remembered that her name was Claire.

"Are you back to stay?" she asked.

"Just a visit."

"You ought to swing by and say hello to Jim. He'd love to see you."
While she was scooping change from the cash register, she added, "He's
back from Afghanistan."

"I didn't know he'd gone."

"Soldiering is in his blood. Band of brothers, that kind of thing."

"Good for him."

She handed me my change. "Actually, not so good. He's been pretty
down."

"Where's he living?"

"Our old house."

I drove there with stout and Doritos. Parked across from Jim's house,
wheels turned toward the curb, was a Lincoln Town Car, one of the last
of the big sedans—paint job failing, fenders mismatched, plenty of dings
on the bumper. Once known as a car for the senior set, it was now filled
with young men whose music and voices I could hear as I parked well
behind them. The music was rap, celebrating, so far as I could make
out, the poetry of punching women in the face. The deportment of the
young men went with the song, for they were a lively bunch, calling to
one of their number who was just leaving the Hutmacher porch. They
were cheering him, and two of them got out, raising beer cans. They
drained the cans and threw them into Jim's driveway.

"What the fuck you looking at?" asked the young man coming from
the porch, testosterone leaking from his ears. He'd hooked his thumbs
in his belt. He wore a muscle T-shirt and romantic jeans. I absorbed
his question without comment. He was young and entitled to a certain
amount of swagger. And I was here to see Jim, not mop up the street.

His two friends, having thrown their beer cans onto Jim's lawn,
turned their attention to me. Their friend had already used *What the
fuck you looking at?* so they were forced to think of something else. In
lieu of thought, one of them grabbed his crotch and rocked it toward
me. The other one, after performing a quick scan of his mental contents,
came up with "Eat me, motherfucker," but he knew it lacked a certain
something, so he turned around, lowered his pants, and mooned me.
His friends in the car applauded by slapping their hands on the roof.

I waited until they bundled themselves into the Lincoln. One of them remained long enough to shake his beer can and spray the grill of my Acura. He'd probably been born here and was under the influence of mine gas. What would be the point of handing him a beating? He was already beaten. He was like all the tough guys I'd known here who had gone nowhere and were still here, breathing mine gas. When their car reached the bottom of the hill, I got out and walked to Jim's door. I pressed the bell, but it was dead. I knocked on the door. There was no answer. I bent down to the mail slot and called in, "Jim, it's Tommy Martini. Open up."

Jim Hutmacher had been our quarterback in high school—sure-footed and fast, with a head on his shoulders, and a powerful throwing arm. The sound I heard approaching was the slow shuffle of somebody else, someone who had never called a signal, or faked a handoff as he dropped back to pass. Jim Hutmacher could stand in the backfield, calmly looking for a receiver, finding him, and then throwing over the heads of the defenders, dropping the ball where he wanted it. But in college, he only made the practice squad, because our state university had recruited one of the best quarterbacks in the country. After two years on the bench, Jim quit because soldiering, as his sister said, was in his blood.

The door opened and there he was, disheveled, eyes as quick as ever but lodged in a face ruined by booze. His skin was yellow. He had a large green garbage bag in one hand and a shotgun in the other.

"Martini."

"Don't shoot."

He turned and put the shotgun in an umbrella stand but kept the garbage bag in his hand. It dragged along the floor as he shuffled down the hall in ratty bedroom slippers. I noticed the kitchen door had been torn off, along with the hinges. It rested against the wall.

We moved into the living room. The television was on and a baseball game was in progress, with the sound turned off. He sat down in front of it, then put his face in the garbage bag and retched. When his head came out, sweat covered his forehead. "Detoxing," he said.

"That's a good thing, right?"

"If your heart doesn't explode." He put his head back into the bag. When it came out again, he said, "When you get off the sauce, everything you've been avoiding comes back and speeds up your heart. Watching baseball with the sound off slows it down. Proven fact."

"You been through it before."

"A number of times." He sprawled back in the chair, letting the bag fall to the floor. The beautiful athlete was gone, in his place this bloated substitute from the bench.

We stared at soundless baseball for a while. "Need anything else?"

"Gatorade. For the electrolytes." He pointed to a pile of empties. "I thought I had enough."

There was a convenience store at the bottom of the hill. I went there and looked through the cooler, selecting some Smartwater along with Gatorade. I thought cold bottles would be more bracing, though I had no experience detoxing from alcohol or anything else, unless you count dangerous women as an addiction.

When I returned to his living room and silent baseball, Jim picked up the Smartwater. "The fancy stuff."

"Nothing too good for old Jim."

"Everything's too good for old Jim. Even this place." He gestured, indicating the ramshackle house. As I looked around, I noticed that under the stairs leading to the second floor a cot had been jammed in. Following my gaze, he said, "Terry Taliban put me there." Seeing I didn't understand, he added, "They're still after me. It comes from being blown up. Or as we said in Kandahar, blowed up."

He put the Smartwater to his lips. His hand was trembling. We went back to looking at baseball with the sound off. The game had a dreamlike quality that way, the batters' compulsive little habits at the plate more sharply outlined. But with the sound off, their strange inner calm was also visible, along with their amazing attentiveness to the guy on the pitcher's mound. Even when the ball flew silently past them, their corkscrewing bodies had a beauty I'd had never fully seen before. "I think I prefer it this way."

"It does it for me," said Jim. He'd finished the bottle of Smartwater and started in on a Gatorade, but he paused to retch in the bag. Looking up at me, he said, "I'm down to the green bile."

"Is that a good sign?"

"It beats having a seizure."

"How long were you in Afghanistan?"

"Too long."

"Sorry, stupid question."

"I don't mind. I'm not there any longer." He turned toward his bed under the stairs. "Except at night. Then the T-man's in my dreams."

I noticed there was a handgun alongside his pillow. Jim would not be someone you'd want to shake awake. "Who were those assholes outside your house?"

"Local boys."

"I got that, but what else?"

He shook his head and went back to retching in his garbage bag. After which we watched more baseball with the sound off. Finally, he said, "I've got cable. I can always find a game somewhere."

"They threw their empty beer cans into your driveway."

"I've seen worse." He paused. "Rocket-propelled grenades—now, *they* can really chew up a driveway."

"Have these assholes got some sort of beef with you?"

He opened another bottle of Smartwater and drained it. "I'm feeling smarter already, how about you?"

"I haven't had one yet."

"I highly recommend it."

"We were talking about the assholes."

"Maybe they don't like my face. I don't care much for it myself."

On the TV screen, a ball sailed silently out of the park. When the batter had rounded the bases and was approaching home, he pointed to the sky and blessed himself. Taking note of this, Jim said, "I heard you became a monk."

"I did. It probably won't last."

"But it was fun for a while?"

"I'll take it over rocket-propelled grenades. But I miss the female sex."

"I had one of its members living with me recently. You might find traces of her in the bathroom."

"She left?"

"I think so."

On the TV screen, the announcers were discussing the home run. With the sound off, they looked more idiotic than usual. Jim said, "The problem with the assholes is, I'm going to kill one of them."

"Take it from me, that's a problem you don't need."

"They follow me around in that pimp wagon of theirs. They come up close. Sometimes they tap my bumper. You saw the shotgun. I carry it in my truck. And you can see I'm not in my right mind."

"They seem like the crazy ones."

"No, they're just assholes. The strange thing is, I have no idea why they picked me. But they did. And I sure as hell will kill one of them. A kind of spontaneous reaction I won't be able to control." He put his head in the bag for a while, and the sound was impressive. Finally, he brought his head out. "Furball."

"How did it start with the assholes?"

"I talk to myself in public." He picked up a bottle of Gatorade and studied its color. "For example, I might talk to this bottle before purchasing it. Did you talk to it before *you* purchased it?"

"No."

"There you go." He opened the bottle and brought it to his lips. After a long swig, he said, "Where would we be without electrolytes?"

"So they heard you talking to yourself."

"They're like children. Anything out of the ordinary inspires them." He drank again. "I'm still going to kill them."

"Does it feel like you have a volcano in your guts?"

"More like a phosphorus grenade. A result of my work environment. How about you?"

"I was born that way. I used to take pills for it."

"The VA give me some of those." He pointed to the garbage bag. "They're in there."

I was remembering handoffs in the backfield, when he'd smacked the football precisely into my gut, where the volcano had burned and where it burned now. "We should coordinate something."

"Like what?"

"A ride in your truck."

His eyes met mine. "They're *my* assholes. You don't need to get involved."

"Too late."

He continued gazing at me with those quarterback eyes. He'd seen more violence than me, seen it large-scale on the battlefield. I felt dwarfed by his experience, but at this moment he needed me, or he certainly would kill an asshole. He would be put in a maximum-security prison where his battle readiness would get him endless stretches of solitary, and he would come out—if he came out at all—more broken than he was today, and that was saying something. I said, "We've got to show the assholes the volcano and the phosphorus grenade in all their terrifying color."

He smiled. "At the moment, I'm indisposed." He put his head back in the bag.

For the rest of the day, we watched baseball with the sound off. He was right, you can always find a game somewhere on cable—big-league or college, including women's college ball, which has finer points you don't see elsewhere. We watched replays of Little League World Series games. By the time he put the green bag aside, announcing that phase was over, I was hungry. He had menus from several restaurants, and I called out to an Italian one and ordered too much food. An hour later, I picked it up. "Enjoy," said the cashier, pushing a large cardboard box toward me.

"What have I done?" I asked her, looking at the supersize order.

"Happens all the time," she said.

"Is there life after meatballs?"

"I don't think so."

I carried the box to the Acura and drove slowly to avoid upsetting the spaghetti sauce, which was packed in a separate cylindrical container.

Thus protecting my precious cargo, I returned to the Hutmacher house on the hill. The foundation had been constructed in the shape of a wedge so that the house would sit level, and the driveway had also been wedged into a level plane. But the backyard, where Jim's old man had labored to produce something like a lawn, followed the steep slope of the hill. It was a crazy place to build a house, but Jim's wasn't the only one. The slope of the valley held many such houses and made you think people lived tilted lives. Maybe we all do, no matter what street we live on.

Jim met me at the door and appeared steadier on his feet, though his skin was still yellow. "I'm not as bad as I look," he said when I observed that his flesh tone was the color of a summer squash. As if in proof of this, he made up a plate for himself from the contents of the box. I followed suit, and like our brothers around the world, we sat down to eat it on a couch facing a TV screen filled with sport. The sacred meatball was consumed.

Jim ate sparingly at first, but as the night wore on he returned to the cardboard box for more. I was eating my way through it fearlessly. We reminisced about games we'd played, the remembered game as dreamlike as baseball with the sound off. It's why athletes sound so cliché-ridden when questioned by reporters. The game they've been in has happened for them on a level that can be expressed only in dream images, and these are hard to articulate. So they smile stupidly or get surly in a hurry.

After running through several seasons, we were out of dreams. Jim said, "You know how a few lines from a song can run through your head for days?"

I told him I'd had the experience, and he said, "I have it, but it's not a song." He paused. "It's small-arms fire." He stared at the TV set. We were looking at a bygone World Series game. "Light machine guns. Even some old Lee–Enfields. Stuff Terry Taliban used. That's the song I hear. And if I'm out shopping and I hear it, I start talking to myself so I won't hear it. Because if I keep on hearing it, I'm liable to freak out." He pointed to the kitchen door that had been torn off the hinges.

On the screen was a baseball game from the fifties, and the black-and-white video made it seem as if ghosts were playing. It was easy to see the older playing style, especially in the pitcher's windup and delivery. Elaborate wasted motion but mysteriously beautiful, as if the pitcher were masking some profound secret. I said, "I lived with a difficult woman who recited poetry to me."

Some interesting action was going on in the game, and it was another inning before Jim asked, "Remember any of those poems?"

"One by Yeats. *I carry from my mother's womb a fanatic heart.* I felt she was trying to tell me something."

"How did it work out with her?"

"With me looking into the barrel of her gun."

"That puts a strain on a relationship."

A ghostly centerfielder chased a long flyball, climbed the fence to catch it, and seemed to hang there for a moment like a butterfly, wings outspread.

"On the other hand, when some bad dudes came looking for me, she brained one with a paperweight."

"Yes, but could she cook?"

When we finished eating, we shared the last bottle of Smartwater. "I'm about smarted out," said Jim. He stood. "Time for our battle rattle." He went to a closet and took out a pair of Kevlar vests. "In case the assholes are carrying, let's be prudent."

I had difficulty fitting the vest around my chest, but when it was fastened it was a secure feeling. I looked at Jim. "Are you up for this tonight? We can wait until you're feeling better."

He was tightening his own vest with the ease of one who had done it many times. "There's a strange thing about detoxing. When I stop puking green death and my heart comes back to normal, I feel supernaturally calm."

We walked toward the door. He stopped at the umbrella stand and looked at the shotgun. "Do I take it?"

"The effect will be better without it."

21

Jim backed his truck out of the garage. I asked him if he knew where to find the assholes.

"They'll find us." He wasn't a big man, but he had the presence of a torpedo—a stored-up will to destroy. "The woman who lived with me—and may still be living with me, for all I know—has great patience. I've tried being patient with the assholes."

"It won't work."

"I thought they'd get tired of fucking with me."

But we both knew they wouldn't get tired of fucking with him. They were drawn to Jim, sensing in him something they lacked, and lacking it, they were jealous. They knew that his mumbling was not that of some babbling old fool; what they couldn't know was that Jim's mumbling was an incantation to the gods of war.

"That guy on your porch today—did he say anything?"

"He said, and I quote, *We know what you're up to, man.*"

The asshole swaggered through my memory, his slightly bowlegged walk expressing the purest kind of stupidity. Jim continued. "He was talking through my door. He didn't see the shotgun."

"Does he know you own one?"

"Maybe, but he can't imagine getting both barrels in the chest."

We were in the one-way labyrinth out of Jim's neighborhood—a route that forced us to circle blocks out of our way, but our destination was free-floating. He said, "I'll be off the sauce for a while. The temptation will come when my liver stops hurting."

I was sleepy from meatballs. It would be a while before I was restored to full consciousness. We passed the usual barrooms, their windowless walls calling me to drink. I wondered if I could wind up like Jim, with my head in a garbage bag. Anything was possible, especially if I stuck around this town. "Ever think of getting out of here, Jim?"

"Talking to myself in a different town doesn't seem like a solution."

We entered the downtown area, with its blank facades, the old businesses now advertising nothing but the inflated egos of teenage graffiti artists. And I saw the name RUBY again, in red letters six feet high. The girl got around.

At Parade Square, the sex workers were working the bicycle lanes. "A little attitude adjustment, guys?" She walked in her high heels and fishnet stockings alongside the truck, and when we passed on by, another one took her place, then another. It was like a beauty relay, and it seemed a shame to disappoint them.

The corner boys were out, providing fuel for desire or delirium. We drove past the square and out of the downtown area. We kept going until we reached the walls of the football stadium. It had been wonderful to come onto the field, our forms exaggerated by shoulder pads, big numbers on our backs, our breath visible in the cold fall air. Invincible. There to play our hearts out, adolescent energy bouncing us up and down. "It was lovely while it lasted."

"Yes, it was," said Jim. "My prelude to war."

He put the truck in gear, and we rolled slowly past the stadium. "How long will you be in town?"

"Until I find out who killed Finn."

"That could be a while."

"Probably."

"I was pretty boozed up when it happened."

"He was shot in the back in his yard."

"It's like killing Jiminy Cricket." Jim steered us back into the downtown section. "I mean, why do it? He was just singing a song."

"Some people didn't like the tune."

"He gave me a ride in his Corvette once. I thought we were going to wind up on the moon."

"He liked speed."

"So do I, but this was absolute fucking nuts, and I thought, *This guy wants to die*. Did he want to die?"

"He had romantic ideas about it."

"You lose that in your first firefight." Jim swung in beside some Circle K gas pumps. "As the rockets came in, I prayed to Jesus I was elsewhere."

"Which is where you are now."

"The power of prayer has been proven." He filled his tank. Across the street was a gym where I'd fought a few amateur boxing matches against guys who'd been trained by serious managers. My opponents were heavyweight power punchers like me, but they were intent on breaking into the profession, and I was just a tough college kid. But then I did something none of them had done with their best punch: I killed a man in a fight.

Jim drove on past the roller-skating rink, closed now and boarded over, nobody going round and round. Just us, round and round the town. "I've got to pick up a job somewhere," said Jim.

"Anything in mind?"

"I welded stuff in Afghanistan. To fortify trucks that had no armor. We'd slap on any scrap metal we could find. I can do that."

"You could armor this truck."

"It's a start."

We came up on the county jail. Razor wire gleamed under the glow of security lights. "When I was a kid I thought I'd wind up there," said Jim. "I still worry about it."

"This is why you don't want to shoot an asshole, even though they're in season."

"Shoot one and stuff him. Stand him up in my driveway."

"A good security system comes with a little sign you can put in your driveway."

"A stuffed asshole sends a stronger message."

The jail fell behind us. I had pretty much recovered from the meatballs. I was thinking clearly again. Or perhaps I never think clearly. If I did, I wouldn't be in Coalville.

We drove past an old movie theater. Its doors were boarded up, and the marquee was advertising a local law firm specializing in injury claims. "That's a movie I don't want to miss," said Jim.

His eyes went to the rearview mirror, and he looked at me. "We have company." He pulled over. "You may hear me talking to myself. It's usually just field manual stuff. *Six tasks which are common to all echelons*, stuff like that."

I opened the door and stepped out. Jim stepped out from the other side.

The big Lincoln was pulling in behind us. It was large enough to fit five assholes, and all five got out. The chief asshole took a step toward us. He was the bowlegged one who had swaggered off Jim's porch. He said, with mocking friendliness, "Jim, you're out kind of late."

Jim didn't respond. He was mumbling.

The asshole came closer. "Speak up, Jim. We can't hear you."

I was smiling to myself. He was going to remember the next few minutes for years to come. I said, "Hey, fuckwad."

He seemed surprised by this form of address, so I repeated it with a slight variation. "That's right, fuckwad, I'm talking to you."

"Then you're making a big mistake."

"Why, is there some other fuckwad here?" He was letting me walk right up to him, within range of what was going to be overwhelming force. Of course, he didn't know that. He was high on some bad chemicals. Maybe they caused him to think I was two feet tall.

He was a heavyweight—young, reasonably fit. As on our first meeting, he was wearing stylish jeans, but he had changed from his muscle T-shirt into a Hawaiian shirt with gaudy palm trees printed on it. A cigarette pack was outlined in his breast pocket. He had a gold earring in one ear. If I bit off a piece of his ear, might I accidentally swallow the ring? Possibly.

His haircut was the kind to increase intimidation—a close shave around the ears giving him the look of an escaped convict. With no sense of self-preservation, he had allowed me to come into his personal space, confident that being outnumbered five to one, I wouldn't last long. I was remembering a drug lord saying politely to the man he was about to stab in the heart, *Did you enjoy your meal?* I asked Mr. Fuckwad if he'd enjoyed *his* meal.

"What meal?"

"The one you're about to lose." My hands were at my side, and he couldn't imagine how fast one of them was about to enter his vital region. He quickly found out. My fist went up into his stomach and stopped at the diaphragm but still lifted him off the ground. I stepped back quickly because he brought up a sizable portion of the meal I'd inquired about. He collapsed in his Hawaiian shirt, the palm trees falling into a puddle of puke.

Jim rushed past me, charging into the ragged formation the other assholes had formed. They were expecting the shuffling, muttering drunk they'd seen earlier in the day. Instead, they got a tire iron in the face, the first asshole feeling it unhinge his jaw, the second one getting it just above his eyebrows. He stiffened, eyes wide open in disbelief, the night going wrong fast.

"Easy, Jim," I said, stepping in beside him because he had raised the tire iron, preparing to cave in the guy's skull.

He glanced at me. "Am I over the edge?"

"Just a little."

He threw the tire iron at the Lincoln's back window. The window shattered into a cobweb of vintage glass. He turned back to the other tire-ironed asshole, whose forehead had grown something like another little head without eyes. Jim rushed him backward, the guy's arms flailing wildly, his body off balance, his night continuing to go wrong. There should have been a pile-on, five against two, and instead streetlights were revolving, the pavement was coming up to meet him, and then he was pinned to it, Jim on top of him, muttering, ". . . primed, fused, armored, or otherwise prepared for action . . ."

The asshole with the unhinged jaw was exploring its new flexibility, saying, ". . . What's this . . . what . . ."

Which left two assholes for me. One of them was a skinny little rat who took off running. The other one charged me, posing as a fighter. He was a pretty good size, but this was not his night. To have your legs swept out from under you while emitting your war cry is demoralizing. Then to have two hundred pounds fortified by a Kevlar vest drop on top of you completes the feeling of defeat. As he struggled underneath me, I felt all the sorry shit that made up his life: the posturing for women, the clowning around, the aimless bullying, the disordered thoughts of an unschooled mind, all of it packed into this body whose strength came from miners buried a hundred years ago. I felt it all seeping into me and jumped off him like a dog that has tasted a poisonous toad. He gazed up at me, puzzled, having resigned himself to a beating. I yanked him to his feet. He put up his arms to protect his face, and I slapped them down—a little bit of action that almost set me off again.

"Do it," he said. "I don't give a fuck."

He really didn't. The resignation in him went back a long way. It probably started in grade school when he realized that along with being poor, he was also stupid. I shoved him from me. "Get lost. We're taking the Lincoln."

He gazed at us for a few moments, then turned and walked away. Broken Jaw and Swollen Head followed. They'd had enough. They weren't a hard-core gang after all, just loosely affiliated losers, without firepower, and no territory.

Fuckwad, in his Hawaiian shirt, had remained on the pavement, hoping perhaps to be overlooked. But he was the one I wanted. I yanked him to his feet. "Take off your shirt and get in the car."

He removed his pack of cigarettes and studied the puke-covered fabric of the shirt, then threw it away. "Where we going?"

I shoved him in on the passenger side and spoke to Jim. "Follow in your truck."

I got behind the wheel of the Lincoln. The Town Car had been one of the glamour rides of its era. It was moth-eaten now, the Scotch grain leather cracked, the deep pile carpet worn. But the feeling remained, of a great American dream, to arrive at your destination in two tons of carnal delight. The keys were in the ignition, and I put us in motion.

Fuckwad asked where we were going, and again I ignored him. He reached into his pants and took out a cigarette. The dashboard had a lighter and he used it. Blowing smoke, he asked, "Jim a buddy of yours?"

When he got no answer, he took another long drag. "He's like a mental case, right?"

"He's a fucking war hero. What the fuck are you?"

"Just an interested party, man. I check up on him now and then."

"By throwing beer cans in his yard."

"I'll retrieve them. No offense meant."

The V-8 engine breathed deeply under the hood, like a dragon in its cave. When Ford wanted to get serious, they could do it right, and they'd done it right on the Lincoln Town Car. As a monk, I had put my love affairs with automobiles on hold, but this one filled me with thoughts of sin. I could buy a secondhand Town Car and take a luxury ride to Alaska. That should be far enough away from this valley of tears.

Fuckwad looked across at me. "We thought, *Get a rise out of Jim, do him good.*"

Since I'd punched him only once, he was starting to relax a little. He continued to speak through mouthfuls of smoke. "You know, help a guy get out of himself." He liked this line of thought and pursued it further. "Promote interaction, you see what I'm getting at?"

The seats in this car had once been an embrace of soft leather, but now the hard bits underneath were starting to come through. Well, nothing lasts forever, but the engine still made its low animal noise, ready to eat up the road if given a chance.

Fuckwad continued his portrait of thoughtful caring. "When we have a little time on our hands, we go to Jim's. We try to talk him around."

Smoke drifted toward me, gave me the desire. "Give me a cigarette."

"You got it." He tapped another cigarette from his pack, and I lit up. I was back in the valley, smoking in a pimp car.

"But Jim," continued Fuckwad, "he's hard to reach. It's a fucking shame. You mind if I play some music?"

I didn't stop him. I wanted to hear the JBL sound system. The Town Car was one of the first to offer a CD player in the dash. A thundering bass shook the front seat. A female rapper, whose time was not that of a vintage Lincoln, broke in defiantly. To the accompaniment of synthetic instruments, she explained her position in the world, which was not one I'd care to question should I ever find myself on her turf.

Fuckwad tapped on the dashboard, just above the glove box. He'd said his piece about Jim, and now it was time for aesthetic pleasures. He'd paid with a punch to the guts and figured he was in the clear. If I stole his Lincoln, he'd steal somebody else's. He was a big enough guy, but he'd realized I was bigger. In Coalville, that was grounds for negotiation. He reached to the radio volume knob, turned it down. "You can drop me anywhere."

"I want you to meet somebody."

He flipped the butt of his cigarette out the window and lit another one. "You're the man."

He trusted to the tide that carried him from day to day. If I could go far enough back in his family tree, I'd probably find a simple Irish potato farmer, wedded to the land, dependent but ever optimistic. Then a son strikes out for the new land, gets here and winds up in the mines, producing children in the dark and dreaming in the depths beneath the city, finally resulting in the asshole sitting beside me.

I puffed on my cigarette and he puffed on his, and smoke hung heavy around us. He asked, "What do you think of my Lincoln?"

"It's nice."

"I like a big ride."

In his big ride, we rolled along the empty streets, the soul of the town appearing bleak at that hour. Of the two of us, my companion was the optimist. Maybe he'd gotten it from that farmer forebear of his. So he expounded on the virtues of a big ride, as if it weren't being forced on him; he didn't seem worried about its outcome. He didn't know where I was taking him, but being shuffled around against his will was not strange to him. He was wearing cheap cologne and a Timex wristwatch, and the hour was one familiar to him. Nighttime brought amusement and occasional opportunities for income. "You and Jim are tight, I get that," he said. "Couple of war heroes."

"He wanted to blow your head off."

"Overreacting, but I see where he's coming from."

"Tell me."

"Words fail me, man." He gestured with his cigarette, as if outlining a difficult geometric problem.

We were on the south side of town. I pulled into Uncle Silvio's parking lot. Jim pulled in behind me in his pickup truck. Several much bigger trucks were hulking in the shadows cast by huge security lights. Silvio's outfit worked around the clock. One of his drivers was standing near the office door. "Silvio around?"

"On a job. Should be back any minute."

I rolled the window back up. On both sides of us was the presence of big machines—dumb, severely masculine, waiting.

Fuckwad looked around, mildly curious, with the air of one who has been dragged to odd spots before. "Mind me asking what we're doing here?"

"You'll find out."

Perhaps it was the heavy shadows of the trucks that surrounded us with their suggestion of brutal force, but Fuckwad seemed suddenly less optimistic. "You got, like, earthmoving stuff here?" The idea of being buried alive had dawned on him. "What do you say we get out and stretch our legs?"

"What do you say you stay right the fuck where you are."

"I'm sitting, man. Fully cooperating in every way."

"Give me another cigarette."

"You've got it. On the way."

I smoked and waited. Eventually we felt the ground rumbling, and a huge bank of lights swung into the driveway, like the eyes of medieval dragon. It was Silvio's biggest truck, the one he used to pull broken-down city buses off the streets. It came into the parking lot, a second vehicle lumbering behind it, wheels cradled by large iron brackets. The air brakes squealed, the truck shuddered to a stop, and the door to the cab opened. Silvio swung down. I got out to meet him. He was looking at the Lincoln. "Windsor V-8 engine." Having identified it, he looked at me. "Where'd you get it?"

"It belongs to the asshole inside. He and some asshole buddies were bothering a friend of mine." I pointed to Jim, who was getting out of his pickup. "Afghan vet. Had a bad war. I had to keep him from killing the asshole."

Jim came over to us and they shook hands. I told Silvio, "I want to teach the asshole a lesson he won't forget. I was thinking about your car crusher."

Silvio nodded toward the adjacent parking lot. I got back into the Lincoln.

"What's up?" asked Fuckwad nervously.

I drove the Lincoln into the adjacent lot and parked alongside the car crusher, which was stationed there like a devouring monster waiting for a victim. I told Fuckwad to get out.

"Still cooperating, man," he said, opening the door of the Lincoln. "Fully with the program."

Silvio and Jim joined us. Silvio shoved Fuckwad into the back seat of the Lincoln. "Sit there, and don't move."

"Not moving," said Fuckwad. "Sitting here, as required." But his eyes were jumping around, staring out one window and then the other. Silvio rejoined him with a length of rope. "Give me your arm."

"Restraints aren't necessary, man. I'll go quietly."

"You'll go the way I say." Silvio tied his arm to the back seat safety belt. "Other arm."

Silvio tied it to the other safety belt. "Now, stay there."

"I'm not going anywhere, man." He tried to raise his arms as if to demonstrate. "But I'd like to know what the fuck's going on."

Silvio engaged the childproof locks on the Lincoln, shutting Fuckwad in. Like a child, which in some sense he was, Fuckwad would now be unable to open the doors. Silvio climbed up onto the seat of a crane used to lift cars and position them over the crusher. He positioned the jaws of the crane around the trunk of the Lincoln, then engaged them. Like a hungry dinosaur, they bit into the trunk, seizing it firmly. Silvio lifted the Lincoln and dangled it over the car crusher. Then he climbed back down to the pavement.

Suspended by safety belts, Fuckwad tilted forward toward the front seats. The windows were up, muffling his cries.

Jim and I looked down into the interior of the car crusher. It held eight rows of hinged steel rollers rotating against matching rollers. Anything that fell between them would be slowly crushed and swallowed. Silvio powered the crusher up and the monster rollers began to rotate. Their menacing sound drowned Fuckwad's cries of alarm. We could see his open mouth moving, like a fish in a tank. Silvio climbed back up onto the crane and began to lower the Lincoln. As it touched the grinding rollers, the Lincoln bounced violently, Fuckwad bouncing with it. Then the rollers caught the grill and gobbled it up along with the headlights. With a hideous rending noise, it devoured them.

The noise was deafening, and Jim and I stood back to spare our eardrums. Fuckwad was not spared. He shook in the back seat, his screams lost in the crunch of metal and glass. The crusher began to eat the hood and then the Windsor V-8 engine. The solid engine block buckled in the bite of those terrible jaws, and mangled pieces of the car were disgorged onto a conveyor belt that carried them into a dumpster.

I looked up at Silvio. Concentration marked his expression as he fed the Lincoln deeper into the crusher. It had now devoured the engine, motor oil coating its slurping fangs. It began eating the windshield, which splintered into a thousand pieces, the frame around it buckling inward. It was like watching a road accident in slow motion. Fuckwad was still hanging downward, with the jaws coming closer to him.

The steering wheel was devoured along with the dashboard. Then the jaws bit into the front seats, ripping the Scotch grain leather, combining it with the pile carpeting and rolling it all into a ball that disappeared in the churning mouth of iron. The seats disappeared, and Fuckwad was next, hanging just above the rollers.

Silvio paused the crane, letting Fuckwad dangle. He swung the crane boom and lowered the rest of the Lincoln to the ground. Jim and I opened the doors and untied Fuckwad. He crawled out, pale and trembling violently. He reached for a cigarette, but his pack had fallen into the crusher. I said, "If you or any of your asshole buddies ever bother Jim again, you're going the rest of the way in. Is that clear?"

Again his lips moved like those of a fish, but no sound came out. He staggered away bent over, as if still being lowered into the crusher. He made a guttural noise, which sounded like *gack*. Silvio lowered what remained of the Lincoln into the crusher. The beast ate it completely. He climbed down and turned off the crusher. Fuckwad had reached the end of the parking lot and was looking up and down the street, bewildered and still muttering *gack*. He walked on, bent over. Silvio said, "Usually, we don't let them out of the car."

I said, "Jim needs a job. He can do welding."

Silvio looked at Jim's hands and saw evidence of manual labor. "Ever drive big trucks?"

"I drove a tank retriever in Kandahar."

Silvio nodded, looked at me. "You know what that is?"

"No, sir."

"It's the biggest tow truck in the world." He looked back at Jim. "When can you start?"

"I just need a shit and a shave."

"I'll see you back here." Silvio returned to the second-largest tow truck in the world and finished the job of bringing a broken-down city bus into his parking lot. Jim and I got into Jim's truck and drove. We passed Fuckwad, who was weaving along the street, disoriented by shock and terror.

Jim said, "It's too bad about the Lincoln."

"Had to be done."

Fuckwad grew smaller in the rearview mirror. The crusher had eaten his car, but he'd avoided being eaten himself. The sun would be rising soon, and he'd be there to see it. When its rays came over the edge of the hills surrounding the valley, they would warm his face. The little shred of optimism that kept him going would surface. He'd find a McDonald's, have an Egg McMuffin, and resume his journey to nowhere. I was glad I'd kept him alive for another day. We've got to help our fellow man when we can.

When we got back to Jim's house, he said, "Keep the Kevlar. With what you're doing in this town, it could be a handy thing to have on hand."

22

A possum was out raiding neighborhood garbage. When my car approached it, its snout was buried in a stack of garbage bags and its prehensile tail was wrapped around one of them. A living fossil and symbol of Coalville, another living fossil. The odd thing about the possum is that if you scare him, he plays dead. Falls on his side, shows his fangs and gumline, and then emits an odor of advanced putrefaction—a form of death you would not want to ingest. That's Coalville too.

Putting the possum behind me, I drove until I reached Mirror Lake, to which Queenie had recklessly invited me. At her family's cottage, she handed me a selection of bathing suits from the Jack O'Malley Sporting Goods store. "Find one that fits. You can change in the spare bedroom."

The bedroom had the smell of wood smoke, damp air, and time. I sorted through the selection of suits. Some still had the price tag attached. One was decorated with a pattern of little seahorses. My own little flotilla. I left my clothes behind on the bed, and the seahorses and I returned to the porch. Queenie was in a bikini. Our high school sketch artist was a vest-pocket Venus.

In the middle of Mirror Lake was a small island, and we swam toward it. Queenie was a strong swimmer, having grown up on this lake. When she climbed out of the water ahead of me, her wet bikini clinging tightly to her jarringly lovely body, I remained in the shallows, looking upward. It's my understanding that when girls begin to develop breasts, they're sometimes uncomfortable with this farewell to childhood. I wondered if it had been the case with her, a young Catholic girl schooled in modesty by the nuns. I further wondered about the moment when the size of her breasts exceeded the nuns' expectations, becoming the eye-filling rack that was exceeding my own expectations.

"Swallowed a tadpole?" she asked, standing over me, hands on her hips, aware of her power over me and any other male who might swim out to Circe's Island. Then she stretched out on the sandy shore, pretending to examine her painted toenails. In spite of her teeny-weeny bikini, she, too, was unsure what to do next. "I guess," she said with a sigh, "we should've kept our clothes on."

"Don't say that. Sunshine promotes vitamin D."

A heron flapped on by us and landed in the reeds, where it assumed the fishing position, eyes fixed on the water. Queenie said, "We should swim back."

"Let's wait and see if the bird gets lucky." The heron took one slow step through the reeds, vigilance in every feather.

"They're so beautiful," said Queenie. "I always wanted to be tall."

"You're perfect the way you are."

"I wasn't fishing for compliments."

"I know. The only one fishing is the bird."

We sat there, watching the heron. Finally, she said, "I keep dreaming Killian and Connor are chasing us."

"Their brother Mike has been chasing me for years. You get used to it."

"Are you sorry you came back to Coalville?"

"Not at the moment. At the moment, I'm right where I want to be."

"Me too. But it's complicated."

"There's no denying that."

The heron's head and neck plunged swiftly downward, and it came up with an eel. The eel was crosswise in the heron's beak and wriggling desperately to get free; by masterful snaps of its beak, the heron gradually turned the eel around and sent it down. It next appeared as a quivering motion in the heron's neck. "Can it swallow that thing?" asked Queenie.

I was asking myself the same question. That had been one big eel. But the heron kept working at it, neck slowly undulating. I had to assume it knew what it was doing, but its neck was bulging out disturbingly on both sides. Then, with one significant gulp, it swallowed the eel. Without missing a beat, it went back to gazing at the water, body frozen in concentration.

We took that as our cue and slipped back into the water. "Once around the island?" she suggested.

And so we circled the isle of Circe. I looked at Queenie, then back down into the blur of the water. The water played with my eyes, as if I were a nearsighted fish. But when my face came up, there was Queenie, looking at me. She pointed away from the island, and we swam toward the shore. She knew what I knew, that if we stepped back on the warm sand of the island, we'd be flesh against promised flesh. So back toward shore we went, past the public dock where kids were cannonballing into the water.

We walked through the shallows toward the shore, the mermaid and her captive sailor, neither of us knowing how we were going to explain ourselves to her father. Jack O'Malley had arrived from work and was sitting on the porch of the cottage, drinking a beer. Queenie had gotten her black hair from him; his strong nose and chin had been softened in her, but the eyes were the same burning Irish flame, green as the Emerald Isle. As the owner of a sporting-goods shop, he kept in good physical shape, possessing every workout toy known to man. He raised an eyebrow in my direction, wondering what his safely engaged daughter was doing with the monk from out of town. "What's the word, Tommy? How's your uncle Silvio?"

"Waiting for you to tee off with him, Jack."

"He can drive, but the putt is not in his power."

"Give him time."

"He's had fifty years."

Queenie and I walked into the house. I could feel Jack's eyes on the back of my neck. When we were inside, Queenie said, "If he starts with you, get him talking about the Red Sox."

We changed clothes and met again in the living room. She was wearing cutoff denim shorts and a white T-shirt. We rejoined Jack on the lawn. He had lit the charcoal grill. "Like every sportsman, I like my hot dogs crisp."

"He means burned," said Queenie.

"It increases their nutritive value," said Jack, carefully rotating the dogs. My first baseball glove came from his store, Uncle Silvio bargaining with Jack over the price and insisting that Jack throw in a free baseball, which he did.

The hot dogs came off the grill at a moment precisely determined by Jack, and then the toasting of the buns. We added mustard and sauerkraut. "I'm not into hot dog–eating contests," said Jack as we sat on lawn chairs facing the lake. "The spirit of competition is there, but the dog as a culinary masterpiece . . ." He held his up. ". . . is undervalued."

The late afternoon sun had turned the lake into a shield of gold. The sound of children's high-pitched voices came from the public dock. My ribs were still hurting from the beating Brian Fury had given me. I would eat his heart like a hot dog.

"We saw the heron swallow a big eel," said Queenie. "It was amazing."

"In training for a hot dog–eating contest," said Jack.

"I don't know how he got it down."

"When you get an eel in your beak," said Jack, "it's only going one way."

"The eel struggled bravely," said Queenie, "but it was outmatched."

And suddenly, the heron was coming toward us, a gray-black silhouette, big wings flapping as it hunted an underwater snack before bed. It flew down the lake and passed out of sight, but I heard the impact of its long legs on the water at a different fishing spot, perhaps known for action at this time of day.

"Can I give you a beer, Tommy?"

"Sure, Jack. Just the thing."

"Queenie?"

"I'm fine."

We were all fine. The heron was doing its tai chi, and I was on my second hot dog, trying not to admire Queenie, but Jack saw right through me.

"Tommy, you know Queenie's fiancé, Richard Mittleman?"

"I've seen him around."

"Dad—"

"Yes, darling daughter?"

"Shut up."

"Copy that." Jack went back to his grill, rotated his hot dogs as the golden shield of the lake began to fade and the water turned flat and featureless. The magic of the day was done.

Queenie said, "Tommy and I are going to the pavilion." She got up from her chair and I followed, to a path that led through the woods. "Dad's jumping to conclusions."

"What about you?"

"I'm just jumping."

A speedboat came tearing up the lake and was soon bearing down on the shoreline. At the last moment, it turned, churning a tremendous wake. At the wheel was a young man, slender and tall, blond hair rippling in the wind.

"Reed Hamilton," said Queenie. "Do you remember him?"

When I was in my teens I'd been to a party at Reed's house, taken there by Finn. It was on the highest hill above town, and Reed had been lounging around dreamily, looking at the guests indifferently, occasionally taking a champagne glass from a caterer and then raising a toast to himself. And now I remembered:

"Finn called him the Blond Shadow."

The waves continued to slap on the shore as he roared away. "Disturbing my heron," said Queenie.

"You don't like him?"

"I like him well enough, but there's no getting close to him. There's nothing there. And I think he might be a heavy drug user."

I watched the receding wake of his speedboat. There might be nothing to him, but he had a feel for the lake, in a twin-engine ride worthy of Neptune himself. The waves were lapping on the shore like his laughter, which I could hear above the roar of the motor. He spun the boat around and headed toward us again, head back, blond hair blowing, and as he got closer I saw the grin on his face. It was a cosmic grin. When he swept along our end of the lake, he waved, I don't know who to—maybe the whole world.

Again the waves broke on the shore as the Blond Shadow spun the craft around, giving us the roar of the engines and then bubbling off back down the lake. We continued up the path to the pavilion. It was a big redwood construction with a massive stone fireplace. It was empty except for us, as if it had been keeping others away so an illicit kiss would stay hidden in the dusk. Her lips were coming toward me. My Irish handful, my partner in crime. And then my phone rang. I answered automatically in case it was about Bridget.

It was Bridget's mother, asking me if I had any news.

"When I have news, I'll call you right away."

"You have no idea how worried I am. Something terrible has happened to her. Otherwise, she would've been in touch with me. Her tragedy has aged me ten years. You should see my skin . . ."

While I was cursing myself for answering, and at the same time trying to placate Veronica, Queenie stood up. I quickly ended the call, but she was looking at her watch, a million miles from the kiss she'd almost given me. "Go back to town."

"When do I see you again?"

"Call me at the station."

"And then?"

"And then we'll see."

23

I had last seen Shirley Kaminski on the Coalville football field, in a sweater with a big *C* on it. One of the Centralites, as they were called—a team of high school girls creating graceful formations on the fifty-yard line. Now she was working the bike lane in shiny black boots that went to the middle of her thighs, and beyond that was a skirt that could have passed as a handkerchief. "Shirley . . ." I couldn't think of anything to say but her name.

"Tommy Martini," she said quietly, and we just stared at each other. Then I put my arms around her.

"That costs money," she said.

"Let's go somewhere and talk."

"I don't go anywhere till the sun comes up. Like Dracula." And there *was* something ghoulish about her makeup—wildly overdone and completely unnecessary. She'd been an attractive girl and still was, but in the bike lane you had to have eyes like stoplights.

I said, "I remember you with a big *C* on your sweater."

"Now it's a big *H*."

And then I saw, in the midst of all that eye makeup, her pupils were like pinholes.

"I'm a heroin misuser, Tommy," she said with a sardonic smile. "Who woulda thunk it?"

"I'd like to help."

She steered me along the bike lane. "I don't want to be helped. Anyway, not by you."

"Why not?"

"Because you're from my other life."

I stifled the impulse to play it my way, forcing her hand with offers of hotel, car, cash—whatever she needed to kick her habit. So I said, "You probably heard about Finn Sweeney getting killed."

"No, I didn't. I don't watch the news. I don't watch anything except cars going by. But I remember him. Good-looking, talked a mile a minute. That's a shame. Who killed him?"

"No idea."

"I went to one of his parties in my previous lifetime. He threw great parties."

"He married Bridget Breen."

"That's right, he did. Beautiful Bridget. She could've had anyone."

"Including me."

She looked away, back toward the cars. "Here comes my fancy man. Tommy, do me a favor and get lost."

I turned away before he could see me, but I heard his voice, and every word was a display of his power over Shirley. I'd seen her on a football field on a fall day, when the air was crisp and her life was her own. *Follow him. Crush him like a fucking bedbug*, said my anger demon. But that wouldn't help Shirley; some other fancy man would just latch on to her. I put the demon back in his bottle, where he grumbled a while but finally resumed just tending the eternal fire. I started asking people about Finn. He was remembered, the TV guy with the microphone, asking questions nobody wanted to answer, and at two in the morning I left the square. Misery lights started turning behind me, like bright evil bubblegum being chewed. I thought about making a run for it, but my Acura had a ten-year-old engine and was essentially a family car. The police cruiser was a Ford Interceptor—zero to sixty in six seconds. I pulled back to the curb. A cop came to my window; another one stopped at the rear of the car. I heard my taillights breaking. The cop at the window said, "Get out."

He cuffed me and walked me back to the patrol car. It was police harassment, but it would be buried in some other dimension. The cop standing by the back bumper of the Acura said, "You've got no taillights." The nightstick he'd broken them with was loosely gripped in his hand.

They shoved me into the back of the patrol car. It had the usual hard plastic seats for easy washing up after puking drunks. But there was a thoughtful indentation in the backrest to accommodate cuffed hands. Legroom was minimal to reduce leverage should the passenger be inspired to attack. I was not inspired. I was staring through a metal screen. One of the cops said over the radio, "I've got him." And the crackling answer in return was, "Proceed to rendezvous."

"Acknowledged."

And away we went, past those citizens of Coalville who were glad not to be in the back seat of a patrol car. Those who should have been in back were especially glad. When we started up Quarry Road, I knew that the bodies of the Muldoon brothers had surfaced and I'd be going to jail for a thousand years. Queenie would be marrying her vegetable man, and Phil Branca would pay off a prison guard so I'd have a good cell, but I would not be chanting with monks at midnight. I'd be trying to sleep with a pillow crammed around my head to keep out the voices of the brothers of doom, one of whom might want to build his street cred by shanking a Martini.

But when we parked behind the abandoned Martini office, I noticed there were no forensic people around, no security tape, none of what you would find at a crime scene. And there was something odd in the way the cops were handling themselves. They were under orders they weren't particularly happy about. Not that they cared about me. I was a burden they didn't want, but the order had gone out and they were following it. It was hard to get on the local force, and it was a good-paying job, but with the job came unwritten rules of loyalty, and they weren't directed toward the Martini family.

Then a familiar Plymouth hardtop, circa 1961, showed up out of the past. And Brian Fury stepped from it. I didn't know whether to laugh or cry. Laugh because the Muldoon brothers were still in seventy-five feet of water, or cry because Brian Fury was bad news wherever we met.

"Out," said the cops, roughly assisting me off my plastic seat and onto the gravel of the old Martini parking lot. Brian came toward me. My sworn enemy had me at a crime scene and didn't know it. Of course, there was going to be a crime, and it would be against me. I could see the eagerness in his eyes, just as I had seen it when the snake, prior to being toasted alive, wriggled in his malevolent young fingers.

"I thought this was an appropriate place for our second meeting." He nodded toward the old Martini office building. "Your home field, shall we say? What happened to the quarry business? Run out of stone?"

"There's stone left."

"But it's flooded, right?" He pointed toward the quarry. The surface of the water was visible through the trees, moonlight sparkling on its calm surface. "Too bad for the Martini family, but Mother Nature has spoken."

One of the cops was fiddling with the belt on which his many tools were hung. He was signaling Fury to get moving with whatever bullshit was going to go down. Fury said, "You've been asking questions, Martini, concerning a criminal investigation that's none of your fucking business."

"There's no investigation. You shut it down."

He was untroubled by the accusation. "What's your problem anyway, greaseball?"

"I haven't got one."

"Yes, you do. *I'm* your problem." He nodded toward the cop who now had what he needed from his belt. The next thing I felt were my arm and leg muscles contracting violently, and I collapsed, hitting the gravel face-first. Tasered.

The other cop yanked me to my feet. He was an older guy, undoubtedly chosen for long service in bending the law. Fury poked me in the chest. "Six quadrillion electrons have just danced through your body. That's what the training manual says. I read it before we came out here, because I wanted to know exactly what you'd feel. Care to comment?"

An electric eel had slithered through my nervous system, and I had no comment.

"Two probes fired at a hundred and sixty feet per second. Little barbed thingies." Fury was examining the probes in my back. Then I felt them being pulled out of my skin and heard them retracting into the gun. "Turn around and face the officer," said my own personal sadist. Everyone should have one.

The cop looked at me, his eyes saying, *He's nuts, what can I tell you?*

"Hit him again," snapped Fury. "In the neck. We'll see if his eyes bulge."

The cop raised the Taser, aimed it carefully, and fired. As the probes sank into my neck, my head went violently backward. I felt little electric worms burrowing through my vocal cords. My legs locked in a painful contraction while my arms flopped around like a puppet struck by lightning. One of life's memorable moments.

When I opened my eyes, Fury was peering at me closely. "Are we having fun?"

My lips felt fuzzy, but I managed to speak. "I'm remembering . . . the snake."

"What snake?"

"You roasted it alive."

"I roasted a lot of them. You were there for one? I don't remember you hanging around."

"I avoided you."

"But you can't avoid me today. Today I roast *you*."

The cop removed the probes from my neck and retracted them into his gun. I was wondering how many rounds his battery could deliver. But he probably had another battery. And the other cop had a Taser too. Enough hits from a Taser can kill you. They looked at Fury with professional curiosity, wondering where he was going to take this.

"I could have him fire those little hooks into your eyes, Martini."

The cop was loyal, but he wasn't going to blind me. He fired into my stomach. My body contracted, the electricity deep in my muscle tissue, and again I hit the ground face-first.

Fury spoke to the cop. "Have we achieved complete incapacitation as described in the manual?"

"Looks like it to me."

"Ben Sweeney ordered this meeting, Martini, and I was happy to oblige him. He says you ruined his son's life." The Taser fired again.

The probes sank between my shoulder blades, and I *did* feel like the snake in the fire pit, wriggling for my life.

Fury addressed me from above. "Do you wonder why I don't kill you?"

It had crossed my mind, but I was facedown in gravel, six quadrillion electrons having just passed through my body, and once again I was not inclined to comment.

He put the toe of his shoe under my chin. "You thought you were hot shit. Because you could run . . . with . . . a . . . football." He punctuated the pauses by moving his shoe up and down under my chin. Then he must have nodded to the cop, because I got Tasered in the ass, which made my cheeks clench so tight I thought they'd be permanently fused, and my electrified hips caused me to begin fucking the gravel.

"Priceless, Martini. Fucking beautiful. The way I've always wanted to see you and hope to see you again."

Then the probes came out of my ass, the wires were retracted, and I heard the gun being holstered.

"But get this. You can arrange our next meeting. All you have to do is keep asking questions. And you will see me again. Are we clear on that?"

My throat was constricted, and my *fuck you* resembled something a frog might say.

Footsteps crunched back across the gravel. Car doors slammed, and I listened to the vehicles as they roared away.

I rolled onto my back. My face stung from being imprinted into the gravel. But I managed to smile at the sky. Incapacitation had been achieved, but the truly incapacitated were under seventy-five feet of water, wedged against the roof of their ride. Killian and Connor were never going to rise from the abyss, and District Attorney Brian Fury would never be standing here with his fucking forensic team.

My skin was on fire where the electric fangs had bitten into me, and my muscles were still twitching. I slowly got to my feet. At first my legs didn't work too well, but I took a deep breath and pointed myself in the direction of downtown Coalville. Gradually, I found my stride on Quarry Road, road of my ancestors, road of Martini Stone and Sand.

24

"I've got to change rides, Uncle. The cops keep stopping me." I showed him the broken taillight. I didn't tell him about being Tasered. He worked with the police on emergency calls; maybe he knew the guys who'd Tasered me. No sense putting him in the middle.

He led me into his office, and from his pegboard full of key fobs, he selected one. "The Acura's too tame for you anyway."

"What have you got in mind?"

"The Terminator's own ride." We left the office. Jim Hutmacher was in the main garage, under a welding helmet, a torch in his hand, kneeling beside one of the big trucks. He waved the torch at me as I walked by. We stepped into the alleyway. Violets grew up through the cracks in the pavement. As a little kid, I picked violets for Grandma Martini, feeling full of myself when I gave her my modest bouquet. She had fussed over the offering, finding a tiny vase and arranging the violets carefully. The shadow of violence was in me, but to her I was a bambino with flowers in his hand.

"You posing for the cameras?"

"I'm remembering the violets."

"Just don't do it on TV." He opened one of his many small garages. My next ride was parked inside, military and angry-looking, the Hummer in its lair. "You'll go broke buying gas, it's difficult to park, and environmentalists will hate you for driving it."

"I can't wait."

"Wait no longer." He handed me the key fob. "I'm glad you'll be in this thing. The doors are reinforced against gunfire."

"Who owned it?"

"Retired cop. He thought there was a contract out on him."

"And?"

"There was."

He opened the tailgate of the Hummer and pointed inside. "Comes with a seventy-five-piece toolkit, pry bar, nice work belt, flashlight. What else do you need?"

"Saint Christopher medal?"

"Behind the visor."

I got in and backed the beast into the alleyway. He tapped on the window, and I opened it. "How's it going with Queenie O'Malley?"

"I'm taking her to a ball game."

He pointed a thick finger at me. "*Testa di minchia.*"

"Which I think means dickhead."

"So try not to be one."

When I pulled into the parking lot of the TV station, Queenie was waiting for me. She'd changed from office clothes into an outfit that left her midriff and shoulders bare. "You like?"

The silver-colored skirt and blouse were made of silk that moved when she moved. The skirt was cut on one side, and I liked it very much. I presented her to the Hummer and handed her the keys. "You are the Terminator." She'd certainly terminated the Muldoon brothers. "Let's see what you can do with this."

She scrambled up into the driver's seat and clutched the wheel. "It's lovely, like a big bad troll." She switched on the ignition and drove us away from the TV station, her little hand on the gearshift. "You and your Hummer."

"What's wrong? I thought you liked it."

"It's another eye-opener."

"On what?"

"On settling for less."

"Well, you don't have to settle for less with this thing. It weighs eight thousand pounds."

"Don't play dumb. You know what I mean."

"Is this about you and Richard Mittleman?"

"No, it's just about me. Forget I said anything."

The slit in her skirt was on my side, and nearly the entire length of her leg was visible. It helped me forget.

Coalville had a decent stadium where a AAA team played. It was built on a high hill overlooking the valley. Judging from the parking lot, there was a good crowd for the game, and Queenie slotted the Hummer neatly between a pair of pickup trucks. Using the Hummer's grab handle, she lowered herself from the driver's seat to the pavement. I lent a hand, and she was soon firmly planted on her platform sandals. They had silvery straps that matched her skirt and blouse. I followed her silver footsteps to the entranceway. She handed in our tickets and headed toward the staircase that would take us to our seats. "We're right behind the home team dugout."

We took our seats and I looked at the scorecard, wondering if any major-leaguers had fallen from the Show and wound up here in purgatory, but there weren't any. And then a familiar name jumped out: *Robert Romano, left field.*

"Bobby Romano's playing here."

"You didn't know that?"

"I've been away, remember?"

"He got traded here last year. It's nice for the town. One of our own."

Bobby Romano, a slugger from Cathedral High School who would bless himself at the plate before driving one over the fence or striking out beautifully. He'd gone on to bat for Notre Dame, and that's where I lost track of him, only to find him again tonight, back in town. Queenie said he'd never gotten to the Show. "He works for his father in the winter."

Which meant he did plumbing. If you wanted somebody to carry a lead-lined sink under one arm, Bobby was your man.

"He was awfully serious when I knew him," said Queenie.

"Keeping his eye on the ball."

"He kept his eye on the girls too."

"You?"

"Once, a double date."

"He struck out?"

"Wouldn't you like to know?" She straightened her skirt, covering up the bare part of her leg.

The radar gun said Bobby was facing a ninety-mile-an-hour fastball. It was being thrown by a guy who'd previously thrown for the Hanshin Tigers in Japan. His first two pitches whistled by our hometown boy. The Hanshin Tiger was pitching Bobby tight, nearly taking off his chin, but on the third pitch, Bobby's trunk and shoulders bunched up like a roped steer and then, *crack*—the ball went straight down the left field line, just inside the foul pole and into the stands. It looked as if he had hit it off the handle—not a favorable spot for contact, but he'd powered the ball anyway because he was big, strong, and fearless about fastballs under his chin. May he get to the Show.

We were cheering when he trotted toward the dugout and tipped his cap to Queenie.

I said, "He hit that one just for you. I know how these things work."

As I turned to sit down, I checked out the box seats. District Attorney Brian Fury and Ben Sweeney were sitting back down after their own bit of cheering, and I thought, *From a chance at the Olympics to a kick in the ribs on the courthouse floor, followed by Tasering*—this was the Show I'd gotten to.

When the game was over, Bobby came out of the dugout and motioned us to join him at the chain-link fence.

"Congratulations, Bobby," I said. "You're getting paid to swing a bat."

"They don't pay much," he said. "It's a short season."

"Come on," said Queenie, "you love it."

"I live on beans and dreams." He took off his cap and wiped his forehead. "What have you been up to, Tommy?"

"A monastery in Mexico. The religious life," I added, though that hardly clarified anything.

He looked at me, puzzled but too polite to inquire further. We talked about the team's schedule, and I learned that for playing the entire season he would earn just under ten thousand dollars. "I'm working below the poverty line." He said this with a laugh, and the laugh told me he would play for nothing. "I thought I'd see you in the NFL by now," he added, looking at me.

Talking about my failure to reach the NFL would be a mirror of his failure to reach the Show, so instead I said, "I had a couple of mixed martial arts bouts in Vegas. They went okay."

He liked hearing that. Sport was all he knew and all he cared to know. You had to feed your dream constantly so the fire wouldn't ebb, because once it ebbed, you were finished. I still had one spark burning in the ashes, and to let Bobby see it seemed the right thing to do. "You probably remember my cousin Dominic. He's managing wrestlers in Vegas now."

"It's good to have family around you. It's why I like playing at this field." Another mark of politeness. He didn't *mind* playing at this field, but *like*? No pro likes the minor league. We chatted a while longer, and then a local reporter came for an interview. Bobby told us he hoped to see us again. "You'll know where to find me." He nodded toward the home team dugout.

When I turned around, Brian Fury and Ben Sweeney were coming down the steps toward us. Queenie saw murderous rage rising in me and touched my sleeve. "Not here, not now."

She kept me moving, but Fury stepped in front of us on the staircase. He smiled and I was reminded of the possum baring its teeth in among the garbage bags. "How're you feeling, Martini? Any abnormal brain activity? Having difficulty processing information?" He looked at the two marks on my neck where the Tasers had struck me. "Those look like love bites. Vampire been sucking your blood?"

"I have," said Queenie, her own anger rising.

Ben Sweeney ignored her and stepped between us, his face only inches from mine. He'd ordered me Tasered and beaten, *and there's more in store*, said his eyes. Moving behind *my* eyes was the old familiar phantom, Saint Death, ready to quite happily finish Ben Sweeney with a single punch. But then, looking at him, I saw he was already dead, gone into the dark with his son, down in the grave with him. The rage drained out of me, and I just listened as he said, "The sight of you disgusts me." He turned to Fury. "This man should be in prison."

"I'm working on it," said Fury.

As they headed toward the exit, Queenie said, "You exercised admirable self-control."

"But you almost lost it."

"That was Finn's father, wasn't it? What's he got against you?"

"He blames me for Finn's death."

"That's hardly fair." She put her fingers lightly to the Taser burns. "What *are* these marks on your neck?"

"Spider bite."

"Cut the crap."

"Fury Tasered me."

"Why?"

"For old times' sake."

She drew back in concern. "Is he suspicious about Killian and Connor?"

"Don't worry. He pulled me in because the sight of me pisses him off. He doesn't know anything about us and the Muldoons. Killian and Connor are right where we left them. Now can we go to dinner?"

But she was rattled by the memory of how Killian and Connor had put themselves into the quarry, and said, "I want to go home."

I was suddenly facing that impenetrable fortress known to men the world over, where no amount of pleading or flattery will change a woman's mind. I knew better than to try.

25

I maneuvered the Hummer into the city parking garage, sending up the red wooden arm as I drove through. I parked and walked slowly down the ramp. The street greeted me with its empty eyes. And then five shadowy figures stepped into the feeble light of the entranceway and approached me with the unpredictable gait of the street, that strange mechanical dance of teenage hoods. Their not-yet-fully-developed brains made them believe that my truck would provide them with a powerful ride for the night.

I watched as they approached, their hips and shoulders gyrating as if attached by strings to an epileptic puppeteer. Their finger signs to each other, to the world, and to me were fairly simple renderings, suggesting a violent social position. They didn't realize just how prepared I was to crush their evil ambitions into the ground.

The loudmouth led, of course. "Hey, bro, can you light me up?" He bobbed in front of me, to the misbegotten beat in his brain. I assumed the little bastard was armed, so I took the initiative.

"Fuck off, piglet." I drove both fists into the sides of his head, and he collapsed inside his hoodie, his finger signing over as he sank to the pavement.

This gave me the opportunity to grab a second one, mauling him around until I could pin his arms behind his neck. "How about I rip your fucking head off?"

His constricted throat gave him the voice of a dying duckling. "Take . . . it . . . easy . . ."

I pointed his lowered head from homey to homey. "Anybody else?"

Written on their faces was the ageless question, *What the fuck just happened?* I pushed the duckling toward them and he flapped his wings, but the lift wasn't there and he collapsed into their arms. They steadied him, then picked up the homey I'd put on the pavement and shuffled away, having failed for the moment to gain a foothold in this rough-and-tumble town. But the night was young.

I walked to the Top Hat bar. It had been built in the 1930s and had kept many of its art deco touches, but Valentina wasn't one of them. "What'll it be, big guy?" she asked from behind the bar.

"You work here?"

"First night. Popov is hard master." But Valentina's only master was Valentina, and she was joking. She had her blond hair pulled back into a ponytail, but she still looked like Bridget, and she asked me, "Find your girlfriend?"

"I'm still searching."

She wiped the bar in front of me. "After work, I take you home."

"Not tonight."

"Why not? I'm soft Russian moonlight. You have car? I tell Popov he don't have to pick me up."

"I'll take you home. But not tonight."

"Girlfriend on the brain."

"Swimming around and around."

She made me a whiskey sour and walked back down the bar, cheering her other customers. Her little black skirt showed her long legs, and she had the gift of making easy conversation, unlike me. I'm built for solitude. But then there's Queenie. We seem to get along; after all, we killed the Muldoon brothers. What more can you ask of a romance?

The other barmaid was the girl whose hair Kip had shaped. "I am Natasha, remember? Tell your friend how much he help me. Wrong-way hair kill woman."

The double doors of the bar swung open, and three men entered.

Two of them were professional muscle, and I recognized their boss as the pimp who managed Shirley Kaminski. Valentina refused them service and pointed toward the door.

The Top Hat bouncer came out of the shadows, a young guy in a T-shirt with a top hat printed on it. The bodyguards looked at him, but their boss decided he didn't need this place. He gave Valentina a dismissive wave and walked back toward the doors, followed by her invective. When she came back to my end of the bar, she said, "Grisha is Moscow hood. Try to steal our business."

We chatted for a while, but then her phone rang. She answered it, frowned, and immediately came out from behind the bar. "Popov in trouble." She hurried toward the door, and Natasha and I followed. Outside the bar, Grisha was holding a gun to Popov's head. His bodyguards were holding Popov's arms. Popov, half their size, was trying to reason with them.

Natasha and Valentina began shouting at Grisha. He gave them an indifferent look and went back to drilling the barrel of his gun into Popov's ear. But when Valentina kept shouting, he slapped her with the back of his hand.

Wobbling on her high heels, she screamed at him in Russian. As she screamed, her ponytail swung dramatically. He watched it swinging back and forth, then reached out and grabbed it. She shrieked as he twisted her head, using the ponytail like the short leash on a bad-tempered dog. I'd noticed that along with his exquisite summer suit, Grisha wore shoes I'm sure he adored. The leather looked soft yet reflected the streetlight with a luminous glow. Only expensive shoes give you that type of gleaming presentation. So I spit on them.

As he peered down in amazement at this gross insult to his footwear, I wrenched his gun away from him and gave it to Valentina. His bodyguards were looking at me as if I were an idiot or a pacifist because I'd just given a gun away. One had cheaply dyed golden hair. The other had red hair and a wildly unkempt beard. They tried to bum-rush me. Bad move.

When I was in Vegas for a fight, the promoter had a device for measuring the impact of a punch. Mine came in at a thousand pounds, and tonight Big Red got every bit of it on his thick head, enough to twist his brain inside his skull. He went down without a sound.

Blondie was wailing on me, but it didn't matter, because I was more than willing to take a few of his shots so that I could deliver one of my own. When I finally hit him, his dyed-blond hair flew backward and the rest of him followed as he sagged to the pavement.

Popov sprang into action, quickly relieving both men of their firearms. Then he leaned toward me. "You never pay in my place again. Fuck free for life."

Valentina was pointing Grisha's gun at him as if it were a sex toy, waving it suggestively in the direction of his balls.

The Top Hat bouncer had come out during the confrontation and was standing beside me now. "You're Martini, right?"

I told him I was, and he said, with professional courtesy, that he knew I'd been involved in a fatal punch-out while on the job. "I worry about it myself. In the heat of a fight, I could easily croak someone."

We both looked down at the bodyguards. Big Red was gingerly touching the thousand-pound welt on his forehead, and Blondie was slowly pushing up from the sidewalk. The bouncer said, "They'll be after you somewhere down the road."

"Let them try."

Valentina threw Grisha's gun into the sewer drain. We heard a clank followed by a splash. Grisha stared at the sewer drain, then shrugged a farewell to his pistol. Popov threw the bodyguards' guns into the same drain. Two more splashes.

Grisha and his bodyguards walked toward a Mercedes convertible. Before they got in, Grisha blew a kiss to Valentina and Natasha.

As we watched them pull away, Valentina asked me, "Where you learn to fight like that?"

"Vegas," I said, which seemed as good an answer as any.

"Las Vegas," she said as if whispering a holy name. She turned to Popov, and though they spoke in Russian I heard the word "Vegas" repeated as if it were a religious destination.

We all went back inside. Valentina and Natasha resumed service, and the bouncer joined me at the bar. "You fought in Vegas?"

I told him I had.

"How did that work out?"

"Victory was mine."

"I'd like to get into the UFC."

I gave him Cousin Dominic's number in Vegas. "He might be able to help you."

He bought me a whiskey sour. Valentina knew how to mix a good one. We could all start a new life in Las Vegas.

26

"You'll get real Sicilian arancini," said Phil when I told him I was going to eat at his restaurant in the hopes of impressing a young woman. "And you'll have a table where nobody can shoot you in the back."

It was on a slightly raised platform, closed off on three sides from other diners. Queenie and I had the whole of the restaurant in front of us, in a pool of candlelight. Phil's plan for my romantic evening continued with the appearance of the chef, sweeping his white chef's cap before Queenie. Alessandro was a small man with a pencil-thin mustache. He acknowledged me with another slight bow. "I gave you your first good spaghetti."

"I remember. I was with my grandfather."

"May he rest in peace." He made the sign of the cross. As if in response, a waiter appeared behind him, tray in hand, and salads were placed before us. Alessandro leaned toward me and said softly, "I see your cousin Angelina now and then. When I mention your name, she curdles the cream five tables away."

"We've had a falling out."

"I'll talk to her on your behalf. A family squabble helps no one." He tipped his cap and walked away.

Every eye in the place was on the recipients of this supreme benediction, and Queenie had to be impressed, but her heart was troubled.

"My father sees me marrying Richard as two businesses getting together, sports and vegetables. Football and zucchini."

"End it with Richard. Put yourself in the loving embrace of the Martini family."

"If only it was that easy."

"I'll tell you how easy it is. When Richard wakes up in the morning, he's thinking about produce."

"And not me? You may be right. But that's not the point." Her eyes swept the room. "There's Reed Hamilton."

He was alone, one arm hanging languidly off the back of his chair. His tailoring was upper-class best—nothing splashy, just marvelous material cut to perfection. He gave Queenie a little wave, fingertips tickling the air. She returned the gesture.

"Secret signal?"

"From childhood."

"What's it mean?"

"Nothing much. Comforting sign." Her eyes were still resting on him. "Reed goes around that way, playing with the world. Emotionally, he's about four years old."

"How old would you say I am, emotionally speaking?"

"Three and a half."

The waiter glided back, twisted the label of a bottle toward us. "Mr. Branca would like you to have this."

It was a Masseto that would have cost Phil seven hundred plus if he'd actually bought it. After it was poured and the waiter had left, I raised my glass and said, "When a don blesses you with his wine, hell opens its arms."

"I'll drink to that," said Queenie, and we clinked glasses.

Another waiter brought rice balls covered in breadcrumbs and stuffed with cheese—the famed arancini. Phil was right, they were the real deal, made as my grandmother used to make them. "All this cheese," said Queenie, "will go right to my hips."

"The more of you, the better."

"I'm only going to eat one."

"Alessandro will be insulted."

So we ate them all. Shards of splintered light from the candle were dancing in Queenie's eyes, and the chemistry between us was so strong, I thought the whole restaurant could see it. But where had that chemistry been when we were younger? Eclipsed by long-legged Bridget, who collected young men as if playing a hand of cards, discarding some, choosing others. I'd been a discarded card.

Alessandro returned with the main course. "Pork chops Italiano with a secret sauce." With another flourish, he instructed the waiter to place it before us. His final appearance was at the end of the meal, when he presented us with tiramisu in little glass cups, "to properly control the cream." He paused, then added, "Forgive me if I speak plainly. In Italy, tiramisu was used as a tonic in brothels."

"Well, that's it," said Queenie, inserting her spoon. "I'm done for."

When we'd finished our coffee, the waiter informed us that the meal was compliments of Mr. Branca. "We loved it," said Queenie, and then dragged me over to say hello to Reed Hamilton.

He unraveled himself from the chair and stood, brushing blond hair off his forehead. He was certainly stoned out of his mind. He could have been lying sideways in an opium den. The corners of his mouth creased in an easy smile. "I'm a little high."

"We're not feeling any pain either," said Queenie.

"Yes, pain is to be avoided at all costs." He looked at me. "You're Finn's friend. From the gangster family." He said it without embarrassment. It was a handy classification. "That must've been fun."

"It had its moments."

"I'm devoted to fun. Finn was the same way; his parties were marvelous. Everything anyone could want."

"He called you the Blond Shadow," said Queenie.

"How perceptive of him." Reed again pushed blond hair back off his forehead. "I *do* prefer keeping in the background."

He was a voyeur of the harmless kind—into drugs, watching the world go by as if it were a streaming movie. His eyes came back to mine, and I saw him dropping into the clouds of memory. He resurfaced. "And you were Finn's shadow. The protector. Wait, that's not quite right." He tickled the air again, just two fingers by his temple. Agitating his memory. "You were his . . . friend." He said this with a touch of wonder in his voice, as if the concept was totally alien to him—something other people did, just another classification.

"Friends for life," I said.

"Naturally. I saw that. I'm sorry for your loss. Of a friend." He floated back down into his chair, and with a little tickling of the air he bade us good night.

Outside the restaurant, Queenie took my arm, pressing her breast against my biceps. "Blame it on the tiramisu." On her other arm was a huge handbag, containing the many things the female of the species uses, including potions that work on men's minds.

As we walked around the building to the parking lot, her pressure on my arm increased, but this promise of intimacy died as a car came by, stopped, backed up, and then stopped again. Russian Blondie and Big Red got out.

I gently undid Queenie's fingers. "Go back to the restaurant."

"No way." Her eyes had turned as mean as a Coalville possum.

I whispered to her more urgently, "These guys are bad news. Beat it."

"I'm not going anywhere." The curvy little possum, standing her ground.

Big Red came first, steroid madness in his brain. The signs of juicing were there. The muscles that attach to the shoulder joints get so bulked up, it looks like an ox wearing a plow. He was yoked.

Moving slowly toward him, I raised my hands. "How can I make it right?"

"I . . . fuck . . . you . . . up . . . is . . . how." He wanted to get into it again. Honor must be served. Maybe he was Russian military.

I heard an electrical snapping sound from behind me, followed by something like a swarm of hornets going past me. Big Red's body convulsed. Two little wires had appeared in his chest, dangling down in metallic coils. He fell at my feet, chest heaving, a strangled gasp in his throat. Then he went completely still, his eyes suddenly staring into the Russian afterlife. Queenie's voice was climbing wildly. "I picked it up at Dad's store. It's for hikers going into bear country."

Blondie ran to the car. The engine rumbled, the tires screeched, and he sped away.

Queenie was staring down at the guy she'd Tasered. The fiendish instrument in her hand was as big as the one the cops had used on me. She said, voice still climbing, "It's for stopping a big animal."

"It stopped one, all right." My Olympic trainer had lectured me on how steroids can thicken the muscle wall of the heart and screw with its rhythm. Big Red's heart must have been beating out of time when Queenie's electrical charge hit him, and fatal arrhythmia had followed. His dead eyes were looking up at the night sky, expressing shock beyond the six quadrillion electrons that had stopped his heart. It was the shock of the great divide he was crossing. I opened the back of the Hummer and heaved his earthly remains inside. Then I got Duke on the phone. "Meet me at Phil's restaurant. The parking lot. *Now*."

As soon as the call ended, the phone rang again. "Duke?"

"Tommy, it's Veronica. I'm all dressed up and I have nowhere to go."

"I wish I could help you, Veronica, but I'm busy right now."

"What about later?"

"I'm sorry. I've got things I have to do tonight."

"Did you eat the cookies I gave you?"

"Every one."

"Where are you? I want to be able to picture you."

I looked at the body in the back of the Hummer. "I'm moving some furniture for a friend."

"Do I know him?"

"He's a new friend. He's not part of the old crowd."

"Bring him around for cookies."

Big Red's mouth was open, but he would not be eating cookies.

Duke couldn't have been far away, because I could hear his big Cadillac approaching. "I have to run now, Veronica. You take care."

I disconnected as Duke parked and stepped out of the car. "Queenie O'Malley," he said with a smile. "I've known you since you were five years old. I pulled your pigtails and you kicked me in the shins."

"I just killed the guy in there," she said, pointing to the back of the Hummer.

"So I got off lightly." Duke glanced inside, then looked at me. "Who is he?"

"Russian muscle. Works for a pimp."

Duke saw the dead man's gun in my hand. "I'll take that. It's probably from Little Odessa and certainly hot." He went to his car and brought a blanket. He looked at Queenie. "I like sleeping underneath the stars." He covered the body, turned to Queenie again. "Want me to drop you off somewhere?"

She shook her head.

He put his arm around her. "Live for the moment, right? That's the Irish in you. We're always ready."

I asked him where we were going and he said, "The elephants' graveyard." We followed him, Queenie in the front seat with me, and the Russian hood taking his last ride in back.

Her eyes were filled with tears. "I just want to have a home and some kids."

"Sorry, not tonight."

"A little garden in back, with a wading pool. One of those rubber things you blow up."

I looked in the rearview mirror, first at the road behind me and then at the blanket beneath which the dead Russian lay. I looked across at Queenie, who, in a white silk blouse and matching skirt, seemed like a female warrior from the moon, the faintly luminous silver straps on her feet having brought her to Earth. I said, "Outside Paloma, Arizona, is a sinkhole. Two hundred feet down is a man's body. He's probably just bones by now, but he's there and I put him there."

"Did you kill him?"

"I only buried him."

"Was a woman involved?"

"Why do you ask that?"

She lowered the visor and looked into the mirror attached to it. I thought she was going to re-create her face with the time-honored application of mascara and lipstick, but she just stared at herself as if at a stranger. "I just killed someone else. He's under a blanket in back of us. Where the child safety seats should be."

She put away her tissue and took out the big stun gun. "They have little ones that look like a tube of lipstick. Why didn't I have one of those? But that's Jack. He's got a treadmill in his bedroom that's smarter than he is. It has maps of entire continents. He's walking around the world on it."

We followed Duke, not around the world but just across town and then out into the hills that ringed the valley. After twisting and turning through the hills for a while, the Cadillac left the pavement. We were on a dirt road. There were many roads like this outside town, left over from logging and mining days. Hunters used them now, or lovers. On both sides of us, low-lying vegetation grew out of hillsides that had been formed by early mining efforts. As kids, we used to call these *man-made mountains*, as if the men who'd made them long ago were in some way mysterious. They weren't mountains really, only high hills of rocks and dirt, created by earthmoving machinery. But a feeling of mystery still emanated from their ugly shapes.

The road became a grassy indentation. I took it slowly, but I could see Duke's car parked ahead. Beyond it was a dilapidated mining tower that once lowered a cage of miners into the earth. Scattered across the ground were piles of discarded mining equipment. Parked nearby the old machinery was a small Toyota truck. The door opened, and into the headlights stepped Stashu.

We walked to the tower. It had been sealed off with six-foot-high steel plates. These were joined to another steel plate that formed the top, turning the whole thing into a cube of steel. One of the plates was hinged and secured with a heavy-duty chain and padlock. Stashu opened it, after which Duke handed him an envelope. Stashu put it in his pocket, got back in his truck, and drove away.

"I know that guy," I said.

"No, you don't. And he doesn't know you." Duke and I carried the body to the tower, and Queenie followed.

"Number one torpedo," said Duke, and we tossed the Russian in. Apart from an initial scraping sound, there was nothing more, the body just falling silently through long darkness. The shaft had to be a deep one, because there was no sound of the body landing. Queenie was behind us, whispering prayers. I added a few of my own and Duke muttered, "Done and fucking done."

Queenie asked, "Why did you call this the elephants' graveyard?"

The headlights of the Hummer were still shining on us, and Duke's eyes reflected the light, giving him the look of a gray-haired old Druid speaking to his apprentices. "There used to be a zoo in town. This was before you were born. It wasn't much of a zoo, but it had an elephant. Her name was Ella, and she lived a long time. When she finally died, they didn't know where to bury her." He pointed into the shaft. "So they dumped her here." He called down into the darkness. "How're you doing, Ella?" Then he led us back to his car and the Hummer.

"Show's over. I'll see you lovebirds again sometime."

"We're not lovebirds," said Queenie.

"Could've fooled me." He reached out and gave her hair a gentle tug. "Queenie O'Malley, the toughest kid on the block."

He got into his car and drove away. I didn't try to catch him.

"We're not lovebirds," repeated Queenie.

"I'm not insisting."

We got in the Hummer and drove back to the road. She said, "I can't break with Richard."

"Fine."

"You're supposed to ask me why."

"I know why."

"No, you don't."

"I was raised by a crook, and I'm not much better. How's that?"

"It's not a complete picture."

"What did I leave out?"

"You're scary."

"You're scarier."

Having just electrocuted somebody, she couldn't argue the point.

27

"How did you like the arancini?"

"I've never tasted better."

"You ate as a guest at my restaurant. You walked outside with your date and these guys jumped you. I can't erase what happened. But from here on, you eat free at my restaurant. With a guest."

So I had free service at a cathouse and free food at a fine restaurant. Life was going my way. I said, "I apologize for bringing you this trouble. The departed worked for a Russian pimp."

Little Joe was breathing heavily in the corner. "Grisha Volkov. He has good friends in Brighton Beach."

Good friends, in Little Joe talk, meant that Grisha Volkov was connected to power players in the Russian mafia.

Phil sighed. "It's not like the old days where we'd to go to war over something like this. I'm running a white-collar operation and I don't want any heat. You understand?"

"I do."

"Volkov will recruit somebody to whack you. He has to or he loses face. My advice is, go back to Mexico."

"I can't do that, Phil."

"Fine, but I can't protect you."

"I understand."

Little Joe stood, and I stood with him. He held the door with his massive hand, and once again I went past the Phil Branca photo gallery of grandkids smiling, their grandfather scowling down from above them, cigarette forever stuck behind his ear. And then a photo of Misty in her wedding gown.

The photo came to life as she greeted me from the living room, where she was watching women discussing the ins and outs of a situation beyond their control. "Tommy, come and watch with me."

I looked back over my shoulder toward Little Joe. He nodded. I took my seat beside Misty on the sofa as directed, and the pressure of my body on the cushion sent her my way, her big warm thigh saying hello. She was in a house coat and curlers. The ladies on the TV seemed to be in the room with us, because I felt an overwhelming female presence.

"So how is our monk today? Saved any souls?"

"He was a real creep from the first and I knew it," said a TV lady. "But I married him anyway because it was *time*."

"Misty, I should be going."

Her hair was wound up tight, and her curlers were coming closer. "You're no more a monk than I am. You should come and work for Phil. He's really a lovely man when you get to know him."

"I'm sure he is, but I promised Primo I'd stay out of the life."

"The life is different these days. We're into legitimate businesses. We own a funeral home. We work with insurance companies; we even run a rehab clinic and straighten people out."

"I hate to say no, especially to you, but I really am a monk."

"If you're a monk, I'm the *Mona Lisa*." She adjusted one of her curlers and went back to watching her TV show.

———————

Fuss, a.k.a. Jeffrey Goldfuss, the young nerd who worked for WVIM, was seated beside me in Finn's old office. In front of us were a computer screen and a glass-topped humidor belonging to Finn. In it were Cuban cigars, four hundred dollars a box. Finn's vintage Zippo lighter lay beside the humidor. On one side of the lighter, Saint Michael the Archangel brandished his fiery sword. Was that how Finn thought of himself? On the other side was an inscription: *I light the way*. I lit one of his cigars with the flame of Saint Michael.

For the past hour, Fuss had been showing me through Finn's computer files, but so far I'd seen nothing that might give me a lead to his killer. The coffee machine was making noises, and Fuss poured two cups. His cup said *I'm Attacking the Darkness*. Mine said *Crypto Man*. The coffee was hideously strong. He tempered his with six teaspoons of sugar. I could see the sugar behind his eyeballs, a growing little pile that fed his nervous energy.

He sat back down at the computer and brought up a new file. "This is Ruby." The screen showed a photograph of a young girl in a tight red miniskirt and blouse. She wore heavy eye makeup, and her hair was red and long. "She calls herself Ruby the Forbidden Fruit." He magnified the picture, and now it was possible to see through the makeup. Ruby was a very pretty teenager in grown-up clothes. "She saw Finn on TV and came here wanting to tell her story."

"What kind of story?"

"Underage prostitution. Bridget and Finn took her in. She lived with them for a couple of months, but they tried to reform her, so she left."

"Where is she now?"

"No idea," said Fuss, in the deadened affect of a cyber pilot. He had shown me Ruby and now he'd slipped away.

"Anything else?"

"Like what?"

"Like what else is in her file?"

"Oh." Pause. "This."

I peered at the screen. On it, standing at a drinks table and slightly out of focus, as if the photograph had been taken surreptitiously, was Brian Fury.

I expressed my surprise. "In the Ruby file?"

"Hanging out."

I gazed at Fury's face in profile, his button nose not his best aspect, but he hadn't been posing. He'd been talking to Ben Sweeney.

I looked at Fuss. "What else?"

He brought back the photo of Ruby. "She'll never know how much I love her."

———————

Kip was doing Queenie's hair under the studio lights. "Nothing serious," he said, scissors flashing. "Just some nasty ends."

Queenie's fabulous look was Kip's creation—the dead-straight bangs, the slow curve along her cheeks. She reached up to give Kip's hand a squeeze. "Thanks."

She turned to me. "What do you think?"

"We're expected at Phil's restaurant, compliments of the house."

She raised her hand. Her engagement ring sparkled under the studio lights. "Dinner with Richard." She stood. "And I'm already late."

"Is he picking you up in a pumpkin?"

"Walk me down the hall." As we reached the reception area, she said, "When I go out with Richard, nobody dies."

"It was an accident. And that Russian guy was just like the Muldoons. You did the world a favor."

"I don't see it that way."

"It's the only way to see it."

She looked up at our image in the security monitor. The camera distorted us the way those things always do. She said, "I Tasered that guy because I couldn't bear the thought of you being hurt." And then she was gone. A pumpkin did not await her. There might have been pumpkins inside it, because it said *Mittleman Produce* on the side. I couldn't see Richard clearly, but I didn't have to. He was in the driver's seat tonight.

Kip joined me in the reception area. He said, "The promo for vacuum cleaners is up next. After you watch it a hundred times, you start to see the hidden message."

I asked him if he knew Ruby.

"Finn was making a movie with her."

"What about?"

"Child prostitutes."

"She was on the street?"

"She was."

"She's beautiful. How did she wind up there?"

"Let's take a little ride."

We got into Kip's convertible. I gazed at the clouds overhead as we went. Big and fluffy pillows, carrying summer with them. I said, "You could cut hair anywhere. Why don't you go to California? The weather's better."

"I've built up a clientele of lovely women here. I do house calls." The way he said this made me wonder if he did more than hair on those house calls.

He drove to Parade Square, waved to one of the corner boys, and bought a gram of meth. As we drove away from the square, he said, "I was the fastest little corner boy you ever want to see. Saving up for hair school. The higher use of the razor."

Then he drove me to a part of town that had always been poor, only now the poverty was more visible, the porches peopled with loafers, drug users, and drunks. These were ugly, old houses where the upper apartments were reached by outside staircases, the steps holding garbage bags, baby strollers, and other assorted artifacts of crowded city living. The looks we were getting were hostile in a way that reminded me of what I felt around Mexican cartel members: that the slightest annoyance or inconvenience could be answered with a blast from a handgun.

We headed toward a staircase that angled three times to the top floor, each landing crowded with empty take-out containers and plastic bottles, some containing what looked like piss. Every door was covered with graffiti, and the one on the top floor spelled RUBY in big red letters. "Am I going to meet the Forbidden Fruit?"

"If we're in luck. But you'll certainly meet her mother." He knocked, and we waited.

The woman who answered had the sunken eyes of a meth user. She tried a seductive smile that quickly collapsed, her cracked lips opening to show yellow teeth. She was still young, but her badly wrinkled skin made her face look old, and the sores that covered it didn't help. Her twisted housecoat hung half open, and I saw more of the sores caused by constant scratching to chase away the feeling of bugs under the flesh. Completing her look were stiletto heels, at odds with the blousy housecoat.

"Kip? It's Kip, right?"

"Right, and this is my friend Tommy."

She put out her hand. "Nice to meet you, Tommy. I'm . . ." She paused a moment, as if trying to remember who it was that lived in her body. "Willow," she said finally, "like the tree."

Her hand was dry as paper. The apartment reeked of cigarette smoke and decaying food. She said, "Come on in. It's a little messy at the moment. But the bedroom's nice. Want to see the bedroom?" She pushed against the door. There was a man in the bed—asleep, drugged, or dead. "Oh," she said. "I forgot about him." She closed the bedroom door.

Kip handed her the gram of meth. "I couldn't find flowers."

"Thank you, Jesus," she said, and immediately picked up her meth pipe. When she exhaled the vapor, the sweet smell of burning meth reached my nose, as if a scented cleaning product had been opened. And a sweet smile came to Willow's lips, showing her yellow teeth again. "Thirty-eight pounds of this would keep me high twenty-four hours a day for fifty-eight years." Her eyes blinked slowly as she reviewed the pleasant calculation. "How about that? Ain't that a thought?"

"We were wondering if Ruby was around," said Kip.

"Gone." She gestured toward the window, as if Ruby had flown out of it. "She says she's dating somebody really important, but she might've been lying. I lie all the time. You have to." She slipped her arm through Kip's. "Cut my hair? Make me look beautiful?"

He sat her in a chair, put a towel around her shoulders. Then he wet her hair and began cutting.

"I tried to keep Ruby here," said Willow.

"You did," said Kip.

"But she's strong-willed. You know her."

"I do."

"I set a bad example, sure. I won't deny it." Her eyes closed, and a faint smile crossed her cracked lips as the meth settled nicely into her brain. "I . . . won't . . . deny . . . it."

"Does she check back in?"

"Who?"

"Ruby."

"I haven't seen her. My little girl that I totally raised. On my own." She opened her eyes and looked at me. "Do you know my daughter?"

"I've seen a photo of her."

"Gorgeous, right?"

"She is."

"Her father is gorgeous too. He never comes around. Never contributes a dime. His habit is worse than mine, and mine's no joke." She closed her eyes again. "We used to be a knockout couple." She threw open her housecoat. "Look at those legs."

"World-class," I said.

She dangled one of the stilettos. "We could go to the bedroom after my haircut."

"There's somebody in there."

She closed her eyes and seemed to fall asleep. But then her eyes opened and she pointed to the floor. "See the bullet hole?"

There was, in fact, an exit bullet hole from a high-caliber weapon.

"Right up through the floor. If I'd been standing there, I would've gotten it right in the hoo-hoo." She turned to look at Kip. "You know the kid who lives down there?"

"I've never had the pleasure."

"He's okay, takes care of his little brother and sister. But he doesn't know how to handle a gun."

We gazed at the bullet hole, a clear indication of poor gun handling.

Willow closed her eyes again, the faint smile returning to her lips. "When she was little, Ruby and me used to wear mother-and-daughter outfits. We were adorable." She opened her eyes and was looking at me. "You should've seen us."

"I would have liked that."

"Up at the mall, before it shut down, somebody said that exactly: *How adorable.*"

"I'm sure you were."

"I sold our mother-daughter outfits for a couple of days' worth of crack. Now somebody else can be adorable."

Kip removed the towel. "Got any product?"

"In the bathroom. Ruby bought tons of it. Unless she took it with her."

Kip found something, smoothed it into Willow's hair. He had also brought back a hand mirror and held it up to her. She smiled, and said, "Well, look at me."

"Many will," said Kip.

"I need a *lot* of covering makeup for my uneven skin tone." She touched at one of the sores on her cheek. "Then I can get back to making a living." She turned toward me. "I provide commercial sex." She pointed toward the bedroom. "I wonder if you could help me get rid of him."

I walked with her toward the bedroom. She said, "When a buyer falls asleep on me, it's difficult unless I'm working with a pimp. Which I don't like." She sighed. "If you don't make your quota, they kick your ass."

I opened the door. The guy in the bed was a fair size. Willow said, "I think he's packing, so be careful."

I shook him by the shoulder. "Rise and shine, big boy."

He was deeply out on some kind of tranquilizer, so I lifted him off the bed. He swayed back and forth, then looked at me. "Who the fuck are you?"

"Room service."

"I'll give you fucking room service," he said, and tried a head butt, using considerable thrust. I quickly lowered my head so that he butted the top of my head, which did nothing to me but brought his nose against the anvil of my skull. He staggered backward. "Fuck . . ." I turned him around, removed his piece, and marched him across the apartment to the door. He went fairly quietly, clutching at his nose.

"Come back again," said Willow.

28

Santiago flagged me down at the entrance to the trailer park. "Don't go in, Tomás."

"What's up?"

"Some guy is watching your trailer from across the river."

"Watching how?"

"He came through the trees and bushes. Like this . . ." Santiago mimed stealthy movement, twisting his body back and forth, his arms showing branches and bushes being pushed aside. "Then he flattened himself out and is hiding there."

I was hoping it was a birdwatcher. Or just a drunk trying to find his way home. There were so many bars in the neighborhood, you could lose track of where you were, and take a shortcut through the trees.

"He's here to blow you away," said Santiago, with the authority of one familiar with wildlife along the rusty river.

The far bank of the river had been a string of vacant lots cleared for another trailer park, but the deal had fallen through, and the lots had been taken over by opportunistic sumac trees that now formed a dense thicket. "Okay, Santiago, I'll take it from here."

"You need me to go with you, Tomás. I'm a sneaky little fuck."

"You'll get hurt and your mother won't cook me any more tamales."

He looked disappointed. "I'm trying to earn a bicycle here."

I was thinking that I could make my way across the river on submerged refrigerators and automobile parts. To a hit man it would appear that I was walking on water. That would shake him up. But if I lost my footing and went under, it meant ingesting toxins not yet known to science. Instead, I walked through the trailer park until I came to the bridge. I crossed it on the pedestrian walk, and on the other bank of the river, I entered the thicket of sumac. But I was not a sneaky little fuck. I was the two-hundred-pound gorilla in the bush, dead branches crunching beneath my feet and green branches snapping as I eased past them. I stopped, knowing I wasn't going to get the jump on the hit man. I felt someone behind me, turned, and found Santiago holding up the Marksman slingshot I'd bought him in a moment of weakness. We had shot a lot of BBs at floating cans and bottles the river brought. He whispered, "I'll drive him toward you."

I couldn't deny him. The sneaky little fuck made not a sound as he went off on his mission. I suffered second thoughts about recruiting him, but really, he'd recruited me. And we had to take out the hit man before the Mother of All Tamales was killed at her stove by a wild shot from the far bank. Then I heard, through the thicket, the snap of the slingshot, and a man's voice yelping, "Son of a bitch . . ."

The slingshot snapped again. "Cocksucker . . ." I heard the ratcheting of a rifle round, but the slingshot beat him to it. "Fuck me . . ." came rasping through the sumac. Getting hit with a plated steel ball at two hundred feet per second is a strong deterrent to birdwatching.

Santiago did a war dance in front of me. "I got him, Tomás! Twice in the head!"

I pursued our assailant through the sumac, but it was slow going and by the time I reached the end of the thicket, the hit man was jumping into his car. Santiago came up beside me with a jagged rock in the pouch of his weapon. He stretched the rubber to the max and fired. A little blossom of ruptured glass appeared in the windshield.

The driver slammed the car into reverse. He backed up at high speed with extraordinary control, narrowly missing parked cars as well as moving ones but never slowing. And then I knew who he was. If you were a crew of bank robbers, car thieves, or a boss just wanting to get somewhere in a hurry, you hired Vic Zamboni, known professionally as Wheels Zamboni, once the greatest street driver in the business, now retired, or so I'd thought. He backed around a far corner where oncoming drivers honked angrily as he steered past them in reverse. And then he was gone.

"We lost him," said Santiago.

"Not really. I know who he is."

"And I cracked his window."

"Duly noted."

We walked back through the vacant lot, got into the Hummer, and headed toward the bike shop. The slingshot was folded in Santiago's lap. His pocket bulged with loose BBs. I said, "The Mother All of Tamales must not know what happened today."

"Ten four."

At the bike shop, we bought a six-speed Rocket Rider with bottle holder and saddlebags. The salesman said the seat was "adapted to the morphology of children," for which Santiago might have given him a plated steel ball between the eyes, but instead he feigned patience. When we lifted the Rocket into the Hummer, he said, "How much of the cost did I work off today?"

"You flushed a hitman. You're fully paid up."

"What do I tell the Mother of All Tamales?"

"You did some extra work for me."

"Two in the head, one in the windshield."

I left him off at the trailer park and paid a call to Duke. There was a large bar in his living room, with an even larger TV screen between gigantic floor speakers, all of it resting on a thick, white living room carpet. Off the living room, I could see a pool table. "Game of eight ball?" he asked. He could clean a table in two minutes, and my wallet along with it.

"Where do I find Wheels Zamboni?"

"What do you want him for?"

"To give him my love."

"He pulled something?"

"He was hiding in the grass across the river from my trailer. He had a rifle and he wasn't hunting water rats."

"So what happened?"

"He fucked it up, is what happened. And now I want to see him."

"I better go with you or you're liable to kill him."

"So what? He tried to kill me."

"To scare you, maybe. Not kill you."

"That remains to be seen."

"Wheels isn't a hit man. It's not his thing. Anyway, you can't kill him. Phil wouldn't like it. He throws Wheels a bone now and then. He feels responsible since Wheels retired."

"Why is he retired?"

"He says it's his heart. I think he's lost his nerve. If somebody's robbing a liquor store and you're the wheelman, you have to sit there like a fucking icicle."

So we drove in Duke's car to one of the old neighborhoods, where the houses were in various stages of neglect. "Wheels wanted to race for a living, but Primo loved him as a driver, so that was that. He was a driver, not a racer."

We stopped at a house that had been stuccoed as an afterthought. The stucco was falling off, and I could see old wooden siding underneath. Parked in the driveway was the car Wheels had escaped in. It was in better shape than his house. Duke looked at the cracked windshield. "You?"

"The kid who lives next to me did it with a slingshot."

"Don't mention that to anybody. It would ruin Wheels. He'd never live it down."

We went up the sidewalk to the house, and Duke rang the bell. Wheels came to the door. He looked at Duke, then at me. "If you're here to kill me, Tommy, get someone to take care of my bird."

"Your bird?"

"My parakeet."

Duke said, "He's not here to kill you or your bird. Now, let us the fuck in."

Wheels led us into a shabby living room, all the furniture worn down the way he was. But the walls were filled with framed and gleaming antique racing posters from the Monaco Grand Prix. And there was a beautiful watercolor of a sky-blue '57 Thunderbird.

"What can I get yuz?"

"Couple of beers," said Duke.

"You got it, my friend." Wheels hurried off to the kitchen. I heard his bird talking the sort of parakeet talk such birds engage in, a strange little language all their own. Wheels returned with a plastic tray bearing three bottles of Guinness, without glasses. He set the bottles down on a coffee table whose faded surface was stained with many rings. "First let me say, Tommy, I'm sorry I took the contract. Big fucking mistake." He had lost most of his hair, and I could see the welts where the two BBs had hit.

"I'm going to let it ride, Wheels."

He grabbed both my hands. "God bless you." Then we all sat down in threadbare chairs. "And the contract was just to fire a round your way, not hit you. I swear that on my mother's grave."

"Who hired you?"

He looked at me with sad, tired eyes. Beneath them hung thick, heavy bags that made him look like an aging basset hound. "This is the hard part. This is like a disgrace." He took a swig of Guinness. "Your cousin, Angelina."

"She give you a reason?"

"She said you stole a house from her and her kids. Father Vittorio was in there somewhere. I knew right then, this is fucked, stay out of it. But then I figured, one shot past your head, no big deal, you'd get over it."

We sat there, looking at each other. My own family was shooting at me. Wheels said, "I knew you when you were a little wiseguy."

"I remember."

"And your grandfather was good to me. I'm going to have a mass said for him. And put flowers on his grave. Will that square us?"

I looked at the aging wheelman whose days as a driver were done, who was stuck here with his parakeet. "We're squared."

"I'm relieved as hell. I've done lots of shitty things in my time, but this one's right up there near the top."

"Did you tell Angelina the hit was a bust?"

"She said that was okay, you still got the message."

Duke asked me, "*Did* you steal her house?"

"Vittorio left it to me. I was supposed to give it to Angelina?"

They agreed that I was under no obligation to give her the house, and we drank our beer. Duke said, "Angelina should run a crew. I always told her that."

We examined this thought as men will when they sit around drinking beer, feeling we understand women. Duke said, "You've got to talk to her."

"I intend to."

"But not at her house—you'll freak her out. I'll bring her to my apartment tonight."

Wheels took out his wallet. He laid five hundred-dollar bills on the coffee table. "This is the action she gave me. Take it, Tommy."

"Keep it. Get a new windshield."

"Take two bills anyway, for my sake."

I took them. Duke told him to give New View Glass a call. "Ask for Max. He owns the place and kicks back to me. He'll replace your windshield, no charge."

"Thanks, Duke. And thank you, Tommy. If you ever need a driver, just let me know."

We finished our beers and he showed us his bird, a pretty little thing talking to itself. Duke asked if it could say anything in English.

"Fuck yes. Mostly stuff she picks up from the TV. Say something, baby."

She said nothing we could understand, but Wheels seemed pleased. "She's company, you know what I mean?"

I said I knew. And then we left.

"You saw; his nerve is gone?"

"Then why was he crawling through the bushes with a rifle?"

"To feel alive. Someday it'll be you and me crawling through the bushes."

29

Duke had primed Angelina with my own favorite drink, a whiskey sour. The bourbon and lemon juice were sweetened with sugar, but there was no sweetening Angelina. She didn't rise to greet me, just stared. Her eyes were ice in a whiskey sour. She was a Martini—born angry, with a taste for action.

Duke said, "Kiss and make up or I shoot the both of you."

I said, "Angelina, I didn't write Uncle Vittorio's will."

She was seated in an armchair, her tanned, sandaled feet resting on Duke's white carpet. Her hair was a mass of black curls. She wasn't beautiful, but she had allure, with a way of angling her head and shoulders that I'd always found fascinating—a sinuous motion that showed there was something coiled in her and ready to strike. Her voice was a female version of Primo's, raspy and deep. "You influenced Vittorio."

"I was in a monastery. How did I influence him? Through the power of prayer?"

"You worked on him long-distance. I don't know how."

"He was a complicated man. I saw the complication. It's the same one I have."

"Yeah, what's that?"

"Choosing between the spirit and the chase."

She was still eyeing me coldly. Duke said, "You know what he's talking about. You're just like him."

"Stay out of this."

I asked how old her kids were.

"None of your business."

"I want to do something for them."

"Like what?"

"How about I pay for their cars?"

"They're five and six. Their cars have plastic wheels and go *toot toot*."

"Okay, something else."

"How about a house? Like the one you stole from them."

"That's gone, Angelina. Forget the house."

"I'll never forget it. Those high ceilings, and a mountain practically in the living room."

"Five people tried to whack me there."

"And what did you do about it?"

"I killed them."

This shut her up, and she gazed at me through narrowed eyelids, trying to gauge how much of the Martini madness ran in my blood. "And," I continued, "I put their bodies in a sinkhole. There's room for one more."

She turned away from me and looked out toward Parade Square, its trees and sidewalks lit by lampposts that had been there a hundred years. But she was a modern woman of fashion, from her false fingernails to her false eyelashes. She'd fought the downward pull of the town with beauty treatments and ego. "Don't fuck up my payoff, Tommy."

"What payoff is that?"

"I finessed the gaming commission until they gave me the green light on the casino."

"To do what?"

"To run the place, *idiota*."

"They gave the license to *you*?"

Duke said, "To get a crook like Angelina a casino license ain't easy. There are seven people on the gaming commission. Five lawyers and two professional politicians, all of them bent, all appointed by the governor, who's bent as a dog's back leg. But they're all guys. Bring a pair of tits into the room, and they lose focus. Am I right, Angelina?"

She smiled. She was wearing a dark-blue floral dress so thin it could have been a nightgown. "They focused, all right."

I stared at the new casino owner. She ran a numbers racket, did some fencing, but that was small change compared to what it would take to build the casino. "Whose money is it?"

"Phil's. And a few other members of a business consortium."

I could imagine these members, from Carmine Cremona in Vegas to Nick Piazza in Miami. The newest casino in the Northeast would be run by mobsters, with Angelina fronting for them.

Her graveyard stare played over me, as if measuring me for a tombstone. "And after everything is tied up in a bow, your stupid fucking friend starts a campaign to blow the casino out of the water. What an asshole." She kicked her sandals off and rubbed her feet in Duke's thick white rug. "This feels nice."

The first female genitals I ever saw were hers. She'd shown them to me one day, saying, *You ought to know about this.* And seeing my shock, she'd smiled and said, *Now you know the truth.*

She rose from her chair, walked on her bare feet across the carpet, and stood at the window. Nearby, a neon bar sign flickered. Its light was reflected on Duke's window. The reflections played on her face. She turned toward me. "What did Finn Sweeney ever do for you? He was just a rich twit."

I could see her checking herself out in Duke's wall mirror, one of those old-fashioned convex ones with an eagle spreading its wings on top of the frame. He must've had it for years, and she was a tiny twinkling figure at its center. "And you were nuts about his wife. From what I hear, you still are." She looked at Duke, who must have told her about our search for Bridget.

She came across the carpet slowly, her feet creating tiny sparks, increasing the feeling I had that she was an electric being. In Paloma, when our uncle's will was read, she was out of her depth, but here she was in her element. She stopped in front of me, looked up with those grave-yard eyes. "Finn Sweeney had the hots for me. You didn't know that?"

"I must've been gone by then."

"You were always gone. You never saw things straight. It's the altar boy in you." She was standing only inches from my face. "Asshole Finn didn't have time for the girls his family wanted him to marry. Their la-di-da bullshit bored him. He wanted to get down where it's real, so he hit on me. I told him to take a hike."

"Do you know where Bridget is?"

She looked toward Duke. "He doesn't know when to quit."

"He's in love," said Duke.

Her icy eyes held mine. "Tommy, you can fuck Bridget Breen and a rubber doughnut, but don't cross me, ever."

"Why did you hire Wheels to take a shot at me?"

"For the fun of it." She reached her hand out and with her long, shiny red fingernail tapped the bridge of my nose. "Just for laughs."

"And that's it, nothing else?"

"Nothing else." She gently patted my cheek, her gold bracelets jingling.

"This is the kind of sit-down I like," said Duke. "Everybody gets loaded and nobody gets plugged."

She moved away from me, back to the window. Gazing at the dark courthouse lawn, she said, "Your friend liked our gangster image. Lots of squares are that way."

I was remembering something I hadn't thought of in years: Primo telling me to *bring that rich kid around; I like him.*

The neon bar lights played on her face again. "Finn Sweeney was cracked. The way he never shut up." She slowly retraced her steps across the carpet, producing another little trail of sparks. She picked up the shaker, handed it to Duke. "Again."

He shook up another batch, poured for the three of us. The sweet-ness of a cold whiskey sour works wonders on a summer night. Angelina stood in front of me again, glass in hand. "Poor little Tommy, Bridget didn't love you."

"I'll live."

"Not if you keep pissing people off. The casino legislation is fragile. Don't fuck it up."

"I don't give a shit about the casino."

"Good." The graveyard stare left her eyes, but there was still no way
to read her, because her cosmetic mask not only enhanced her features,
it made her inscrutable as a statue. "And by the way, Queenie O'Malley
is worth ten of Bridget Breen."

"You don't miss much."

"I talk to Phil. You took Queenie to his restaurant."

"Did you ever hang out with Bridget and Finn after they got
married?"

"The minute the ring was on her finger, she became Lady La-di-da.
I didn't even get a tour of her new kitchen."

"Would you have wanted one?"

"Bridget could be fun because she knew what a load of shit guys
are. You should've heard the things she said about you."

"Like what?"

"That she didn't want a Saint Bernard for a lapdog." Angelina gave
a little laugh and sipped her whiskey sour. "We used to do sleepovers.
We'd spend all night reviewing men. Fast-talking Irish bastards turned
her on. That left you out."

Angelina resumed rubbing her feet back and forth in the carpet, her
red toenails going in and out of the plush weave like a school of tiny
sharks. "Bridget said you were a Saint Bernard and you'd climb a mountain of ice to save somebody. But you didn't turn her on. You weren't a
glib Irish bastard."

It was a bit of a gut punch, the image of myself galumphing through
the snow with a keg of brandy around my neck. I walked to the window
to get away from her mocking eyes. There were shadowy figures moving
in Parade Square, going in and out of the round lamplight, earning a
night's pay. I looked for the flash of a red dress, for Ruby on the prowl.
And then I saw the Blond Shadow, swanning in his tan summer suit and
wide, floppy collar. "You know that guy? Reed Hamilton?"

Angelina sparked back across the carpet and looked out the window. "I've been at his house a couple of times. A classy mix of drug fiends."

"Is he trying to score down there?"

She shrugged. "If he is, he's hard up. When I was at his place, we were snorting German pharmaceutical, the best in the world." She looked at Duke. "I don't suppose you have any. No? Then I'm going home." She slipped into her sandals and headed toward the door.

"You're over the legal limit," said Duke. "I'll call a cab."

"Since when did you worry about what's legal?" She paused in front of me. "Don't cry over Bridget Breen." She ran her fingernail from the bridge of my nose to the tip. "Be a good dog."

30

I was three whiskey sours into the night and feeling the promise whiskey gives. In Coalville, if you aren't half drunk by nine o'clock, you're out of step with your ancestors. I crossed the street and entered the shadows of the park, its long row of trees interspersed with benches. On one of them sat the Blond Shadow, Reed Hamilton. He was quietly singing to himself, a tenor that was almost a falsetto.

I sat down beside him, and he turned slowly toward me. "Finn Sweeney's friend." He seemed to say this to himself rather than to me. He produced a flask from his light tan suit, which he wore with the indifference of the rich, as if it had fallen around him from the sky and happened to fit perfectly. He extended the flask to me. "Bolivian brandy."

The flask was highly polished silver, bearing his initials elaborately woven together by the engraver. I undid the lid and had a taste. "Fruit and flowers."

"From the Andes." He took back the flask.

I said, "I'm trying to find out who killed Finn."

"You were close to him. I tried to be." He put the flask away. "I hope you succeed."

"I'm getting nowhere."

"Murdered in his garden. I've been to parties there. Tiny little sandwiches and fabulous champagne."

"Can you tell me anything that might help?"

"Not really." He opened the flask again. "Instead of watching his portfolio grow, Finn bought a TV station. I don't think his family was too happy about it."

"Ever meet a girl who calls herself Ruby the Forbidden Fruit?"

"The devil child."

"Sounds like her."

"I used to think I knew the world. Educated in Switzerland, that sort of thing." He put his head back, a length of blond hair falling across his brow. He seemed to be remembering Switzerland fondly.

I brought him back. "And Ruby?"

"Educated by Lucifer." He turned toward me, his pale blue eyes those of a summer sky. "She hasn't been seen for a while."

"I wonder why."

"She could be running a sex seminar. Actually, she probably will someday." He chuckled to himself at the success he imagined for her. "I've met many smart people. Friends of my father. One of them was a chemist, knew the formula for everything." He shook his head at the memory of such prowess. "But Ruby is like a Russian chess protégé. If you know what I mean."

In the light of the park lamps, shadowy players were hunched over the chess tables. He was looking their way.

"She's a protégé?"

"Most definitely." He smiled fondly. "It's her eyes. Feral. But with a shifting something in the background, a form of intelligence I'd never seen. Certainly not in Switzerland."

I looked up the street, hoping to see Ruby the Forbidden Fruit coming down the long catwalk of the concrete path. Hamilton said, "She's right out of Darwin. In Switzerland we read a lot about Darwin. He would've called Ruby a new variant of the human teenager. It's why the limousines stop for her."

We walked toward the street. "Here's one now," he said, and I watched it pull in alongside him.

"Mr. Hamilton?" came the voice of the driver.

Hamilton paused at the door to look back at me. "I hope you find her. For your higher education." He turned his gaze toward the shadowy chess players and other figures in the park. "Read your Darwin. It's all in there."

The limo door closed, and there was nothing but black glass rolling away. I had three whiskey sours and two brandy chasers in me and felt that the night still had something to tell me. I circled through the park, in and out of the lamplight. Moths were chasing the light in every one of them, trying to find their true love, the moon.

"Honey, I have what you want." She blended with some illuminated bushes that lined the square, so that there was light spilling onto her blue high-heel shoes. The rest of her was sequined blue sheath. "Ravish you to death?" she said, wriggling up to me as I walked.

"I'm looking for Ruby."

"What do you want with her? I'm the full-grown version." She twisted her hips toward me.

I said, "She's my sister."

"Yes, and I'm your aunt Sally." The sequined sheath came closer. She was packing something in that dress that I wasn't expecting to see on a woman. She saw I saw. "It's the wig, isn't it?" she said, pulling at it angrily. "It doesn't do a goddamn thing for me."

"You look fine. I used to be a bouncer. I had to train myself to see through the bling."

"No, it's the hair. It's not right; it's not me. And since we're talking trash, what do you want with Ruby?"

"Do you know her?"

"She's a walking electric chair." Blue high heels clicked beside me. "I wouldn't get near the little demon if you paid me." She rearranged the string of pearls that fell into her cleavage. "Self-discovery is my thing."

"What's so dangerous about Ruby?"

"She's a manipulating little bitch with the mind of a video game." She paused. "But her act is perfect. She puts me to shame."

When we arrived at the next pool of lamplight, I said, "I saw a picture of her with the district attorney."

"Of course you did. She's a snitch. A treacherous informer." She opened and closed her purse with a snap. "I have a very interesting gentleman I see on a fairly regular basis. I give him a little kiss by the fountain. Ruby took him for her own. She isn't sixteen yet, so he'll get fifty fucking lifetimes in prison if they catch him with her. And he's not terribly prosperous. I may be his one adventure a month. She's blackmailing him, but he won't admit it."

She snapped the purse open and closed it again, like the mouth of a small, angry alligator. "And he's not the first. Anybody who fucks that little demon is hers forever. Because her very own district attorney is waiting in the wings and he loves to bust sex offenders. He gets off on it." The wig shook, perhaps in disgust, near my face. "And how did you get a picture of her with the district attorney? Are you a private eye? Do I fall in love with you in the third reel?" She peered closely at me. "You're undercover. I won't tell anyone."

"Actually, I'm a monk."

"Everybody in deep religious drag. Maybe I should try it." She stepped into the next pool of light as if considering a costume change. "But who would I give all my Jimmy Choo shoes to? And why is a monk looking for Ruby?"

"She may have something to do with the death of a friend."

"I said she was poison."

"She didn't do it. But she might know who did."

"Well, I haven't seen her around for a while. Maybe hell had a recall on her model."

"Aside from snitching and blackmailing, have you left anything out?"

She considered this, twirling one of the waves of her wig around her little finger. "I'm probably jealous. She's invented herself. At the age of fifteen." We clicked on into the next pool. "Confidence, poise, with childhood madness mixed in. I just want to be a regular girl, make a small living out here until I retire."

"And what does Ruby want?"

"Her own line of cosmetics, I don't know. If you saw her strutting around, you'd see the little bitch has star power. You sure you don't want a lovely blow job in the bushes?"

192 | WILLIAM KOTZWINKLE

We were back at the bench where I'd met Reed Hamilton. The whiskey sours were running down, and the brandy was gone from my brain. "I'm going to call it a night."

"All this fuss and bother and you're *leaving* me?" The sequins made tiny clicking sounds as she ran her hands over them.

"Afraid so."

"Well, you can have this for nothing: Don't believe a word the little monster says. She lies with every breath." She made her way back through the pools of lamplight, and I went to where I could see Shirley Kaminski working the bike lane, without her seeing me. Like Knucklehead Nowitzki, her Polish ancestors had probably worked in the Adeline mine, battling stone and darkness so their daughters could live in the light and wear pretty clothes. If one of them came back from the grave, he would grab her pimp by the neck and, with hands made strong from swinging a pick, strangle him.

I walked away. Dialogues with the dead get you nowhere.

31

Barnes & Noble had cappuccino and Darwin. The cappuccino was delicious, but Darwin was slow going. After several hours of skimming through animal husbandry, orchids, and how long it takes the ocean to turn a cliff into sand, I gave up and put Darwin back on the shelf. I walked a few blocks to the doors of the Top Hat bar. The painted hats loomed over me, so that entering, I felt like a rabbit being put into position for the magician's act, in which I would be pulled out and put on display, and the audience would clap and ask good-naturedly, *How did that rabbit get in there?*

And then I was inside the magician's hat. Many animals were stuffed inside for the audience's entertainment—old drunks and young people, among them Queenie and Richard Mittleman, who was sitting across from her in a booth along the wall. I recognized him from his size. He got up at four in the morning to wrestle fruit and vegetables, ready to do the heavy lifting.

Valentina's voice interrupted my meditation. "Hey, big guy. Where you been?"

"Looking for you."

She ran a rag lazily over the bar top in front of me. "I wear my flowered Russian panties just for you. But you don't care."

"I care very much."

"Give proof."

I ordered a Russian mule, which she accepted as proof; then she caught me looking Queenie's way. "You like that little rabbit? Big guy like you? You kill her in bed."

"We haven't been in bed."

"Short girls turn big guys on. Know why?"

"I'm hoping you'll tell me."

"Old story. Protect little package."

I couldn't tell her Queenie had killed a guy while protecting *me*. Three guys, actually, if we counted her sending the Muldoon brothers to a watery grave. I said, "She's tougher than she looks."

"She make you happy?"

"Not tonight."

At which point another big guy came through the door. Unlike Richard Mittleman, he was not a gentle purveyor of vegetables. The smoke signal from the top of his head read *I'll kick your ass, whoever you are*. Beside him was the sort of scrawny little bird that follows oxen around to eat ticks off the back of the ox. I think they're called oxpeckers. This little bird was definitely an oxpecker. His feathers were colorful—a Cuban-collar shirt with roses printed on it. The ox wore a sweatshirt with the sleeves cut off to show his biceps.

He swaggered his muscles to the other end of the bar, and I saw Valentina check beneath the bar to see that the baseball bat was available. But she served him and the oxpecker with her lazy smile because business is business. When it ceased to be business, out would come the bat.

The oxpecker was looking around. He lived on blood the ox spilled. His eyes fell on me and traveled up and down my form, and a satisfied little smile crossed his lips. He would keep his scouting report to himself for a while, but inevitably he would perceive, with his little oxpecker brain, a wordless insult emanating from me.

After they'd been drinking a while, the bouncer stepped in beside me at the bar. "I usually know when trouble's going to start. How about you?"

"Pretty much."

"You getting that feeling now?"

I remained where I was, bathing in the aqueous light of the room, the various lamps mixing a sea-green glow that spilled over booths and bar. Valentina was joking with the oxpecker and the ox. A pretty woman behind a bar can play with dangerous men all night long, amusing herself and them without inciting violence. The bouncer moved to a better angle of attack should action erupt. Valentina refilled my glass. The bite of the ginger beer in my vodka was settling my digestion enough that I could almost swallow the sight of Queenie with Richard Mittleman.

"I take you home after bar closes." Valentina was once again making lazy movements in front of me with her rag.

"I can't tonight."

"I give you fuck of a lifetime."

"I'm sure you would."

"I tell you the truth," she said, leaning toward me and lowering her voice. "In Russia I had chance to marry big shot. But I marry Popov instead. Know why?" She tossed the rag beneath the bar, then looked up at me, her false eyelashes like little black butterflies she kept as pets. "Big shot make me cry."

She saw that I doubted her. "No, is true. Big shot was prick, hurt my feelings."

She adjusted a large dangling earring. "Popov buys phony gold light switch for our shit house in Bellefontaine, says, *Valentina, you are light of my life.* You see difference?"

I admitted that I did. And perhaps I was careless as I looked toward Queenie and Mittleman, their booth being directly beyond the ox and the oxpecker. Maybe I squinted, maybe I tilted my head a certain way. The oxpecker was roused. He pushed away from the bar and closed the distance between us. "You got a problem, fella?"

I laughed. He was such a little fucking oxpecker.

The ox behind him came off his bar stool. I felt murder enter me like a phantom that had access to my body. It stretched out luxuriously, increasing the blood flow to my muscles. And then it floated up into my skull, where it settled in behind my eyes.

And then I heard Duke alongside me. Even when he just says hello to

196 | WILLIAM KOTZWINKLE

you, his voice is like an icicle in the ear. The oxpecker automatically folded his feathers because an old lion had come to drink at the waterhole. As for the ox himself, barroom fighters expect bruised knuckles and a split lip, but a bullet between the eyes is another matter entirely. He said something to the oxpecker, and they moved toward the door. The great muscular arms of the ox were like cannons. He'd been born in the wrong time and place. He belonged in a private medieval army, or on a pirate ship. In Coalville, he would always be a man whose raw power brought him no profit, only chaos, and his oxpecker was almost a guarantee of that.

My view of Queenie was now unobstructed. I could walk over there, ask her to run away with me. We could drive across the country in the Hummer, live in high desert country, watch the monsoon together.

Duke put his hand on my shoulder. "Don't waste your time mooning over Queenie O'Malley. You're not the marrying kind."

"What kind am I?"

"Your old pal Finn gives you a phone call and you hop on the next plane from Mexico."

"It was a call for help."

"A married guy wouldn't answer that call. The wife would ask him where the fuck is he going and why isn't he taking her."

Queenie and Richard Mittleman got up from their booth. They chatted with some other couples and then headed toward the door. Duke said, "She's a homebody. You don't see that?"

"I don't know what I see."

"You see a great body. Not the same thing as a *home*body. You've got to learn the difference." The bar lights were shining on his rocklike face. "You know why you live in that monastery?"

"I've often wondered."

"It's your bachelor hideout. From which you emerge for fun and games. It's *action* you love, Tommy. Not the holy cross before you. And not Queenie O'Malley beside you."

We made our goodbyes to Valentina and left the Top Hat. "I'm looking for a girl in a red dress."

"Ain't we all."

"She calls herself Ruby the Forbidden Fruit because she's only fifteen."

"Are you trying to get yourself arrested?"

"I'm digging for information."

"Six feet should be deep enough. Just add an inexpensive coffin for yourself. Phil will give you a discount." He turned down the street that led to the four-leaf neon sign of the Shamrock bar. I watched him go, his hunched figure like that of a vampire.

I walked to Parade Square. The chess players were concentrating on their game, sliding pieces on the concrete table. They played with a digital clock alongside them, its face showing a tiny glow. I watched, but their moves were too fast for me—local wizards whose nights were spent here, perfecting the art of war in miniature.

And then there was a soft voice at my shoulder. "Back for more? What do you think of my new wig? Does it go with my eyes?" Her eyelashes were longer than Valentina's.

The chess players tapped their clock, indifferent to her presence. "*I'm* the queen," she said to them. "The most powerful piece on the board." They continued to ignore her, so she said to me, "Let's walk."

Her large pile of hair cast its outline on the sidewalk, outshadowing mine. She said, "Artistic perfection is what I'm after."

"Seen anything of Ruby?"

"Her again? If I dressed like Barbie doll, would you love me?"

"I might."

"Well, the little fiend still hasn't come to the square. The vice squad is looking for her."

"What for?"

"Oh, who cares? How about an unforgettable blow job? I usually charge forty, but I'll do you for twenty-five and you'll remember me forever."

I declined and watched her go through pools of lamplight, swinging her beaded handbag, the click of her high heels slowly fading.

Reed Hamilton was sitting on the edge of the fountain, strumming a ukulele. He was a good musician, the little instrument putting out much more than I thought possible. And I listened to the song he was singing in his high tenor, "*Oh, show us the way to the next little girl. Oh, don't ask why; oh, don't ask why. For if we don't find the next little girl, I tell you we must die . . .*"

When he saw me, he stopped singing. "David Bowie did it better."

I said, "I hear the vice squad is looking for Ruby."

"And if they don't find her . . ." He stroked his ukulele. "I tell you they must die."

A corner boy came over. "Gentlemens, I have some choice tranq for your power nap."

"Yes, give me . . ." Reed handed him several bills. ". . . however many that comes to."

"Come to twelve caps exactly." The boy counted them into a small silvery packet.

"Will they give me seizures and a heart attack?"

"Hasn't so far."

"I've had them before?"

"Several times."

"Splendid." Reed laid the little packet into his ukulele case. The corner boy walked off and Reed said, "I like to support local businesses."

"I looked up Charles Darwin."

"And did you find Ruby?"

"Not yet. I'm a slow reader."

"*Occasionally some creature has been saved from fatal competition by inhabiting a protective station. That's Ruby. And Finn was her protective station. He loved her."

"And you? Do you love her?"

"Madly. Tragically." His eyes expressed a hope that I might understand him. I couldn't say that I did, but I liked him.

He closed his ukulele case. "It has nothing to do with those tight dresses she wears. It's because there's still something of the child in her. When she looks at me, it's with a gaze of deep, cruel sharing. That's how children see the world. Now I must say good night. I have what I came for." He patted the case contentedly. "The total disintegration pill."

I saw his limousine coming up the street and walked with him toward it. Once again the window of the limo opened and the driver asked, softly and politely, "Are you ready, Mr. Hamilton?"

Reed slid the ukulele case inside, then turned back to me. "You're doing splendidly with Darwin. I can tell." He got into the limo, and it rolled away.

32

In hopes of running into Ruby, I returned to Parade Square the following midnight and watched a skateboarder balancing on the rim of the fountain until he flew off and landed near Reed Hamilton, who was again sitting on a bench, strumming his ukulele. When he saw me, he broke off with a quick flourish. "Martini, Finn's friend . . ." He smiled his cosmic grin, indicating he was medicated for the evening. ". . . and friend of Darwin. I hope you read his section on ants. Those nasty little ones who take slaves."

"I preferred his take on the bees."

"Well, who wouldn't? Such efficient use of wax." He set his ukulele into its case. "Quite a little hive we have here tonight. Everyone's buzzing. I love them all. How about you?"

"I'm two drinks behind you."

"We can fix that." From inside his immaculate summer sport coat, he drew out his silver flask. "Hennessey, aged thirty years, like me."

Along with fire, I tasted pepper and chocolate, which is a fine combination when in the garden of evil—child drug peddlers hustling the four corners of the square, and girls in the bike lane taking care of the rest. I handed the flask back to him.

"You said you were two behind. One more to go."

The second hit unrolled another carpet of fire through my chest, and after catching my breath, I asked, "What did you think when Finn came here with his TV crew?"

"I thought he was mad." Reed lapsed into silence, giving further consideration to my question. "But like many overprivileged people, he suffered from nostalgie de la boue."

"What's that in English?"

"Literally, nostalgia for the mud. Getting back to the basic drives." He gestured toward the musicians, the dancers, the drug dealers. "And there they are, on full display."

Angelina's words came back to me. *He wanted to get down where it's real. I told him to take a hike.*

"Actually," continued Reed, "journalism was just his cover. He really came here to see Ruby. Mad either way."

"He interviewed her, right?"

"More than that."

"How much more?"

"Considerably more."

"Even though she was underage."

"I said it was mad."

"And he was married to Bridget."

"He wasn't bothered by convention, as you know."

He'd gone after Bridget, who was bottom-of-the-barrel Irish, but Ruby was below that, living with a meth addict mother and hanging out with the runaways and gang members who lived and loafed in her building. From her photograph, she was dangerously beautiful, and that must have topped it off as far as Finn was concerned. Ruby had been as real as it gets.

I gave the flask back to Reed. He passed it beneath his nose, breathing the escaping vapor. "They were both stars, made for each other, and they knew it." His cosmic grin drooped a little. "So the jealous gods killed him."

"How did she take his death?"

"She showed no sign of grief. Too busy with her plan." He looked up through the trees to the night sky. The Milky Way was directly overhead. "She told me she was going to have twenty million TikTok followers."

I thought of her name in the graffiti murals. In the midst of indecipherable flourishes of egotism, its red aura had caught my eye. Whether she was the artist or had commissioned someone didn't matter. It was a vision of stardom. It was the Milky Way.

"She documents her life," continued Reed. "Ruby the Forbidden Fruit, girl of the streets. She has a prodigious sense of the legendary." Appreciation was written on his fine patrician features. "When friend Finn came around with his camera, she was already developing her legend. Crude snippets on her smartphone. But professional equipment inspired her. She mated with Finn's camera—and with Finn, of course; that goes without saying." He sighed and took another sip of brandy. "All I had was a distinguished name and a ukulele."

Stepping out of the shadows with the bounce of boyhood was Zigzag, the corner boy I'd given the two fifties to. He bumped his fist with mine and I waited for his report, because I could see he had something to tell. Twelve-year-old dope dealers can't hide their emotions like grown-up wiseguys. It's why they're so quick to shoot each other. Well, as long as he didn't shoot me.

"Something come to my attention." He let this sink in. "Blonde you looking for—she with the nuns."

"What nuns?"

"Bitches in black, never say shit."

"The Sisters of Silence?"

"Dem's the bitches." He smiled, waiting for another contribution to the Growing Boy fund.

"You got inside their convent?"

"Pussy only allowed in that place. But I worked it out." He continued to smile, enjoying himself. He had me. I handed him a fifty.

Pocketing it, he said, "Girl I know from the street reposin' there. But she a user." He turned his head, as if other business was calling him.

"Stop dicking me around."

"The whole story come giftwrapped for fifty more."

I gave the little bandit what he wanted. Finally satisfied, he said, "This user, she come over the wall when she hurtin', and I straighten her. Last time she fixed, she tell me some blond lady is all fucked up there because somebody waste her husband." He gazed up at me, a last trace of boyhood in his gaze—a kind of faith in the unseen powers that brought things his way. "Got to be your blonde. Check it out."

I watched him walk away, his small form illuminated by one of the park lamps. It seemed as if shimmering fairy dust lay on his narrow young shoulders, instead of the heavy burden of being an adult too soon.

Reed didn't comment on Zigzag's report. He'd probably guessed the blonde was Bridget, but he didn't want to intrude. And there was something else on his mind. "I've not been completely straightforward with you about Ruby." And then he placed a call. "Ruby, dear, I'm not disturbing you, am I? I met an old friend of Finn's and thought you might want to speak with him. Yes, I'm with him now." There was a pause. He tickled his fingers in the air as he said goodbye and put the phone away. "She's receiving; we're in luck."

I couldn't act on Zigzag's information at one in the morning, so I walked with Reed toward his limo. I said, "I met Ruby's mother."

"The effervescent Willow."

"I had to throw somebody out of her bed."

"Cluttering up the place, was he?"

"Something like that."

"I worry about young Ruby," continued Reed as he opened the limo door. "Her homemade movie is about the sex-trafficking business around here. And the traffickers aren't happy about starring in it. And they certainly couldn't have had warm feelings toward Finn."

"Would they have killed him?"

"I have no idea. They *are* subhuman. I've seen them drive by the bike lane." He gestured me into the limo.

As limos go, it was on the small side, but the seats were certainly luxurious and there were vases on the doors, holding single roses. There was a bar, and Reed made us a couple of gin and tonics and told the driver to take him home.

"Ruby lives with *you?*"

"She lives at my house, but not *with* me. I'm many things, but I'm not a child molester."

The limo purred through town and then up to the better roads and then finally to the best of roads, where the old estates of Coalville had been carved out of the wooded hills. The driveway to Hamilton House was long and winding and lit by bronze post lamps. The house was also lit, by ground lights in the shrubbery. It was three-story brick, much of it covered with ivy. "Built when the family had money," said Reed as we stepped out of the limo.

"You seem to be doing well enough."

"Burning through the trust fund, that's all."

We walked through a brick archway onto a tiled porch and then into the house. Ruby greeted us, and her beauty really was startling. Waves of red hair ran like hot lava to her shoulders. Where the waves peaked, there were tiny touches of what looked like gold but were really reflections from the overhead light in the entrance hall. From my recent course in eyebrows, I appreciated that hers were real with a bit of contouring penciled in.

Neither of us spoke for a moment. She was obviously sizing me up for some use in the shameless way of an ambitious teenager caressed by her own image. The milky whiteness of her skin must have mesmerized her every time she looked in the mirror. Overcome by herself, she felt invincible in certain situations, and this was one of them. She was very much at home in Hamilton House.

"This is Tommy Martini," said Reed. "He and Finn were thick as thieves."

She held out her hand. "I'm Ruby."

"Yes," I said, "you certainly are."

She gave a slight smile, but I could see her mind working to fit me into the somewhat limited picture she had of the male sex. Reed tried to help her. "Martini is a monk, out running amok."

"A monk? Really?"

"Really."

She led us into the living room. The windows and ceiling were high, and the drapes were a thick floral brocade. The furniture was as old as the house, like something in a museum. "Have a seat," she said, pointing graciously toward a pair of antique easy chairs. She sat on a couch facing us, wearing a shiny red dressing gown with pink birds embroidered on it. When her eyes met mine again, I saw a flash of the recklessness she shared with her mother. But Ruby had a strength her mother lacked, having grown up as a little red fox in a chaotic den of drugs and drug users. Spiritually, she had gnawed on bones and sucked out the marrow of intelligence. "How did you get to be a monk?"

"I killed somebody."

I waited for the fox to digest that bone. Why did I throw it to her? To shake her up? She took it between her teeth very calmly and stared back at me. "Was it an accident?"

"It was a punch to the stomach."

"Ouch." She resettled the dressing gown around her knees. Her feet were bare, and of course her toenails were bright red, but with the addition of a tiny rhinestone on each. "Did he have it coming?"

"From the beginning of time."

"That's pretty far." Her fox eyes held no warmth. Her mother's den had been a cold one.

Reed tapped his ukulele case. "Perhaps a little music."

"Sing that one I like, about finding the next little girl."

He opened the case, took out the uke. "*If we don't find the next little girl, I tell you we must die . . .*"

Ruby listened but continued looking at me, the coldness never leaving her eyes, but I could see she appreciated Reed. Like the exotic flamingos embroidered on her gown, he was a rare bird who'd flown into her life. And there I was, built like a prison weightlifter but introduced as a monk. She was turning this over in her mind as Reed sang, "*We've lost our dear old mama . . .*"

Her own dear old mama, like the woman of the song, was acquainted with payment for sex. Ruby couldn't help looking like a little tramp, because she'd gotten her sense of style from her mother, but I didn't think she had worked very long as an underage prostitute. She was too smart for that. She was more like a priestess in a cult of one. I'd seen it before. It had almost killed me in Paloma.

She clapped when Reed finished. "That's our song," she said.

"I've got more," said Reed, "but not until you're fully grown."

Her eyes came back to me. "Tell me about being a monk."

"Just a bunch of guys keeping their mouths shut."

She ran a hand through her luxuriant red hair, extending its reddish flow higher into the light and arching her back. She had the tarty style of her mother, but younger and more vital. "Did Reed tell you about the movie I was making with Finn?"

"*Ruby, the Forbidden Fruit*, twelve episodes on Amazon."

"Only it's not finished. We never got to the best part."

"What part is that?"

"Ruby undercover."

I said, "Somebody killed Finn, and they might kill you."

The flash in her eyes came back—invincibility of the teenager. "I know how to take care of myself."

"Who's in this documentary?"

"Big wheels."

"Doing what?"

"Wouldn't you like to know." I saw what Reed had seen: a child. Even with a silk dressing gown, eye makeup, and all that hair. And Reed was right; Finn had been insane to get involved with her. Maybe she was the reason he'd been murdered. Maybe her aura of invincibility had tempted him to send her too far into the Coalville hierarchy. *I wouldn't get near the little demon if you paid me*, said the drag queen in my head.

Reed said, "I purchased what will probably be vastly inferior product." He took a small packet from his pocket and laid out a couple of lines on an antique Chinese coffee table. Ivory birds were inlaid in it, and the lines seemed to come from their claws. From his pocket he took a sterling silver straw and sampled his purchase. "Yes, it's dreadful."

"You're going to kill yourself with that stuff," said Ruby.

"I'm waiting on something better. Pure, like you."

"Flush that down the toilet," she said, and he did, in a bathroom off the hallway. He returned, smoking a gold-tipped cigarette that smelled like something from the Casbah.

Her concern for him had been real. She was Willow's daughter and knew the score on buying drugs at Parade Square. Sooner or later, you buy the high that's your goodbye. And if Reed croaked himself, she'd be out on her ear. Hamilton House wasn't her last stop, but it would do for now.

But it was my last stop. Ruby wasn't going to tell me what she and Finn had been up to. She was a street kid, suspicious and guarded. Reed said, "There's a pool if you'd like a little swim. No? Something to eat?"

"I'm fine. I just need a ride back to town."

"Of course." He walked me out to the tiled porch and through the archway to the garden. "I'm sorry she wasn't more helpful."

"It was a long shot. But I appreciate the thought."

"Do you think I should have Willow move in here?"

"Mother of the year."

"I could make Ruby my ward. Like Batman and Robin."

We walked to the limousine. The driver was inside, looking at his phone. When he saw us, he got out quickly. He was an older man, probably glad to have the job despite the odd hours. Reed addressed him as if asking a favor. "Can you possibly take Mr. Martini back to the square?"

"Yes, sir, certainly." The driver opened the door, and I got in. Reed waved his gold-tipped cigarette and the limo pulled away. I asked the driver if he knew Wheels Zamboni.

"I believe, sir, he drove for your grandfather."

This took me by surprise. "You're pretty well informed."

"I've participated in card games your grandfather arranged. And I've always had an interest in automobiles."

"Wheels is still around."

"Yes, sir, I believe he lives with his bird."

"Is there anything you don't know?"

"How to stay comfortable with an uncertain poker hand."

We came down out of the wooded hills into the world of the big-box stores—closed now, but several RVs were parked at Walmart, their owners feeling relatively safe for the night. Traveling for their summer vacation. Maybe they'd visit the Adeline mine and, like many tourists before them, wonder how men could have worked underground like moles. Moles with dynamite.

"Did you ever see Finn Sweeney on TV?"

"Frequently."

"What did you think of him?"

"He was a fish."

Gambler jargon, and I knew what he meant. I'd seen the pros at poker tables in Las Vegas, masters with decades of experience and nerves of steel. Finn had neither. He was jumpy, showed his cards too soon, and the pros of Coalville closed him out of the game.

We rolled into the heart of the city, and I had him drop me off at the parking garage.

"Good night, Mr. Martini. I hope I'll see you in my car again."

I watched the limo drive away. A stumbling addict tried to peer through its windows and made peculiar hand gestures, perhaps thinking it would stop and carry him to Crack Castle.

I climbed the ramp to the Hummer on the top floor. Directly behind my vehicle, the elevator door had Ruby's name scrawled on it. I thought I was done with the demon child. Of course, I was wrong.

33

I was seated by the river of rust when my phone rang, the caller identified as *Cathedral*. A woman's voice said, "Please hold for Monsignor Crispin."

Crispin came on the line. "Brother Thomas—may I still address you that way?"

"Yes, Monsignor, I'm still a Benedictine."

"Your informant was correct. If you go to the convent at noon, a sister of the order will let you in. She won't speak, so neither should you. If you have your Benedictine robe with you, wear it."

As I slipped into my cassock and felt myself within its loose, flowing fabric, I had the usual sensation of protection, as if it were Kevlar, not cotton. I was the Black Monk of the Benedictines. I climbed into my bulletproof Hummer and drove.

There are supposed to be five thousand consecrated virgins in the world. Five thousand out of all the women walking the planet. I shouldn't be intrigued by the figure, but I am.

The convent was on the high ground outside town and was only a few miles from the mansions of Coalville. With a little financial help from the first families, it had resisted every attempt by developers to buy it up and chop it into condos. I parked alongside walls made of granite mined a century ago. At the center of the front wall were high wooden doors reinforced with iron. As a boy, I'd ridden my bicycle here, imagining the beautiful sisters beyond these mysterious doors. The mystery resurrected itself now, because the hinges were moving, carrying the doors inward. The nun who'd been awaiting my arrival was young, shy, and silent. She closed the heavy doors and pointed to a path through pruned apple trees, their gnarled trunks showing they were elders, probably planted when the convent was built. The loving attention of the sisters had preserved their strength.

At the heart of the garden was a life-size statue of Mary. A century of wind and acid rain had worn down the delicate features of her face, but generations of nuns had gazed at her in supplication, sorrow, and surrender. They were tuned to a frequency of faith and sacrifice I would never reach.

The young nun pointed to a greenhouse at the end of the garden. I entered it through a glass-paned door. Beside a spray of tall ferns was a woman who seemed to be rising out of them as if she'd posed herself there. And maybe she had. On the football field or in a barroom, Bridget had always known where the light showed her to best advantage.

The breeze from an overhead fan lifted a few strands of her hair like gold being spun in a fairy tale. Her plain black dress could only have come from the nuns. She held out both hands to me. I kept the appropriate distance for a Benedictine monk. We both observed the rule of silence until we'd walked to a pond at the center of the garden. "Who told you I was here?"

"A twelve-year-old drug dealer."

"In this town, that doesn't surprise me."

"I'm sorry about Finn."

"I know you loved him. So did I." She didn't say more. She was the hellcat from South Side.

She cast a skeptical eye over my cassock. "What happened to you? You're supposed to be my old flame."

"You blew it out, remember?"

"Young girls make mistakes."

Goldfish with freakishly distorted heads swam in lazy circles through the clear water of the pond. There were benches beside the water, and we sat down together, keeping a proper distance.

I said, "Since I was a kid, I wanted to get in here."

"Well, it's the last place I'd want to get into." She watched the colorful heads and tails go by. "Those are the ugliest fish I've ever seen."

"It took a lot of breeding to get them to look like that."

"I'm going nuts here. Holy orders aren't for me."

"Duke Devlin thought you were living in a cathouse in Bellefontaine."

"That's just what he would think."

I moved my gaze from Bridget's long black dress to the goldfish with their strange heads. A man involved with two women at the same time has a pretty strange head himself. I asked her how she'd wound up with the good sisters.

"When Finn was shot, I ran from our garden in my bare feet, in the dark. This place isn't far when you're running fast. I told the nuns my husband had been shot and I needed to hide. They said nothing, just waved me inside. Didn't say a word." She looked back toward the somber-looking convent. "They still haven't. Nobody says anything. It's the quietest place I've ever been. I guess I don't like quiet."

"Finn called me right before the fatal shot."

"I didn't notice. I was running for my life." Tears came into her eyes. She turned away. A couple of goldfish were staring up at us. Dark figures fed them regularly, and Bridget in black, along with the black-robed monk, must have seemed like the usual handout.

She stood and looked toward the convent wall, as if she expected the shooter to appear there. Instead, she said, "I miss Finn every minute. He made me laugh like no one else could."

Shedding my cassock wouldn't turn me into Finn Sweeney, who could hold an entire barroom in thrall with an Irishman's mad feeling for fun. I was the galumphing Saint Bernard dog. As if to confirm the image, she asked, "If I leave this place, can you protect me?"

Take care of Bridget. My heart is in your hands.

"You need professional security."

"I don't want strangers around."

"They're trained not to intrude."

"They can be bought. The police in Coalville have already been bought. I can't trust anybody." Her gaze held mine, as it had held me when we were kids and then again as teenagers. "You're the only one I can trust. And you know why."

"The best thing would be to get you out of town."

"I'm done hiding."

"So where do we go?"

"I've got a TV station to run. I can get there safely from my house when I need to."

An imposing figure in nun's habit appeared from the convent doorway.

"Mother Josephine," whispered Bridget.

Mother Josephine rustled toward us, a crucifix swinging from a black cord around her neck. I guessed her age at about sixty. She carried herself with authority, but the closer she got, the clearer it became that she was a contemplative. A rosary was entwined in her fingers. It was the kind handed down from one generation to the next. The beads were smoky gray crystals strung on sterling silver, burnished with a hundred years of devotion. She'd clearly had enough of people talking in her garden, and her eyes were telling me to buzz off. Bridget said, "Mother Josephine, Brother Thomas is going to take me home."

To my surprise, Mother Josephine spoke. "Will you be safe out there?" She gestured toward the stone wall.

"Look at him," said Bridget. "Who's going to mess with *that*?"

34

"I'm dying for some fast food. The nuns eat like birds."

I drove us to the nearest McDonald's window and ordered Quarter Pounders with Cheese, along with plenty of fries. Our orders were passed through to us by a young man who checked out my cassock and the blonde riding with me. "Enjoy," he said in a tone that suggested burger, blonde, and fries, in whatever order I might like.

I parked and we dug in. Bridget had lost her husband and I had lost my friend, but McDonald's is forever. I ate with appreciation for the copious grease in which the world was swimming.

"I needed that," said Bridget as we drove away from the bright yellow *M* that would always be there for us. She had called me her old flame. Women like to keep old flames to warm them when they're sad.

I can usually feel violence approaching, in the same way animals feel an approaching storm. It's an energy that troubles the atmosphere. "I'm hiring a live-in bodyguard for you."

"Who is he?"

"He used to be my grandfather's wheelman."

"A criminal."

"Retired."

"A retired criminal. Wonderful."

I called Wheels and explained the job. Bridget opened the glove compartment, found a pack of cigarettes, and lit one. She lowered the window and blew smoke out into the sunlight. We passed a local bar, drawn curtains revealing nothing of what was inside. Then a boarded-up Catholic church. On the plywood that covered its door were the usual graffiti and, in their midst, RUBY in big red block letters. Bridget didn't seem to notice.

I took the last french fry and headed toward the lofty heights where Finn and Bridget had built their home. Near the top of the mountain, I turned onto Grandview Road and saw the posh property names: *High Haven, Oak Cottage, Flowersburn*. I especially liked *Flowersburn*. Beneath the entire valley, mine fires had been burning for years, the flowers of hell spontaneously igniting. "I wanted to call our place *Wildwood*," said Bridget. "But Finn said it sounded pretentious."

A few more minutes took me to their driveway. It was called, simply, *Sweeney*. I drove into a manicured estate, where brush and spindly trees had been removed, leaving big old pines and birches with plenty of room to spread their arms toward the sun. "When we built up here," said Bridget, "I thought I'd gone to heaven."

The parking lot was big enough for twenty cars. Finn had loved barrooms, and he'd loved parties even more, where he could soar and enchant partygoers with his mad soliloquies. But his house was quiet now, the charismatic Irishman gone to his ancestors.

I parked and we got out. Bridget pointed toward flowering hedges that framed a garden path. "The shooter was over there."

I could see that the hedges had provided easy cover. The shooter had been able to fire directly into the parking lot. "I ran the other way, into the woods. My high heels should be over there somewhere. I kicked them off so I could run better."

We looked for them, but the police must have taken them. "Christian Louboutin," said Bridget. "I paid a thousand bucks for them. I must've been nuts."

We walked past a fountain at the center of the garden, its dancing jets illuminated from below to produce a prismatic play of light, like something out of an Irish fairyland. It might have been the last thing Finn saw as he fell.

She stopped suddenly, staring up at the house. "I can't go back in there."

"You'll come out of this."

"I'll never come out of it, Tommy. Never."

I turned her toward the fountain. "Let's take five."

We stood at its edge, listening to the falling sprays of water. Bees flew by us, working the elaborate garden. A few tiny flower petals were floating in the fountain. She slipped her arm through mine. "Thank you for springing me."

"Anytime," I said, enjoying the faint pressure of her body through the heaviness of my robe, but I felt like an idiot wearing it. In Mexico it worked, but it had no place in Coalville. Faith had left town.

I went to the Hummer and took out jeans and a denim shirt. "The old switcheroo," said Bridget, her voice lighter now. Her panic had dissolved into the fountain.

We climbed a flight of stone stairs to a porch that wrapped around the house, with doors opening out to it on all sides. I imagined guests enjoying catered spreads and fine wine. The white wicker furniture seemed to be waiting for the return of the master of festivities.

We entered the house. Soft, dark paneling gleamed on the hallway walls. "Leather," said Bridget. "Our decorator was really into leather. Do you know Roger Vision?"

Vision was not a Coalville name, and I doubt that it was Roger's name, either. And leather is for baseball gloves.

A leather-topped desk of carved mahogany looked as if it might have come from a Spanish castle. The floor was marquetry, its thin pieces of wood sculpted together to produce the image of an opened flower. And on the desk was a tall vase filled with fresh flowers. "The gardener," murmured Bridget, "carrying on as if nothing has happened. I wish I could."

Wooden stair railings with carved newel posts curved up to the second floor. Bridget flipped a switch, and each step riser had a light embedded in it. "For my movie star entrances. It was Roger's idea; he's very theatrical. Finn didn't care what we did, so long as he had a pool table in the library."

During our many barroom nights, Finn had split his time between shooting pool and shooting off his mouth. He was skilled at both. But the house I was looking at now, with all its antique furniture and feminine touches, reflected nothing of the Finn I'd known. When I would visit him as a teenager, his bedroom had gaming computers that glowed with mysterious interior light. He'd built them and designed software programs to run on them. He had also been an amateur filmmaker, with all the necessary equipment. I imagined a room like that somewhere in this house, which Roger Vision hadn't decorated, where the clutter of a computer wizard and filmmaker awaited their creator's return.

"Want me to show you around?" asked Bridget.

But I heard a car driving up to the house and went to the parking lot to meet Wheels. He'd brought his bird. "If I'm going to be here 24/7, I need to take care of her." I took him to Finn's four-car garage and extended my hand toward a Porsche 718 Cayman.

"I should be paying you," said Wheels. He ran his fingers over the hood. His tone was hushed, as if he were in church. "Massive horsepower."

"Drive Mrs. Sweeney where she wants to go, and don't stop for anybody."

"Thank you for this vote of confidence, Tommy. I won't let you down."

I closed up the garage. We walked around the house and up the stairs to the salon-like living room. I introduced Wheels to Bridget. He said, "I'm sorry your husband got whacked." He opened his suit jacket to show her his holster and pistol. "Anybody tries it again, we whack them back." His suit was shiny purple, and with his bald head he looked like a large turnip. He introduced his parakeet. Bridget fussed over the bird, and I looked at the layout of the living room. The couches and drapes were by Roger Vision and Bridget, but the sixteen-foot oak saloon bar backed by mirrors was certainly Finn's. I could imagine him there, mixing his favorite drinks for guests.

Bridget said, "You know what I need? Badly?"

"A drink?"

"Kip to do my hair." She got him on the phone and explained the situation. She listened for a moment, then said, "That's terrible." She looked at me. "Somebody stole his dog."

35

I like dogs. Primo had given me a mutt named Rigatoni who ran sideways. And I'd liked wrestling with Pigwiggen. So anybody stealing a friend's dog was going to feel my hand. I drove to Kip's apartment. He came out carrying his nunchucks and got in the Hummer. "Dogfighters took him."

The scissors holstered on his belt were gone, in their place a straight razor. I had the feeling it was not going to be used to shape someone's sideburns. "When I'm working late, my landlady takes Amstaff to the dog run. They got him away from her with a Big Mac."

"Understandable."

"They could fight him today as a prospect, or they could train him for months and take all the sweetness out of him." Kip's easy manner was gone. "They'll make him tear cats apart. Then they'll sharpen his teeth and put roach poison in his food so that other dogs won't like his taste."

"I'm looking forward to meeting these people."

But first we met Duke, who was waiting for us on a bench in Parade Square. He was wearing a panama hat and a mellow-yellow summer suit.

"Nice lines," said Kip, trying to sound like his usual self.

"Armani off the back of a truck." Duke slid into the back seat of the Hummer. "I always wear it to a dogfight."

We drove out of town into the countryside. The TV station had gotten a tip, and the informant had given directions to an abandoned farm where the fight was taking place.

"They might cut his ears off," said Kip. "That's to make it harder for another dog to bite and hang on."

"Maybe we should cut a couple of *their* ears off," said Duke.

"I enrolled him in obedience school. A Staffordshire terrier will take you apart if he's not trained." He brought up a picture on his phone and showed it to Duke. "Now, he's gentle with people. But if another dog challenges him, he won't quit."

He passed the phone to me. Amstaff was fawn-colored with patches of white and stood confidently on sturdy legs. He was fifty pounds of muscle, and his low center of gravity would definitely be helpful in a fight.

"A dog who wins fights is valuable as a stud," said Kip.

"Story of my life," said Duke.

I followed Kip's instructions through farm- and meadowland. Duke was looking at the nunchucks Kip had put in the back seat. "I see you brought your devil sticks."

"I just plan to mess them up. I don't want to kill anybody."

"I'm going in heavy," said Duke. "If a dognapper gets himself plugged, tough shit. They should have gone in for crab racing."

"Turn here," said Kip, and I pulled onto a dirt road, proceeding along it until we came to a grassy lane and a faded *No Trespassing* sign. Kip took out his phone, and I waited while he made his call. He exchanged a few words, then put away his phone, and I drove slowly down the lane. A dilapidated farmhouse came into view, with broken windows and a porch that had weeds growing through it. In an adjacent field, cars were lined up. I saw what looked like biker gang security—two guys in bandannas and leather vests, tattoos on their huge arms. They waved for us to park beside the other cars.

We got out of the Hummer and walked toward the bikers. They were friendly enough, ready to admit customers who would add to the excitement. Duke in his panama hat and mellow-yellow suit, and

Kip in a cream-colored blazer aroused no suspicion, but I knew that the devil sticks were hanging inside Kip's blazer.

We received a sporting warning. "Gents, I'm instructed to inform you that being a spectator at a dogfight is a felony offense."

The other biker added, "But don't sweat it. The last time law busted a fight around here, they got all jammed up with paperwork. Too many defendants, and the evidence had to be housed and fed while awaiting the trial." His tattoos were crude, prison style, and he sounded like a jailhouse lawyer. With the smug certainty that comes from an education behind bars, he explained that the county had been stuck with catering for a dozen dogs for six months. "So the county said *fuck this* and now they look the other way."

Kip took out a roll of dough and peeled off three hundreds. "You know a lot about it."

"Pays to know." The biker waved us into the barn. The doors were large enough to admit a hay wagon, but there was no wagon and no hay. Instead, there was a circle of loose-fitting boards that formed the fight ring. Two dogs were going at it, and spectators were shouting encouragement.

A small man turned away from the fight and greeted us. He was wearing a shiny white suit that had apparently been purchased for the occasion; Dalmatian spots were printed in the fabric. A matching tie completed the picture, marking him as the organizer of the event. He had put on all his bling for the event: a Rolex watch that might have been a counterfeit, and rings on every finger. It was the oxpecker.

"All bets are down for this match, but we got another coming right up." He'd been drunk at our last meeting in the dim light of the Top Hat bar and didn't seem to recognize me or care.

The ox was alongside him, grinning happily, pumped like a kid from the excitement, big, stupid, and feeling important. He pointed toward a cooler of beer on ice. "Help yourself. Fighting is by Cajun rules. There's a referee, and if a dog is near dead the ref stops the fight."

"I'm going to look at the contenders," said Kip, and walked toward the cages. The dogs were pacing nervously, their pack instinct aroused by the snarls coming from the ring.

"I'm giving five to one on a newcomer, up next," said the oxpecker to Duke and me.

I said, "I'll take those odds," and took out my wallet. The oxpecker gazed expectantly at it, but I was gazing with even greater interest at one of the rings on his finger—a misshapen hunk of gold.

"I found him!" shouted Kip, over the shouts of the spectators and the snarling of the dogs.

"So did I," I answered quietly, looking at Finn's ring on the oxpecker's finger.

"Something wrong?" asked the oxpecker.

36

The ring had been in Finn's family for three hundred years. Time had worn its detail away, but I could still make out the faint shape of a heart held by two hands. *My heart is in your hands.* It was Finn's dying message to me: *When you find my ring, you'll have found the man who killed me.* Above the heart was a crown, signifying loyalty, and it was my loyalty to Finn that had brought me back to Coalville and that now caused me to reach out and seize the oxpecker by the wrist.

"What the fuck . . ." He gazed up at me, his little oxpecker eyes filled with outrage at this insult to his dignity, his Dalmatian suit, and his very own dogfight.

The ox stepped up to me, his cordiality gone, chest muscles swelling. "You're out of line, pal," he said.

I dropped him with a carotid strike, the hard edge of my hand driving into his neck and disrupting the blood supply to his brain. He was unconscious before he hit the ground.

While the oxpecker was still squirming against my grip, the two bouncer-bikers grabbed me from behind. I caught one in the face with my elbow, but the other biker held on until Duke ripped him away, smiling evilly. He removed his panama hat and spun it toward a safe place. "Come on, sunshine. Give it your best."

The biker was twenty-five years younger than Duke and a product of prison-yard weight training. He dove at Duke and was stopped by a punch he never saw coming.

"Five hundred bucks on the old guy!" called out one of the gamblers.

The other biker had drawn his piece. I swung the oxpecker in front of me. "Plug away."

"Don't fucking shoot," whined the oxpecker. "Find out what he wants."

"I want my dog," said Kip.

Devil sticks came down on the biker's wrist with a *thwock*, and the gun fell to the ground. Then the whirling sticks hit him across the forehead, at which point he decided to call it quits.

"I don't need this," he announced, and pulled a chunk of ice from the beer cooler and put it to his head.

"Hey, man," shouted the oxpecker. "Do your job."

"Kiss my ass," said the biker.

Duke and the other biker crashed through the fence and wound up in the ring between a bullmastiff and a Doberman. The biker was throwing punches prison style, fast and wild, which Duke easily blocked, but the dogs had become confused, and the bullmastiff sank sharpened teeth into the biker's leg. The biker desperately tried to shake off the dog, but the animal was big and had fastened its fangs deep. So the biker pulled his gun, but Duke tore off one of the fence boards and hit him behind the head. The biker went down, with the dog still attached, its neck working back and forth, teeth digging deeper, snout covered with biker blood. The Doberman took off at a dead run, out through the barn doors to freedom, and the rest of the dogs began to howl. Gamblers were arguing about the interrupted match, and trainers were racing for their cages, wanting to get away before worse happened. Duke took all the entry money from the fallen biker's pocket. The mastiff began dragging the biker across the ring, as if to take him back to its den and devour him in peace.

I had the oxpecker's arm up behind his back, just at the edge of dislocating it, and he had ceased his squirming, but the ox was coming to consciousness at my feet. Once again it crossed my mind that he was a man in the wrong century. A horned helmet, shield, and spear would have taken him a long way in the service of his king. Instead, he'd partnered with an oxpecker at a dogfight, and Kip was yanking him to his feet. He swayed groggily in Kip's iron grasp.

Duke joined us, his panama hat in place on his head, brim at a rakish angle. He looked at the oxpecker. "What's up with the Dalmatian?"

I twisted the oxpecker's hand toward him, the ring uppermost. "This belonged to Finn."

Duke glanced at it, then looked at me and nodded, recognizing the ring Finn often wore. He glanced back at the oxpecker. "Every dog has his day."

I shoved the ox toward Duke, who pressed the muzzle of his gun against the ox's broad back while I spun the struggling oxpecker around toward the exit. He was still calling for his bikers, but one was facedown with a dog eating his leg and the other had his hand in the beer cooler to ease the swelling to his wrist. "Hit by a stick," he said to himself, as if unfair advantage had been taken.

Kip, with an agitated fawn-colored terrier tugging on its leash, joined Duke and me and our prisoners, and we walked out through the barn doors, Amstaff in the lead.

37

I called Knucklehead from the farm and explained about the oxpecker, who was wearing Finn's ring. "Can you get a search warrant?"

"What's the address?"

The oxpecker had printed up business cards, identifying himself as a "party event facilitator," which apparently covered dogfights. I gave the address to Magistrate Knucklehead.

"I have authority in that district. I'll meet you there in twenty minutes." I imagined him banging down his gavel, then sweeping out of his tiny courtroom, black robe flapping.

We drove away from the farm. The ox, huge and brooding, was in the front seat next to me. Kip and the oxpecker were in the back seat, along with Duke. Amstaff had calmed down and was in the third row behind the oxpecker, sniffing at his head. Dogs are forgiving. I wasn't. I was imagining Finn's last moments, a bullet in his back, and the oxpecker pulling the ring off his finger. Finn doesn't know the oxpecker's name, but he sees his ring going onto the oxpecker's finger.

The oxpecker thought we were hanging on to him for stealing Kip's dog. "I'll make restitution," he said as we drove through the countryside. "A cash settlement, and I pay for his visits to the vet—something like that."

When Kip didn't respond, the oxpecker said, "I get why you're upset, dogs being man's best friend and all."

In the rearview mirror, I saw Kip's eyes blazing with anger, but he was holding himself in. The oxpecker continued negotiating. "How about this? I have fifty pounds of dog food delivered, your choice, every week for a month."

"You've got to do better than that," said Duke.

"With bones thrown in. Fresh from the meat counter."

"How often?" said Duke.

"Same time frame. Every week for a month." The oxpecker's voice had grown more confident. "And a couple of dog toys."

In the rearview mirror, I could see Amstaff's nose going around the collar of the oxpecker's suit. It must have had the smell of the other dogs on it. The oxpecker turned toward him. "You like me, huh? No hard feelings?"

Amstaff kept sniffing, no hard feelings. Those belonged to Kip, who, I could see, wanted to use the oxpecker for target practice with a throwing star.

"You mind if I pet him?" asked the oxpecker.

"I'd rather you didn't," said Kip.

The oxpecker nodded philosophically. "I violated his boundaries."

The ox, his dull mind still brooding, asked, "You guys undercover or something?"

"We're the militant wing of Pet World," said Duke.

———

The oxpecker's apartment was in a grit-and-grime building put up for workingmen's families during the old mine days. When he saw the police cars in front of it, the oxpecker said, "I'm calling my lawyer."

"Plenty of time," said Duke.

"This is a big fucking circus for nothing," said the oxpecker, echoing the jailhouse lawyer on why a dogfight case would be tossed, that he had a well-documented defense strategy if it ever did come to trial, and that we were wasting everybody's time.

We all got out of the Hummer, Amstaff bounding from the last row and heading for the nearest tree. Knucklehead was waiting for us and handed the oxpecker the search warrant. "This is your copy. The attending officers will make an inventory of everything taken from your property and give you a receipt."

"What a bunch of bullshit," muttered the party event facilitator, a.k.a. the oxpecker. But when one of the policemen removed the big gold ring from his finger and put it in an evidence bag, a panicked look crossed his face.

Knucklehead walked me back to the Hummer. "You guys have to wait outside. Otherwise, the warrant could be tainted." He swung the evidence bag between us, Finn's ring inside it.

I said, "Look for the gun."

"You think he's dumb enough to keep a murder weapon around?"

Duke said, "He's the kind that says goodbye to his turds before flushing. He'd never get rid of a gun he paid good money for."

Knucklehead went inside to join the cops and the suspects. Kip, Duke, and I waited in the yard. Amstaff visited every tree on the block. When Knucklehead came back out a half hour later, the ox and the oxpecker were handcuffed. Knucklehead was carrying an evidence bag containing a handgun. The oxpecker was protesting loudly. "Like I said, you're making a big fucking mistake. I'm connected."

"*I'm* connected," said Duke. "You're a bottom feeder."

"Maybe not." Knucklehead came over to us and said quietly, "He's reeling off some big names, including Brian Fury."

My heart leaped like Christmas morning. "Could we tie Finn's death to Fury?"

"Not yet. But we've got a case against the party facilitator. If the gun matches the bullets that killed Finn, he'll go down. Who he takes with him will be the interesting part."

I nodded toward the ox, who should have been in another century. "He's slow in the head, but I don't see murder in him."

"I'll call you with developments." Knucklehead got into his car, and the police escorted the ox and the oxpecker into their patrol cars. I could see the oxpecker's lips moving as he was being driven away

228 | WILLIAM KOTZWINKLE

in his Dalmatian suit. The ox was staring heavily out the window—a not-too-bright son of the valley, whose freedom had just been taken away.

"All right, gentlemen," said Duke, bringing the money from the dogfight out of his pockets. "You need not report this on your income tax." He counted out three piles, and we each took our share. Amstaff beat his tail on the sidewalk. Duke looked down at him. "You could've been a contender."

We left Kip and Amstaff off at the New Wave Salon, and I drove Duke to his apartment across from the courthouse. I told him I'd found Bridget and she was at home with Wheels Zamboni as security.

"You can probably cut Wheels loose now that we got the guy who whacked Finn."

"He pulled the trigger, but somebody hired him."

"So you'll hang out at Bridget's place? Queenie O'Malley will be pissed. Irish lassies don't like competition."

"I'll be discreet."

"Queenie's a tempting little number. And she's got heart. But you were born under a different star."

"How can you tell?"

"I just know." He tapped me lightly on the cheek. "You draw fire, Tommy. Finally, you'll get her killed."

38

Bridget's pool was in a sunroom whose walls and ceiling were made entirely of glass. The parakeet was in her cage, and Wheels Zamboni was at the door of the sunroom, scanning the driveway and the woods. We were acting on the assumption that Bridget could still be in danger. I'd beefed up the security system and gotten her a couple of handguns, compliments of Duke.

"Car coming up the driveway," said Wheels. And a minute later, "Driver is female."

After another minute, Queenie entered the sunroom and held out her hands to Bridget. "Everybody at the station sends their love."

"I won't be going in just yet. Tommy thinks I have to lay low for a while." She called Wheels over to them. "Mr. Zamboni is providing security for me."

Like my grandfather, Wheels had rough gallantry, and he gave Queenie a little bow, showing his shoulder holster. Then he straightened and gazed into her eyes with full Italian machismo shining. Queenie responded with a smile. "I'm Jack O'Malley's daughter; you've been in his shop."

He drew her attention toward his bird, which was on its perch, head twisting their way. "You gotta meet her. You say something, it goes right into her little brain. She'll come out with it later, while I'm having a beer." Discussion over, he returned to his position by the door. The stance he took, feet firmly planted, shoulders back, gave off the message: *You got problems, look me up. Steady guy, not too old, makes house calls.*

Bridget took Queenie's arm and walked her to a poolside table. "I've thought it over. I'd like you to run the station."

Queenie's mouth fell open and settled into a grin. "Thank you, boss."

"You know how the station works better than anyone."

With those words, I could feel Queenie slipping away from me. *Let me take you to Vegas* is not much of a future when placed against running a TV station.

And then my phone rang. It was Knucklehead. "One of the other jailbirds stuck a homemade knife into the party event facilitator."

"Dead?"

"He won't be facilitating any other party events. The stupid bastard kept threatening to name names. A bad move. It got around town. He was dead the moment he opened his mouth."

"I want to know who hired him."

"Remember your jesuitical teachings. There's the known, the unknown, and the unknowable. Who hired him is definitely the unknowable."

We held the silence for a moment, as if to honor that unspeakable unknowable, somewhere high up the chain of Coalville politics. But I couldn't let it go. "I owe it to Finn."

"Finn's in heaven. He could give a fuck. How's Bridget?"

"Holding up. She's tough."

"I think this guy getting a shiv under the ribs closes it for her. Don't push it any further."

"Wheels Zamboni said the same thing."

"He should know. He's survived a perilous career. Tell Bridget that I'm at her service. Anything I can do, she only has to call me. Now, I've got to run back to the courtroom and send somebody to jail."

He rang off. Bridget and Queenie were still in consultation about the TV station. I walked over to them. "Here's my programming advice for the future. Get some local Italian lady to demonstrate how she makes her spaghetti sauce."

Queenie read my eyes and turned to Bridget, "He's telling us to stay out of politics."

"I know what he's telling us."

I said, "I'm your Saint Bernard dog, Bridget. I'm looking out for you. I know you like that kind of dog."

Whether she remembered calling me that, I don't know. She reached her hand out to me and squeezed my forearm. "It's good advice. I'm not looking for vengeance."

"Vengeance is already yours. Knucklehead just called. The guy who killed Finn is dead. A fellow prisoner croaked him."

She closed her eyes, then slowly tilted back her head, as if sending out a thought to Finn's spirit somewhere. When she opened her eyes, she told me, "I'd like to keep Wheels and his bird for a while. Just to be on the safe side."

"He'll be glad to have the work. I'm going back to the trailer park. Call me or Knucklehead if you need help." I turned to Queenie. "Here's another programming idea. Interviews with local athletes. Develop the male, potato-chip audience."

"Sounds good. I'll start with Bobby Romano."

Did she say that to annoy me? As a member of the male, potato-chip audience, I couldn't tell. I made my farewell to the ladies and gave the latest to Wheels.

"She wants you to stay on."

"How long?"

"Till she calms down."

"Thanks for this job, Tommy. I'll never take another shot at you."

I shook the wheelman's hand and went out the door and across the garden. Finn's ghost was dancing in the fountain, watery fingers reaching up and then collapsing in a shimmering veil. Sometimes fountains can talk, and this one was telling me the oxpecker's murder was only the beginning.

I paused at the spot on the lawn where Finn had fallen. Killed by a guy who ran dogfights. I imagined the oxpecker in the shadows of the foliage, aiming his gun. Rings are sparkling on his fingers as he looks down the barrel. But after shooting Finn, he notices the gold ring of Finn's Irish ancestors. He doesn't know about ancestral magic. He doesn't know that when he removes their ring and slips it on his finger, he's putting on his own death.

39

Bobby Romano hit a ball over the centerfielder's outstretched arm, and I watched it sail over the fence and onto the railroad tracks behind the stadium. The tracks were rusty relics that ran clear across the Northeast, and big-league ballplayers had once traveled on them from stadium to stadium. Bobby had to believe that this home run and a few more like it would help him travel to Yankee Stadium. Pack your bags, Bobby, we want you in New York. I know those dreams; I've had them myself.

My phone played its little tune.

"You'd better get up here," said Reed.

Bobby hadn't reached home plate before I was out of the stadium and into the parking lot. I got into the Hummer and headed for the high ground, where Coalville's wealthy were enjoying their Sunday. It was still summer, with many pleasures yet to be gotten from the sun. I flipped on the radio. Community radio had a show about why we should appreciate pencils, and the commercial stations were all playing music to go deaf by. The one classical station was playing a modern work that would have gone well during a waterboarding session. I longed for the quiet solemnity of a Gregorian chant, sung by monks in an echoing chapel—something to soothe the angry energy held permanently in my stomach as if in some kind of beaker of acids, poisons, and elixirs of pure rage. Even as a child, I had tasted it on my tongue and thought it was normal. I switched off the radio.

Once again I passed the driveway signs on Grandview Road, announcing a comfortable way of living—*Primrose Glen, Chimney Corner, The Burrow.* And after a few more of them, *Hamilton House.* As I parked, Reed came to greet me on the path.

"Ruby's gone."

"No surprise there."

"Come inside." He led me to a vintage kitchen. The dark wood cabinets were still opened with old-fashioned hardware. The sink had antique porcelain faucets. The butcher block had seen much use. But completely up to date was the computer tablet that lay open on top of it. Cartoon characters cavorted on its protective cover, suggesting an innocence that Ruby might have longed for but had never known.

"Her password wasn't hard to guess," said Reed. "Forbidden Fruit. I poked around and found this."

On the screen of the tablet was Brian Fury, naked, slowly lowering himself toward the eye of a camera lens. His brutish form was caught in an intimacy I would rather not have seen, but I couldn't look away. In his birthday suit, he seemed even more sadistic, as if clothing had covered up the finer aspects of his sadism. He was moving up and down on an invisible figure. And then, to my amazement, I saw that it was Ruby.

As the two bodies moved, the images were correspondingly chaotic, which told me there was no mounted camera, no hidden cameraman. I couldn't tell how Fury had filmed it, but however he had done it, it was certainly balls-out madness. He'd always been reckless, but letting Ruby have a copy was beyond reckless. He surely knew she was about as trustworthy as a pet cobra.

And then one of her hands came into the picture, and I saw a large ring sparkling on her finger. I tried to see more of it, but the angle changed again and the limbs were again a chaotic tangle. After more of the surreal sight of Fury's naked back and buttocks, Ruby's face and shoulders came into view. Hanging around her neck was a junk jewelry necklace. This time, the penny dropped.

"Fury didn't make this recording. She did."

The depth of her scheming was impressive. She'd scoped out Fury, seen he was twisted, and played him. I pointed out the ring and the necklace to Reed. "Finn made those. They're cameras. She's going to blackmail the ass off Fury."

It took Reed some moments to process it, but after consideration he said, "I'm not surprised." Then he added, "Darling Ruby has many fine attributes, but a conscience is not among them. However, I shouldn't criticize. I've snooped in her computer."

He was clearly embarrassed by the admission. He was a gentleman, and gentlemen don't snoop. "That's when I called you. I think she went to see him." He hesitated. "I wasn't sure how to handle the situation."

"Have you got a thumb drive?"

He hunted around and found one, and I copied the video file. I'm not a blackmailer, but the bastard was trying to put me away. A recording of him fucking an underage girl would be my get-out-of-jail-free card.

Reed pointed toward the kitchen window. "There's an overgrown path through the woods. Fury's house isn't far. I'm sure that's where she's gone. I'm all for letting people do what they want, but in this case maybe we should intervene."

I agreed and followed him out of the house. "It's that silly film of hers," he said. "She wants a big scene."

"He'll give her a scene," I said, walking toward the Hummer.

"Or are we being overprotective? It's her life, after all."

"Brian Fury kicked the crap out of me in a room under the court-house," I said as I opened the Hummer. "Then he had me Tasered."

"Really? How bizarre."

"Bizarre and illegal. But Fury is the law in Coalville." I reached into the Hummer and loaded Uncle Silvio's tool belt with what I might need for a bit of housebreaking, then added one more item for the interven-tion.

"You're anticipating violence."

"I hope I'm wrong." I started toward the path.

"My driver has the day off, but I'll come around with the limo. She loves riding in it. If we make her feel important, she'll come quietly. Otherwise, you'll be dragging her through the woods."

I entered the fringe of forest that made properties in this neighborhood so desirable, providing privacy and a buffer against intrusion. But a determined teenager with a desire for twenty million followers on TikTok will say, *Screw that*. Fury was going to be the grand finale of her documentary.

The forest path was blanketed in pine needles and leaves from a previous season, making it soft underfoot as I headed toward the little idiot who was going to show Brian Fury that she was in control now, that she had him on camera engaging in love play with a minor. Her teenage brain couldn't compute how fatally stupid this was. Fury wouldn't let her blackmail him. *He* was the dungeon master, and no little twit was going to put him in chains. His political power didn't run deep. He'd admitted that to me in the cellar of the courthouse. Ruby could end his career. Challenged, he would put her down like a bad puppy. When he was twelve, he'd drowned his own puppy in a pan of milk. He'd been unable to resist. The puppy had been so loving, it was asking for it.

I came to a driveway marked by a fancy bit of woodwork reading *The Prosecution Rests*. Brian's touch, a joke for the neighbors. *The DA lives here, watching out for you and yours*. But why had he taken up with Ruby? Had it begun with her being an informer, if she ever really was one? Or did he get off on the insane recklessness of having an underage girlfriend?

His house was an old mansion that had been in the neighborhood from the time when Fury was spelled *Furey*, and an ambitious Irishman had landed the clan on Coalville's shores and made a ton of money on the backs of other Irishmen. Parked in the driveway was an unmarked county cop car, which Brian probably kept for official visits to high-interest crime scenes. Beside it was his vintage Plymouth, still wet, a garden hose on the ground beside it. He must have been giving it a wash when Ruby came to call.

The garden had sculpted hedges and complicated flower beds, several of which had high flowering bushes. They might have won prizes in the neighborhood garden competition, but they created security blind spots. I hurried through them toward framed French doors that were open to receive the summer air, which meant the alarm system was off. So along with the summer air, I just wafted in.

Fury and Ruby were in the living room. She was on a couch with his knee on her chest. He had a gun in one hand and a pillow in the other to muffle the shot. She was looking up at him, certain he was bluffing. After all, they were lovers. She couldn't believe he was about to blow feathers into her brain. Then she saw me and screamed, "Get lost, Martini!"

He turned, pointing the gun my way. I was out of place in his parlor, like a chair that had come to life, and he fired to get rid of the nasty apparition. I took it in the chest, stumbling backward as if a horse had kicked me. He fired again and I was rocked all the way to the wall of the room, but I was still standing, thanks to Corporal Hutmacher's Kevlar vest. The sight of bullets bouncing off me put Fury into flight mode. He grabbed Ruby and ran through the open doors into the garden. He wasn't thinking clearly, only wanted to put distance between us.

By the time I got my limbs working again, he was already shoving Ruby into the county car. It was a tool of law enforcement, a piece of the world he belonged to. He was Mr. District Attorney, after all. Ruby was a pain in the ass, but somehow he would square her, or kill her, and later on get me for unlawful entry. For now, in this moment of blind confusion, he just needed to be in motion, with a cop radio and bent cops on his payroll. Things would work out; he was used to crushing people who got in his way.

I never could have hot-wired a new car in time to catch him, but I had a screwdriver on my toolbelt, and Fury's vintage Plymouth was a simpler beast. I broke the ignition locking pins, and the engine turned over. I spun some upper-crust gravel behind me. Fury was already turning out of the driveway. By the time I reached the road he was flying, but Reed was coming along in his limo. I pointed to Fury's car and Reed nodded and was in pursuit. I pulled out of the driveway behind them, number three in the pack. And that's how we went down the side of the mountain, past all the quaint driveway signs. An owner taking his dog out to have a nighttime piss jumped backward into a driveway as Fury and Reed shot by him. The dog got off a few barks—translation, *This road is mine, motherfuckers.*

And then dog and owner were shrinking shadows in my side mirror. A bicycle enthusiast was next to go, Brian giving him a blast from the county siren. The cyclist's light-reflecting shirt and pants flashed as he twisted the handlebars too fast and spun himself sideways into a ditch.

We came down off the mountain, Brian using the car's cop light behind the windshield and hitting the siren at intersections. Reed and I blew past the frozen traffic and kept with Fury through the center of town. It was the kind of chase I'd been in as a teenager, steering for dominance, and several of my friends had been creamed and crammed into a casket at an early age. This was Fury's mood at the moment, a crazy run for the pure hell of it, and it led us from the heart of town into the older neighborhoods. The streets were narrower, but Fury didn't slow down, just maneuvered wildly, police light flashing. Surprisingly, Reed stayed with him, handling the limo as he'd handled his powerboat on Mirror Lake, with sweeping turns, the rear end swinging wide but avoiding parked cars.

The neighborhood showed increasing signs of deterioration the closer we got to the end of the street, where the houses gave way to the old city dump. As we approached it, I could see something I'd never seen in the days when I shot rats there with my grandfather's wiseguys: Adjacent to the dump, a new spur of the interstate was being constructed. The road crew was using the far end of the disused old dump to store big pipe culverts they were going to need, along with large piles of gravel. That's what Fury was heading for: access to a deserted stretch of the interstate many miles long, out of bounds to all but government traffic. He'd probably already called in on his car's radio requesting his bent cops to meet him there. They would flag us down, block us, and he'd fly on by, with time to figure his next move, panic flight over, and only Ruby to deal with, and she was completely disposable.

He crashed through the dump's wooden barricade and onto its

abandoned road. Reed and I were behind him, bouncing around on the broken pavement. We entered a dystopian world of abandoned furniture, battered stoves, refrigerators, toilets, bathtubs. Adding to the feeling of a failed civilization was a huge crack that had opened at the heart of the dump, a mine fire having burned right up through the surface. The state would put it out and fill it in when the interstate spur was finished. Half the town was built with mines underneath it; why not underneath the access to a superhighway?

At the far end of the dump was a utility road leading to four phantom lanes the highway department had created. Once there, Fury would be long gone. But a line of stoves and refrigerators was forcing him to drive near the smoking crevice. We were closer to him now, and the weight of three cars, one of them a limousine, was too much for a dump floor weakened by fire. Reed slammed on the brakes and I did the same, but Fury's car had already started tilting. The ground gave way and his car went in sideways. I saw Ruby's terrified face staring up and then the car went down, covered in smoke.

I jumped from the Plymouth and scrambled into the crack, sliding down a steep, cinder-encrusted wall and finally coming to a stop on the upturned passenger door. Ruby was looking at me, screaming that the window wasn't working. Breaking a car window with your fist is almost impossible, but I still had the screwdriver on my toolbelt. I rammed it against the corner of the window and the glass fell away. I pulled her out and carried her up the smoking wall of ash and cinders. Reed reached down and yanked her away from the ledge.

Then I went back down for Fury. He'd unbuckled his seat belt and was climbing toward the passenger window, his eyes madly confident that he was coming out of this the same way he had come out of every tight corner a sadist must get himself into. I reached down and he reached up through the smoke. "Work with me, Martini," he ordered as if he were in charge.

A sound of collapse came from below, and the county car fell away in a stream of ash and sparks, with Fury still only half out of the window. The car bounced from one fragile ledge to another until it disappeared, taking Fury with it. I heard it crash into what must have been a large underground chamber created by fires feeding on abandoned coal seams. He didn't stand much chance of coming out of that, and neither would I if the methane fumes got me.

But I lowered myself along a wall honeycombed with cinders and thin as rice paper. I found handholds where the fire had veered off, leaving solid wall. I hated the sadistic bastard, but crazed macho energy drove me downward. I landed on the underbelly of the car, its wheels spinning on four sides of me. I was standing on the roll bar, which was no use now; the car was already upside down. The smoke was thick, and flames were licking up the front of it. When they reached the gas tank, Fury and I would be fried. I lowered myself along the side door and found him. He'd struck a ledge on the way down. Half his face had been torn away and his head was twisted at a grotesque angle. I checked for a pulse, but there was none. Reed was shouting down at me to get myself out. It seemed like a good idea.

I left Fury and crawled back onto the underbelly of the car. I stepped off the bottom of the radiator and grabbed at the paper-thin wall of the mine. I worked my way up the same way I had come down, making handholds in the hot ash. Through the smoke, I could see Reed at the edge of the crack. "I've got you!" he shouted, but I was a long way from his outstretched hand. From below me, I could hear the steel frame of Fury's car starting to creak from the heat. The gas tank would be next. I moved like a mad monkey up the remaining piece of wall. Reed grabbed my hand and dragged me over the edge. Ruby had her phone out, filming my return.

The soles of my running shoes felt as if they were melting into the ground, but I managed to jump into the Plymouth, aim it at the hole, and jump out. The Plymouth rolled to the edge and went over, raising more smoke and ash as it tumbled down into the mine. The explosion came a few moments later, the gas tanks on both cars blowing simultaneously. A huge cloud of smoke billowed into the air.

We could hear sirens approaching, one from the highway corridor construction, another from the dump road. Reed looked at the limo, contemplating a run. A patrician with a drug habit did not want to meet the law.

I said, "Take a walk into the trees, find your way back to the street, and I'll pick you up at Dunkin' Donuts."

"They'll check for the registration."

"Trust me, I'll keep you out of this."

He looked at me doubtfully, but with the sirens coming ever closer, he began threading his way through major kitchen appliances until he reached the row of scraggly trees growing along the edge of the dump, into which he disappeared, a Blond Shadow on the run.

Ruby was brushing ashes out of her hair. I pointed at her necklace. "Did you record everything?"

"Until we went in there." She pointed at the hole.

"Download. Necklace to phone. Now."

"It's there already. It happens automatically. Finn set it up that way."

"They're going to question us. I do the talking."

She nodded, but she might say anything. Headlights and bubble lights appeared from the dump road and from a utility road connected to the corridor construction. The sirens switched off, the cops approaching cautiously. Radio contact had broken with the county car, and they didn't know what to expect. But they could see the smoking crack in the earth and stopped before they came too close to it. Both patrol cars opened and the cops got out.

"Martini, what the fuck's going on?" It was the older one who'd Tasered me.

"Watch your language, there's a child present."

"Where's Fury?"

"Down there." I pointed toward the hole.

He walked judiciously toward it, peered in, flashed his beam into the smoke. The other one said to me, "Put your hands behind your back."

I obliged because they just might shoot me, and as they cuffed me I began to feel the burns I'd gotten in the pit. I said, "Ruby, show them what's on your phone."

"It's private," she said, and started a flow of tears.

"You don't have to worry, honey," said the older policeman. "This piece of shit can't hurt you now."

"Well," she said, brushing away her phony tears, "if you say so."

She held up her phone and they peered into it. They'd seen a lot during their careers, but they'd never seen their boss trying to smother a teenage girl as a prelude to shooting her in the head. The older cop began muttering, "You've got to be kidding me . . ."

They watched the entire sequence, from her arriving at Fury's house, through his attempt to murder her, and finishing as the car took her into the hole. When they looked up at us, I saw their concern for themselves. The quick and easy solution was to take Ruby's phone, then toss us in the flames after Fury. Hurriedly, I said, "There's more like that."

"Where?"

"On a computer, password-protected."

"Jesus fucking Christ."

"Exactly. And everyone knows you two were in Fury's pocket. If she shows this, it's goodbye pension and you'll be lucky if you don't do time for aiding in the corruption of a minor. Now, take off the cuffs."

He unlocked them, saying, "We knew nothing about Fury and the girl." But they both looked as if they'd been Tasered. The older one asked, "So what's our story?"

"The district attorney was involved in a tragic car chase. You joined it and found him in there." I pointed to the hole. "Dig up what's left of him. Turn him into a hero."

They looked at each other. They were old stagers and knew how to finesse a crime scene. The radio log would back them up. Their boss had called for help, they had come a little too late, and the unidentified other driver had gone into the wind. "It'll work," decided the older one. But he was worried. His retirement package was in my hands, and Ruby was a potential nightmare.

I said, "Sure, you're fucked, but you know what? We're all fucked one way or the other."

"I never would have Tasered you, Martini. That was Fury."

"Right, and I was never here tonight, and you never saw *her.*" I nodded toward Ruby.

"Good enough. What's the story with the limo?"

"What limo?"

"My mistake, the light is bad. It's a refrigerator."

I led Ruby away, telling her quietly, "Keep your phone in your pocket. If they see you taking their picture, they'll have to kill us."

"I have all I need," she said with terrifying calm.

40

The next morning, my hands felt as if they were on fire. I sat by the river of rust with my fingers covered in burn cream and bandages. My cell phone rang, and Queenie's name appeared. I cheered up immediately.

She asked, "Can you meet me at the pavilion tonight?"

"Should I bring anything?"

"Just your heart."

"You've got that already."

So when night fell, I drove to Mirror Lake. As I walked the dark path to the pavilion, the aroma of barbecued meat came to me from porches and yards, along with voices of the lake dwellers. I assumed summer was living up to their expectations, with the right amount of fun, exercise, and romance. I suppose I could say my own expectations were being met, for I'd grown to expect murder to follow me through the seasons.

I heard children's voices as I approached the pavilion, but they hardly filled the huge space of the old building. I climbed the stairs and pushed through the screen doors. Some teenagers had their heads together, conferring over their phones. A few younger kids were actually playing a physical game, which involved running around and letting out a scream when a rule of the game reversed their trajectory.

Queenie was sitting by the stone fireplace. She wore a blue shirt with ruffles along the buttons, which gave her an old-fashioned look that went with the time-worn pavilion. She waited for me to sit beside her, then nodded at the children. "I think they made up the game. I can't make any sense of it."

"They probably can't, either."

"And they don't care."

She fell silent then, and I couldn't read her mood. Generations of lake dwellers had enjoyed the pavilion, and there must have been some lovers among them. Warm air, summer smells, and the dim light in the old building had furthered their embraces, of that I was sure, but I wasn't sure about Queenie and me. We'd been through a fatal chase by the Muldoon brothers and buried a Russian hood in a mineshaft, and their shadows still clung to her. They were heavy shadows and would be with her for years.

She looked down at my bandaged fingers. "What happened to your hands?"

"I was on a job with Silvio and got too close to a car fire."

She didn't believe me but didn't push it. "Well, you won't be able to go swimming."

"I brought extra bandages and burn cream. We're going for a swim."

We walked the path toward the cottage. Fireflies were navigating around us, signaling desire with their tiny lanterns. We went inside the cottage and changed. The walls of the cottage weren't insulated, and the moist air of the lake filled each room, along with other smells of summer—spent charcoal, damp towels, suntan lotion, and other scents less definable but part of the comfortable character of the cottage. All this normality to which I didn't belong suddenly seemed very desirable.

I changed into my seahorse bathing suit, and Queenie put on a satiny white one-piece. When she slipped into the shimmering moonlit water, she was a mermaid wearing moonlight. We swam toward the island. I was far from Mexico with its rocky, unforgiving hills and the stubborn plants from which wax is made. The shoreline at Mirror Lake was thick with trees, and the water was free of poisonous snakes. It was a kind of paradise, and it might be mine. I could buy a cottage, spend the summer swimming with Queenie, and cook hot dogs with the neighbors.

We arrived at the island together, and I felt the sandy bottom against my chest. I stood and she came up beside me. Our approach had silenced the bullfrogs, but those farther down the lake could still be heard, along with children's high-pitched voices from the dock. The light of cottages could be seen through the trees. I'd caught Finn's killer, but I hadn't caught Queenie. Though our bodies were almost touching, there was something distant about her, as if she were waiting for her sacred heron to appear and point the way. But the oracular bird was sleeping somewhere in the tall weeds, dreaming of fish.

I put my arms around her. At first, she didn't resist, but then, like a slippery fish, she was out of my arms and back in the water. We swam to where lily pads were growing, their white blossoms closed for the day, but a faint fragrance still greeted us. We floated at the edge of this little water garden, not wanting to disturb it. In the monastery I had this kind of peace, but I didn't have Queenie. I was ready for the trade.

———————

Back at the cottage, we changed into our clothes. She toweled her hair dry, then gently applied burn cream to my fingers. After she bandaged me up, she built a fire in the rustic fireplace, and we sat watching the flames.

"Come to Las Vegas with me."

"You're going through with the wrestling thing?"

"If you'll come with me."

She looked quietly into the flames. "I can't."

"This town is no place for a woman," which was a crazy thing to say especially when the woman in question was as fearless as any man who lived there.

"I've killed three people because of you, Tommy. I don't want to kill anyone else."

"The killing is over. Case closed."

"Trouble follows you, my dear." She laid a hand on mine.

"I had enemies here. I have no enemies in Vegas."

"You'll find some."

"All my enemies will be in the ring."

"I want babies."

"Little wrestlers. Tearing the crib apart."

She took my chin in her hand and turned my head toward her. "You're just talking." She said it in a kindly way. "You have no interest in babies."

"Perhaps not directly."

"There's nothing so direct as a baby."

"I admit I know nothing about them, which is odd because I used to be one." I looked into the fire for support. "It was a long time ago."

"I like working at the TV station. I think I can make a difference in Coalville."

"Coalville will suck the life out of you."

"No, I'll bring new life into it." Now *she* looked into the fire for support. "I'm going to marry Richard."

"Impossible."

"I'm going to marry a decent man who wants to raise a family with me."

"A family of summer squash. Marry me. Tonight if we can find someone. Tomorrow at the latest."

"I don't want fights; I want a backyard and babies."

"Plenty of fighters get married. George Foreman has five boys and they're all named George. We'll have five girls and they'll all be named Queenie."

"I'm afraid of living with you."

"I'm telling you, this town is the problem. I had too many scraps here as a kid. In Coalville, nobody forgets. Once we get away, no one will look at me twice."

"I've lived here all my life and never fought with anybody until you came."

"That's because you're sweet and thoughtful. *I* want to be sweet and thoughtful."

"You want to beat people up in the ring."

"It's just show business."

"And it'll make you happy. It would make me miserable, watching you get knocked around."

"I know a casino owner there. Carmine Cremona. I can work for him."

"Carmine Cremona? That says it all." She gave me a sad look. I could feel it going deep, deeper perhaps than I could go myself. "All those fights you had as a kid were because you could never see further than tomorrow."

She had me there. Long-range planning wasn't in my nature, and marriage is the longest plan of all. Her vegetable man wasn't ever going to give her grief; he had too many vegetables on his back.

"This is our last night, Tommy. You know it as well as I do."

I was thinking of Duke's words to me. *Finally, you'll get her killed.*

She said, "You were my first love. You'll always be my first love."

I poked at the fire, needing something to do. When your heart comes apart on a soft summer night, it's best to say nothing. Out in the darkness, the fireflies winked. How had they ever come up with that strange light?

She said, "Not everyone gets to be with their first love again. I'm grateful."

I left the cottage at dawn, while she was still sleeping. I walked down to the shore. The surface of the lake was like silk. Her sacred heron was standing motionless in the reeds. I thought I had made just one great mistake in my life, when I punched Mike Muldoon too hard, but I had made another: not seeing what was right in front of me, that the quiet girl with the sketchpad was the only girl I could happily spend my life with. Now Richard Mittleman would have that life, and he deserved it because he fell in love with Queenie when she was invisible to me.

The heron lifted off the water and flew to its next hunting place. And I said goodbye to the happy life that could have been.

41

The sensible thing would be to go back to Mexico and pray to the Virgin of Guadalupe for forgiveness of my sins. But because I'm twenty-seven different kinds of a fool, I couldn't leave Shirley Kaminski to her demons. Heroin had trapped her, was ruining her life, would kill her in the end, and I had seen her in her Central High School sweater, looking lovely and bright and, like the rest of us back then, hopeful. I went to Parade Square one last time. I went to the bike lane. I said, "Shirley, let's get you the fuck out of here."

"The monkey follows me wherever I go, Tommy." She looked up the street anxiously. "And I'm due for a fix any minute. If you don't have one, better leave me alone."

"Phil Branca owns a health clinic. You remember Phil?"

"Some kind of connected guy . . ." She wasn't searching her memory. She was walking away from me. I was trouble she didn't need.

The way they did it was highly professional; they'd performed it so many times, it had the feeling of choreography. Shirley was spun around quickly, couldn't speak because of the speed of the spin, and Russian Blondie launched her into the car as gracefully as if he were a member of the Russian ballet instead of the Russian mafia. The other one treated me more courteously, merely smiling, and for a moment I thought I was seeing the corpse of a dead man walking, because he was a copy of Big

Red. He had the muzzle of a nine-millimeter in my ribs. "Move," he growled, "or whore gets it." It was payback for his brother or his clone, but whichever it was, I had put the body at the bottom of a mineshaft. The clone had obviously been following me around town for a while and had seen his chance tonight. Shirley was the pivot. He motioned me toward the back seat of the SUV, where Shirley had awakened from her junkie dream, her made-up eyes even wider because of Russian Blondie's gun nestled against the leather laces of her bondage bra.

"Fine," I said, my good intentions blowing away like discarded candy wrappers, their sweet promise empty now. Shirley was at risk, and I had no play. I got in the car with the Russians. Big Red had the same bright red hair, the same bulbous nose and weaselly eyes as his brother in the mineshaft. Not twins, as I now saw, but close enough to give me the feeling he'd risen from the dead. I was already planning to put him beside his brother if I could. There was going to be some violence, that was a given, and it would be my turn to choreograph where people landed, and how hard. But what troubled me was this business of brothers. Killing Mike Muldoon had meant that his brothers had to kill me. And now this guy, clearly avenging *his* brother. I'd have to stick to killing men who were the only child in the family.

The SUV moved away from the bike lane. The sex workers were looking in another direction, knowing that was the only direction to look if they wanted to stay healthy. Other bystanders hadn't registered anything out of the ordinary; sex workers and their clients got in and out of cars all night long.

We drove past the Railroad Hotel, its illuminated marble pillars inviting the traveler to stay. We would not be staying. We were traveling on. The bridge we took out of town was an example of older engineering: heavy steel girders brooding above the river of rust. It had a solid feel, like the muzzle of Russian Blondie's pistol just under my ribs. I'd knocked him out with one punch in front of his boss, and the memory pained him. He rotated the pistol on top of my liver. "Grisha send greeting."

"I'm the one he wants. Let her go."

He put the muzzle of his gun to her temple. "How about it, Shirl? You go with us, no?"

She nodded her head. Tears filled her eyes. She tried to hold them back; she was a Coalville girl, after all. "Mascara . . . costs money . . ." she said, wiping under her eyes.

Russian Red the Second met my gaze in the rearview mirror. I could always tell which of my grandfather's wiseguys had made their bones. They had a quiet depth; knowing that their enemy was buried too deep to trouble them any longer made them serene. Russian Red had that serenity; in his mind I was already dead. He would take a photo of my corpse on his cell phone, look at it now and then as people look at their grandchildren, and smile.

So we drove out of town, heading toward some prearranged site: a quiet place, a safe house, a field, a piece of woods—hard to tell yet. "I'm . . . coming down," mumbled Shirley, staring at the floor of the vehicle, junkie anxiety in her voice. Two guys grabbing her was scary, but running out of dope was worse.

"Shut up," said Russian Blondie. "You talk too much."

"Yes, Holy Master . . ." She glanced at me, and I remembered how funny she could be in high school, in the hallways, in the moment just before the bell rang for the next period. And maybe she was remembering things about me, the kind of things men don't notice about themselves but women take note of. We were exchanging something, and Russian Blondie was locked out of it.

"Look straight," he said, and tapped her on the temple with his pistol.

She lowered her chin. I was looking at the side of her pretty head, where an earring hung, a glass dewdrop looking out from under her shag-cut black hair; it matched the tear rolling down her cheek. They'd grabbed her to keep me docile and minimize their risk. So here she was, junk sick, probably not caring if they killed her. But I cared.

Fifteen minutes later, we turned off the main road and followed a smaller one, its broken surface indicating it was little used. But they were familiar with it, and so was I. It was the entrance to the old Bellefontaine mine. We came to a *No Trespassing* sign and a heavy chain. Russian Red got out and opened the chain, then got back in and drove onto the abandoned mine road. Tall grass grew on both sides, through which bulky pieces of iron could be seen. The owners had extracted everything they could from the ground and then filed for bankruptcy, leaving the place to their creditors, but there isn't much use for antique mine machinery.

"I'm coming down . . . like a moon rock . . ." moaned Shirley, trying to get her head up, trying to find the next fix and finding only my face. I remembered when she and the other Centralites had used pom-poms to make sparkly fabric dance in the air, and the big golden *C* on their sweaters came provocatively to life. Men will think of these things even with a nine-millimeter pressed to their ribs.

We passed a mine car tipped on its side, then a pile of iron girders, a giant gear wheel, other assorted pieces of the mining operation. We passed several brick buildings whose walls had collapsed, then stopped in front of one that had survived. Its corrugated-steel roof was twisted out of shape, but the building was intact despite crumbling mortar and a door that had been used for target practice. The graffiti artists had been here, using the brick walls to display their art. Ruby's name was written large.

Russian Blondie prodded me to exit the vehicle; Russian Red was already standing at the door and covering me with his own nine-millimeter. Shirley stumbled out, trying to stay balanced on her high heels. "Let's get this . . . over with."

Spoken like a true junkie. Death is better than not finding your fix. She swayed back and forth in front of Russian Blondie. He escorted us into the building and switched on a battery lantern.

"Oh, sweet Jesus . . ." said Shirley, "I used to lay guys here." She was gazing in wonder around the ramshackle room. "When I was sweet sixteen." She looked at me, her eyes seeming to apologize for not having brought me here when she was giving it away for free.

Russian Blondie took our wallets and phones—not a good sign, for it indicated we would have no further use for them. "Now," he growled, "you wait."

"What the hell for?" asked Shirley.

"Boss."

"You guys are pricks. I've always wanted to say that." Trying to stay upright, she leaned against a support beam of the room. "And Grisha . . . is the biggest prick of all."

I smelled fairly fresh blood and checked the walls. Somebody's artery had erupted sideways, sending a gusher of red death into the air. Conclusion: this room was used to eliminate enemies and competitors. Or torture someone late with a payment. Russian Blondie saw I was getting the message. He pointed at my leg and made a scissoring motion with two fingers. "I cut vein. Then pull. Vein come out like string. Whole fucking leg. You scream like bitch." He said this quietly, a sort of reserved malice in him.

Shirley said, "I should have left town on my sixteenth birthday." She lowered herself slowly to the floor, her leather hot pants tight around her thighs as she rolled into a fetal position. Russian Blondie yanked her to her feet and handcuffed us together. Then he handcuffed my other hand to a rusty iron staircase. I gazed upward along its length—heavy industrial construction disappearing into a second floor, through which a bit of moonlight was shining where the roof had caved in.

Leaning against me, Shirley asked, quietly, "What the fuck did you do to these guys?"

"I put Red's brother down a mineshaft."

"Good for you. One of them is bad enough."

"I'm sorry I got you into this."

"I got myself into it. Before you ever showed up."

Russian Blondie and Red the Second were conferring in the language of the Arctic bear. The naked brightness of the battery lamp made their faces seem bloodless, as if we were being held by ghouls. They were professionals, but they were deluded. Being from a vast and mighty country far away, they had disdain for where they were now, as if the entire Northeast, from Brighton Beach to the Bellefontaine mine, were some kind of toy kingdom in which they were the giants. They'd selected this dilapidated building as if it were protected by magic invisibility, but I was listening to a spinning roof turbine above us, rusty and out of trim and making an intermittent shrieking sound. They heard it, but not really, because they didn't understand the spirit of the Bellefontaine mine.

Russian Blondie broke off the discussion with a shrug and walked out of the building. Red the Second smashed me in the head with the barrel of his gun, took the battery lamp, and followed his partner, closing the door after him. Along with the church bells in my head, I heard the snap of a lock.

There was enough moonlight from the open roof to see Shirley's face. It was a mask of junk desire. She cut through it and asked if I was all right.

"He only hit one of the rocks in my head, I'm fine."

She leaned back against the stair railing. "I'm junk sick, Tommy. Sorry about that. Pretty soon my nose will be running."

I told her to put her free hand in the lower pocket of my cargo pants. She came out with three white capsules. They were painkillers Reed had given me for my burned fingers. I identified them for her. "Percocet."

"Christ on a bike, there is a God." She dug a fifty-dollar bill from her leather shorts, emptied one of the capsules onto the back of her cuffed hand, and snorted up the powder. Her eyes closed as relief swept through her. Her eyes remained closed.

"Shirley, are you with me?"

She opened her eyes. "What are we doing?"

"Isometrics."

I got a solid grip underneath the stair railing and waited for the twisted blades in the roof turbine to resume their off-center spinning. Metal against metal makes an almost birdlike screech, and iron bolts being torn out of a floorboard would be quiet by comparison. The bird screeched, and I lifted.

Shirley peered at the staircase, its bottom step now no longer connected to the floor. "If you're Sampson, I must be Delilah."

We squatted together, and she slid the handcuff off the staircase spindle. My right hand was free. I dug a brick out of the rubble piled behind the staircase and handed it to her. She hefted it up and down. "I've always wanted to hit one of those bastards with something."

"They have to come through the door single file. If we hammer the first one, we have a chance." I put my finger against the edge of her eye socket. "That's the orbital bone. Hit it hard enough and it'll break in seven places." I dug for a second brick. As it came free from the pile of mortar, plaster, and wire, I felt the edge of something long and wooden buried deeper in the rubble. A miner's pick would be ideal. I would mine the rich vein in Russian Blondie's forehead. I dug deeper. It wasn't a pick. It was a box. I brushed the plaster dust away.

Atlas Powder Co.
Wilmington, Delaware, USA
High Explosives Dangerous
50 lbs.

I brought the box out of the rubble and carefully pried up the lid. Lying inside were rows of badly deteriorated sticks of dynamite. Kids, vandals, and scavengers had turned this place upside down, but an old building has ways of outwitting those who scrounge around in it. Poor light, the shadows under a twisted staircase, a collapsed ceiling, accumulated rubble—and the evil fairies of the mine await. Their plan is to blow somebody up someday, but it must be the right somebody, not a child at play.

Each stick was covered with wispy hairs. From my childhood adventures around mines, I knew what they were. Old dynamite sweats out its most important content, crystallized nitroglycerin, which is as sensitive to touch as a virgin on her wedding night. We had one hell of a weapon if we didn't blow ourselves up trying to use it.

Shirley, being a girl of the valley, was already on the attack. "I've got a lighter." She reached into her leather shorts. "We'll light one and get them as they come through the door."

"The space is too tight; we'd get caught by the blast."

The screeching of the roof turbine got my attention again. It was saying, *this way*.

I pointed to the crumbling stairs. "Up we go."

With tai chi slowness, I lifted the box. I needed *elegant lady's hand* for what must come next. While handcuffed to Shirley, I had to carry fifty pounds of ripe nitro up twisted, rubble-covered stairs. I prayed to Saint Barbara, patron saint of explosions.

"Just a second," said Shirley, and emptied another capsule on the back of her hand. "I want to be at my best." She sniffed the powder up her nose. "Yes," she said softly to herself, then kicked off her high heels. In bare feet, she came up to around my chin. Her legs gleamed from some cosmetic she'd applied to give them a wet, more naked look.

Held prisoner by psychopaths and holding enough hair-trigger dynamite to turn my body into chopped meat, I could still admire a woman's legs. Darwin would understand.

The turbine bird paused in its screeching, and I heard the sound of a vehicle approaching, its driver taking it slowly over damaged pavement.

"Grisha," said Shirley.

Babying his Mercedes. We had a few extra minutes. The moonlight guided us up the staircase, as if we were traveling on its beam. If I stumbled, we'd be traveling up that beam way too fast. Shirley, in her bare feet, was beside me, but I was no longer checking out her beauty. I was staring down into crystals of nitro, willing them to remain unexcited. In this way, hardly breathing, we went up the staircase to the second floor.

The ceiling had fallen in, bringing with it roofing material and a ventilation duct that once spanned the building. The duct had landed on slats, plaster, electrical cables, and other debris. It had a settled look, having lain like this for years, waiting for a handcuffed couple with a box of nitro to use it as a ladder.

The sections of the duct had been welded together with steel bands. The bands were thick enough to act as hand- and footholds. Kids would have scampered up, no problem. I would have loved that approach, but rapid ascent wasn't possible tonight. When people find old dynamite in cellars, attics, or anywhere else, the bomb squad arrives in body armor, wearing overlapping layers of Kevlar, foam, plastic, and fire-retardant material. Shirley was in abbreviated bondage attire, and I was in cotton cargo pants. If it blew, the nitro would peel the skin off our bones.

"We're going up this thing," I said. I pointed to the hole in the ceiling. "And through there."

"Bombing run," she agreed, grasping the plan. Her wildly made-up eyes were strangely calm. Percocet working its magic. She positioned herself behind me.

Because of the handcuffs braceleting our wrists together, I had to balance the box on my shoulders, with one arm twisted backward, my hand meeting Shirley's on the box's bottom edge. The handcuff brought her tight against my back, so she was almost stepping on me. It forced us to shuffle upward in a kind of snake dance. Each time we moved, the ventilation duct shifted under our weight. If it collapsed under us, the noise would alert our captors, but it wouldn't matter, because we'd be in orbit, going out through the hole in the roof. The question was whether we could get out through it without the aid of dynamite. We'd have to squirm through, like Siamese twins with a packed trunk escaping from the evil circus owner.

The Mercedes stopped outside. The turbine bird was screeching close by us, covering the shifting sound of the duct as we reached its junction with the roof. We were facing each other now, our shoulders pressing against the roof's jagged edge. Together, we eased the box upward. Still pressed together, we eased ourselves and the box over the broken roof slats, plaster, and bundles of wire. Shirley's bondage bra was against my chest, and her lips were almost touching mine. "Kinky," she whispered as we wriggled together onto the corrugated-steel roof.

Still braceleted, we wriggled forward to the edge of the roof and looked down. A battery lantern lit the grill of the convertible. Grisha had driven it almost to the door of the building. He was still behind the wheel, dressed in a tropical-weight suit, enjoying the soft night air. Russian Blondie and Red the Second were leaning against the convertible, giving him a rundown of the situation. Alongside us, the turbine bird continued screeching. We rose together, holding the box. The deadly sensitivity of its contents made it seem alive. It had to be launched without exploding in our faces, and the handcuffs were inhibiting the momentum of the effort. Looking at each other, we silently coordinated our movements and launched it, then flattened ourselves on the roof.

The shock wave of the blast shook the building. After one long second, pieces of the car started landing on the roof, along with Russian Blondie's head, which bounced down next to us, torn neck muscles dripping blood. After things stopped falling, we looked down. The doors of the convertible had been blown off; the seats were gone along with the hood. The motor was smoking. Grisha was no longer behind the wheel. An armless crumpled body on the ground in a fashionable summer suit was what remained of him. Big Red the Second, recognizable only by his hair, had been disemboweled, as if the blast had gone straight through him.

Russian Blondie's headless body was directly below us, slumped against the building. We were looking down his neck.

I said, "Time to hit the road."

She held up her handcuffed wrist. "I'm with you, lover boy."

We slid back down our ladder of rubble and then hurried down the stairs as best we could, the handcuffs holding our wrists together. The locked door no longer presented a problem. The blast had ripped it off its hinges. Shirley retrieved her high heels and we stepped outside. The convertible was on fire now, black plumes of smoke rising from its hollowed-out interior.

We stopped beside Russian Blondie. Without a head, his huge body seemed like an innocent animal that had been forced by its brain to act badly. His shirt had been shredded, but his pants were intact, and from them I retrieved our wallets and phones. Then I called Silvio.

"Get to the old Bellefontaine mine. There's been a big explosion."

"How big?"

"There are body parts all around."

"I take it you're responsible for the body parts?"

"I am."

I heard voices on his scanner. He came back to me. "The cops are already on the move. Get to the mouth of the mine road and stay out of sight. I'm on the interstate about fifteen minutes away. I'll pick you up."

"I'm with Shirley Kaminski."

"It's nice that you're dating again."

42

We moved into the tall grass and felt our way through the scattered mining machinery. Because of the darkness, our progress was slow. The ground was cluttered with sharp objects, and Shirley was in high heels. When I was a kid, I moved around these pieces of machinery with the respect a child has for discarded objects, which give off a mysterious brooding power that protected me then and was protecting us now.

"Our first date," said Shirley, looking back over her shoulder at the smoke rising in front of the moon.

I kept her moving. "The police will probably come to the bike lane tomorrow, asking you questions."

"The girls in the bike lane are in the country illegally and the pimps pay the cops off. So there won't be much fuss about Grisha and those two fuckups."

She knew more about it than I did, so I let it go and concentrated on the police sirens getting closer. They'd soon be barreling up the mine road. It would take them a while to figure out the explosion, but after that they'd be searching the grass and woods. If their bellies were hanging over their belts, they wouldn't go far; even if there was a gung-ho young cop among them, we still had the spirit of the mine on our side. Shirley had laid guys here, and that counts for a lot in the spirit world.

We could smell the smoke now, a dirty mixture of oil, gas, synthetic fabric, and flesh. Two police cars and a fire engine swung off the main road, and we flattened ourselves to the ground. The handcuffs were uncomfortable unless we pressed up against each other. Shirley ran a finger along my cheek. "Tommy Martini . . ." She smiled sardonically as she put her lips to mine. "I saved myself for you."

I wasn't into desperate gangster sex, but I pulled her closer as more police sirens approached. "Your Central sweater used to turn me on."

"It was supposed to. The big C right across our tits was to make the boys play harder." She had her fingers in my hair. "I should've made a beeline for you." Her bare thigh was pressing against mine. "But," she continued, "I had a screw loose."

The police cars passed us, and we waited until their taillights disappeared along the mine road. Then we got to our feet and kept moving, but when fifty pounds of dynamite goes up it sends things far and wide, and the acrid smoke was still floating down on us, bringing with it genetic material from Russia. Blondie and Big Red the Second had been given life's greatest gifts as far as I'm concerned—size and strength. These attributes can carry a man far in this world, and they had carried the men from Moscow to Coalville, but there the mojo of the mine had overcome them. Nevertheless, they'd gone out on a warrior's funeral pyre, so that's something.

I recognized the growling sound of Silvio's wrecker as it slowed along the main road. He had his strobe lights on, flashing importantly, blending his rig with the other emergency vehicles that were showing up. He brought the truck onto the shoulder of the road with the passenger door facing us.

Another cop car arrived, and I heard the garbled talk of police car radios exchanging information. After it passed us, we ran onto the shoulder and then up into the wrecker, Shirley slipping in first alongside Silvio. He looked at the handcuffs, then at me. "She was playing hard to get?"

He pulled quickly off the shoulder and back onto the main road, strobe light still turning. "Anything of yours left behind?"

"Nothing."

"Who do the body parts belong to?"

"Russian hoods who abducted us."

He looked at Shirley in her bondage bra and leather pants. "I can see why they'd want her, but what about you?"

"I insulted their manhood."

"But you didn't wreck my Hummer?"

"It's parked in town."

"My nephew," he said to Shirley, "doesn't think the night is complete unless he wrecks a vehicle of mine. The handcuffs probably held him back."

He waved to a cop car as it came toward us. Shirley took out the last Percocet capsule, sent its contents up her nose, and let out a sigh. Silvio tugged the brim of his cap. "I felt that one."

A slow smile broke across her lips. "Yes, it was pure. Like me." She let her lazy gaze play out the window. "Look at all those little cars."

Like her, I was feeling the big body of the wrecker, rolling high and mighty down the highway. The prestige of a high-end tow truck is undeniable, and men silently acknowledge it as it passes them in majestic attitude, its iron arm unmoved. My own arm had been tested, and three hoods in the wind would announce that fact to the Lords of Karma, and yet another black mark would go down on the Martini report card, kept on file in hell.

Silvio dropped us off near Parade Square. By that time the handcuffs were history, and Shirley had gotten the mud and dust off her bare arms and legs. Silvio looked down at her from the cab of his truck. "Walk around, let yourself be seen, like it's business as usual." He turned to me. "And you and I were out on a job together. You were miles away when the mine blew up. Got that?"

"Got it."

"And we tow this night away." He put the truck in gear and it rumbled off.

Parade Square was showing the usual crowd of dopers, drunks, and the Skateboard Kid, who wheeled on by us, pedaling with his loose foot toward the fountain. He tilted the back end and levered himself up onto the rim, where he glided, balancing with subtle body moves along the inward-sloping face of the rim. I sat on a bench in the square for an hour while Shirley walked around, making sure she was seen, which wasn't difficult since she was fairly close to being naked. The corner boys called to her, but she waved them off. "Goodbye, children, be good." She stopped at my bench. "I want to go into that clinic your relative runs."

"Done." I called Little Joe. When I explained about Shirley, gallantry overcame his annoyance at being awakened past his bedtime and he arranged to meet us at the clinic.

As we walked toward the parking garage, she said, "When Ignaty's head landed on the roof, his eyes were looking at me. And I got the message. I don't want to die with my head down in a ladies-room toilet."

She slipped her arm through mine. "Tonight was a successful date. Back at Central, the girls used to talk about successful dates. They were rare."

"A cheeseburger and some pinball afterward weren't enough?"

Her high heels were clicking on the pavement, and the little rhinestones caught the light from the Parade Square lamps. "I'm never going back to the bike lane." Her voice was determined, but I could feel the tremors beginning in her body. She clung tightly to my arm, fighting back the shakes. "I'm in for three bad days. If I get through them, I'll make it the rest of the way."

"I'll stay with you. I've done it before. We watch baseball with the sound off." I'd parked the Hummer on the top tier of the parking garage and we rode the elevator up. Its doors and walls were covered with graffiti. Ruby's name was there, reduced from its usual size. The elevator was old and slow but managed to make it to the top floor. From the roof of the garage, we could see the illuminated pillars of the Railroad Hotel, along with the bike lane around Parade Square. The girls were still displaying their charms, and the cars were stopping. "Small-town sex work," said Shirley. "You meet such interesting men."

I opened the Hummer and we got in. At the bottom of the ramp, I paid the fee and we rolled onto the street. The bars were mostly closed, but I saw Prince Gran-Gran and his crew getting into a car that probably wasn't theirs. In the middle of the block, a crack addict was conferring with himself about which planet he was on. Shirley said, "I don't suppose you have another Percocet?"

"Fresh out."

She nodded. I saw the perspiration beginning again on her brow. She said, "I'm not worried about the cops. But Grisha was Russian mafia. They'll send somebody to work me over."

"You won't be where they can find you."

"I can't stay in the clinic forever."

"I'm going to give you enough money to do what you should've done when you were sixteen: get out of this town."

"I can't take your money, Tommy."

"I'm not doing anything with it. I'm a monk."

"It doesn't matter. I'm used to earning my own way."

"Then call it a loan."

"It doesn't matter what we call it, I can't take it."

"It's because of me those hoods grabbed you. You think I give a shit about money I'm never going to spend?"

She was withdrawing; she was shaking; she didn't have enough strength to fight me. She asked, "How much money are we talking about?"

"Enough to keep you for a year. I'm the only heir to a crooked fortune."

She reached her hand across to me, put it on the back of my neck. "Tommy Martini, the four-letter man. You know what they spell?"

"Vegas?"

"They spell love."

"My cousin Dominic lives there; he'll help you get settled. You're smart and beautiful. You could work as a dealer."

"I'm not beautiful, just heavily made-up."

"But you'll do it?"

She closed her eyes, let out a long sigh. "Okay, I'll do it. But I'll pay you back."

"Right, fine. Take your time. I won't charge you interest or break your kneecaps."

She laughed, but she was anxious about going into rehab. "I've been through withdrawal before. Around day eight, I'll start getting tender and fall in love with the doctor."

"Lucky guy."

"He's used to whimpering females."

I pulled the Hummer into the Helping Hand parking lot. The building was an old Victorian of the kind that doctors and lawyers like to pick up for their practice—cheap with lots of rooms and a warm, homey look. But the sight of Little Joe at the door gave Shirley pause. "Godzilla runs the clinic?"

"He's Phil's muscle."

She took this in slowly, then smiled. "The Russians won't mess with me here."

We got out of the Hummer and walked to the front porch. I introduced her as an old classmate of mine at Central. "You would have seen her on the field, Joe. White sweater, big gold letter *C.*"

He held out his gigantic paw to her. "Sure, honey, I remember you."

"We all looked alike."

"So I remember all of you. Come on in."

Inside, a nurse was waiting for us—a tough-looking young woman, probably a relative of Phil's. She took in Shirley's bondage outfit without blinking an eye. Her voice, like Phil's, was a throaty rasp. "I'm here for you, okay? No matter what kind of shit goes down, I'm on your side." She pointed to me. "Is this the boyfriend?"

"We're high school sweethearts."

"Well, kiss him, and then he's got to shove."

Shirley kissed me, not probing, not passionate, but creating an intimacy I didn't understand. It was part of the mystery of women, whose feelings are beyond the reach of men.

I watched as the nurse escorted her down a hallway, and then Little Joe and I left the place. "I do remember her," he said. "Tits like that you don't forget."

He walked me to the Hummer. "What's next with you and her?"

"I'll be paying for her stay, whatever she needs."

"Phil said it's on the house."

"Give him my thanks. And tell him Grisha Volkov and his crew will no longer be competition."

"You whacked them?"

"There was an unfortunate accident at the Bellefontaine mine."

"I've been hearing sirens."

"The first responders were not in time."

"You always were a tough kid, Tommy. How'd you like to head up security at Phil's new casino?"

"Not my thing. But I appreciate the offer."

He held the door of the Hummer for me. "Put in a word for me with the Lord." Then he walked to his truck, squeezing his huge frame into it and closing the door with a thunderous slam.

I looked back at the rehab place. In the days when it was built, nobody was rehabbed. A man took the vow or drank his way straight into oblivion.

My shirt was torn from crawling around in the dark, and my pants probably had crystals of nitroglycerin clinging to them, but they would have exploded by now if they were going to, so I drove back to Parade Square. Tomorrow, I'd open a bank account for Shirley, and if they let me into the Helping Hand, I'd sit with her while we watched baseball with the sound off.

I parked outside Duke's apartment house. His window was dark; he was dreaming his gangster dreams. I got out and walked into the square. Zigzag, like a sudden shadow, came in behind me and then matched his step to mine. "Yo, big man, you catch up with your blonde?"

"Your information was good."

"Any other requests?"

"Not at the moment."

"I be around if you need me." He peeled away like Peter Pan's shadow. In a few years, he'd probably be a millionaire.

I walked to the far edge of the square and stopped under a lamp next to the bike lane where three pimps, recently exploded, had made an easy living running girls. They'd selected Coalville, imagining that a small, corrupt American town would be a pushover for gangsters who had cut their teeth on Russia's mean streets. But they'd been unable to see beneath the streets of Coalville, to the tunnels where spirits as dark as themselves, and darker, moved. Six languages had been spoken in those tunnels by somber men who blew the hard veins of the earth with dynamite, protecting themselves with makeshift shields, swearing and cursing the dust that settled around them.

"Martini. Hey, Martini . . ." A car was pulling in alongside me, the window down, and Ruby waving. "I'm glad I caught you. I'm leaving town."

"Where are you going?"

"Hollywood, of course," she said with a toss of her red hair, and she drummed her artificial red fingernails impatiently on the door of the car. It was a modest vehicle. Jeffrey Goldfuss was at the wheel.

I looked in at him. "They say you lose one point of your IQ for every year you spend in California."

"He's got plenty to spare," said Ruby.

He gave me his usual colorless expression, flat as a photograph. "I'll work in Silicon Valley," he said in a toneless voice, as if the words had been artificially assembled from a database. He'd probably do very well out there.

He looked back out over the steering wheel—a human GPS system, fully programmed for the road. The satellites would speak directly to his brain and Ruby would speak to his soul, and by the time they got to California, well, he'd be a changed nerd, that's all I can say.

Ruby ran her fingers through her hair, arranging it behind one ear. Whatever she did with it, she couldn't miss. The genes of Coalville had come together to make one of its rarest beauties, but now must bid it goodbye.

"I've got an agent. She has several producers interested in my film."

"A star is born."

"Thanks for helping me out with that little problem I had."

"Don't mention it." *Not to me or to anyone. Brian Fury is in an urn where he belongs—a bit of quiet ash that does not speak.*

"Well, so long . . ." At her throat was the junk jewelry necklace into which Finn had so skillfully inserted a tiny camera. I had the feeling there would soon be a sequel to her documentary.

She gave a little wave of her hand, in which there was still a trace of the child she'd been.

The car moved forward. Fuss was probably an excellent driver, cautious, averse to risk, steady at the wheel. I watched Ruby's red hair blowing at the window, and then they turned the corner and were gone. It seemed an odd time to start a journey, but they were both children of the night and would be listening to music I couldn't abide. But it was from their world, the world of TikTok, Instagram, and other strange places of exchange. I said a prayer for them and for the three pimps I'd sent into eternity.

43

MacBride's Bar would be my last stop before leaving town. From the bar stool, I looked at the spot where I'd stopped Mike Muldoon's heart. The floor wasn't clean, but you didn't go to MacBride's for a refined evening. I said goodbye to Mike's troubled spirit and drank single malt whiskey from Scotland. It had a heavy flavor of peat—a true drink of the dead. *And here's to you, Mike. Please, leave me alone.*

Not that he ever would. His violent soul and mine were partners forever. The other men I'd killed in Coalville would have to get in line behind him. So I gazed at the floor where he'd breathed his last. Customers walked over the spot, coming and going as I drank. A very large customer stopped there as if waiting for me to look up, which I did, into the eyes of the ox.

I stood up, pushed my bar stool backward. When he was directly in front of me, he said, "It's not over."

"The last time I had a fight in this bar, I killed someone." I pointed past his kneecap toward the floor behind him. "He died right there."

He turned and looked at the floor as if, like me, he could imagine the fallen form of Mike Muldoon. Then he turned back to me. "You hit me when I wasn't looking."

I studied him again, the guy who should have been a pirate, a mercenary, or anything else that would've earned him gold instead of the useless reputation he was protecting. I'd knocked him out at a dogfight, with gamblers watching, and he still felt their eyes on him. I said, "Let me buy you a drink."

"Fuck a drink. I want a fair fight."

"You could wind up dead, my friend. Ask around. I'm not somebody you want to mess with." I was trying to bury some memories so I could leave town. Getting into it with the ox was the kind of pointless macho bullshit that had made Queenie write me off.

He said, "I don't need to ask around. I know who you are."

"Who am I?"

"You're a made guy."

So he wanted a place in the Coalville underworld. His last employer was dead and he was out of a job, but if he took me in a fight, word would get back that he was a useful piece of muscle. Since I'd seen him last, he'd shaved his head, which certainly added to his look of a pirate. If there was a ship in the river of rust to take him to the high seas, he'd be on his way with the tide. But there wasn't, so here he was, looking at me. He had at least twenty pounds on me, and I was his door to fame and fortune. It would be a tough fight on a summer night, not the way I wanted to say goodbye to Coalville. "I'll give you an introduction to Phil Branca. You know who Phil is, right?"

"He's the don."

"I'll call him right now and set up a meeting. Okay?"

He gave me a puzzled look. Friendly gestures were not in his game book. Barroom brawlers in Coalville took pleasure in acting badly, as if it were a duty, and they assumed that friendliness in any form was meant to unman them. He said, "I know what kind of meeting that would be."

"So tell me."

"You and your pals drop-kick me like you did at the dogfight." He took a step closer, and the bouncer walked over.

He had jailhouse muscles and knew how to use them. "Outside, Kunkel," he said to the ox. Then he looked at me. "Not here. Not again." So he knew who I was, but had seen worse on the inside, most varieties of evil having come his way in the cell blocks.

I said, "Fine, I'm out of here. Hold on to Kunkel for me."

I put a twenty on the bar and left. I'd had enough of Parade Square, so I walked through the empty business district, where I used to buy presents at Christmastime. Now all you could buy was crack. The department stores still carried Ruby's name on the plywood that covered their doors. But she was gone with Goldfuss. And soon I'd be gone. But the street held me with its blighted spell. I'd once ridden in a victory parade here, the majorettes up on the float with me, and cocaptain Jim Hutmacher beside me. Bridget had sat on the highest seat of the float, holding her spangled baton like a royal scepter. We sat below her, helmets in our laps, feeling jazzed by the marching band and by the other majorettes who were seated along the edge of the float, their bare legs dangling over the side.

And the float had disappeared into the past, taking with it the cheerleaders, the band, and the heroes. Jim went to war, I went into hiding, and Bridget married Finn. And the street had sunk into its present form, through which I strolled now, unable to break away from the town that had been my home. It was holding on to me with the kind of promise it offered all its favorite sons: of rare opportunity. Another chance with Queenie, the winning lottery ticket, a car dealership.

My phone rang. It was Veronica. "Tommy, sweetie, how are you?"

"I'm okay, Veronica, what's up with you?"

"Bridget won't let me stay with her."

"I think she's busy with the TV station."

"Too busy for her own mother?" The family anger was starting. From Great-Great-Grandfather Breen to Veronica, it ran through her veins the way coal ran through the ground. "She's up there in her mansion and I'm here looking at my bell collection." She rang one of them.

I said, "She's just settling in. She's had a bad shock."

"What am I, chopped liver?"

"You're a chocolate chip cookie, Veronica. You're my favorite other mother."

There was silence, then the sound of ice cubes in a glass. "I feel like smashing somebody's face in."

"No, you don't."

"The fuck I don't." I heard a little bell being thrown across a room. "Now look what I've done."

"Just give her a few days."

There was more silence, but I could still feel her anger. It had a visceral quality and it came right through the transmitter in my phone. This is the curse of the valley, a fire in the mines of the mind that never goes out. She was staring at her bells, or her walls, or the gin in her glass, but wherever she was looking, it was pissing her off. "I've had it with that bitch, Tommy."

"No, you haven't, Veronica. You're just upset."

I heard the hiss of a match, then a mouthful of smoke. "When you see her, tell her I said she can go to hell."

"I won't be seeing her. I'm leaving town."

"Lucky you."

The phone went dead.

I walked to the parking garage. The ox was inside the entrance bay, leaning against the automated gate.

"Here," he said.

"Nobody will see us here. Don't you want somebody to witness your victory?"

"I'll take a photograph."

"Of my bruised and battered face?"

"Whatever's left of it."

He'd have found me no matter where I went, because we had a date, arranged by the darkness or by whatever powers moved inside it, for their own amusement or for no reason at all. But he was the reason I couldn't leave, because he'd worked with the oxpecker, a.k.a. Patrick Blades, which is what it had said on the business card of the party event facilitator. Patrick Blades. A fine Irish name for a scrawny little killer. The dark powers had dragged me to Coalville for their bit of fun, nearly killing me in the process, and maybe that was their plan. Maybe the ox had a punch that would stop my heart the way I'd stopped the heart of Mike Muldoon.

I said, "The light is brighter on the top floor. You'll get a better picture."

He considered this, suspicious of the way the world worked; it was always fucking with him. But finally, he figured why not, here or the top floor, he was going to exert brute force either way. About that, he was confident. I had the same confidence, so we started walking up the ramp. There weren't many cars on any of the levels, because, apart from Parade Square, downtown Coalville had nothing to offer but empty buildings. Until someone sponsored an empty-building festival, the parking garage would always be half-empty.

The top floor wasn't much brighter, because the department stores were out of business and the ambient light of the city was feeble. This cheerless spot was our ring, and he wasted no time, coming at me with his great strength. This first rush was the most dangerous, because he was fresh. I backpedaled and ducked. Blocking was dangerous because he had bones like iron bars padded with fat and muscle. Breaking a brick or my arm would be nothing for him. His fights probably lasted under a minute, at which point somebody would be crumpled at his feet. But unlike them, I knew better than to slug it out with him. He was going to fight my fight, not his own. I made him follow me.

"Pussy," he growled.

Pigeons were watching from the roof of the elevator. A few of them lifted off, disturbed by the brutish forms lumbering around in their world. As they fluttered above us, a police siren joined the night with a rhythmic wail. The wail peaked, then headed off into the distance, growing fainter as I used footwork to keep away from him.

His usual opponents traded blows with hope in their hearts until he hit them with a big one, and then they were looking up at a row of bar stools. Surprised that I wasn't in that position already, he threw away the little caution he fought with, and a few more pigeons fluttered off, preferring a power line while the incomprehensible movements of the bulky forms continued.

"Fucking . . . pussy . . ."

Whatever muscle and bone can give you, he had, but I could tell he hadn't done road work. *Why the fuck should I?* was probably his view on it. Now he knew why. His legs were getting heavier.

The pigeons lifted off the power line and circled for the hell of it, as pigeons will, enjoying the wondrous workings of their wings.

"You fight . . . like an old lady." He got as close to me as he could, which wasn't close enough. He flailed out desperately, anticipating that lovely moment when his fist would make full contact with my head, my eyes would go sideways, and he'd be standing over me.

But he was breathing hard now as I danced away from him. He followed me with difficulty because his legs were starting to feel like wet cement. We got too near the elevator and the rest of the pigeons took off, joining the others that were circling over the empty streets. When the sun came up, they'd start checking for leftovers. But right now it was all about filling the precise spot the aerial formation called for, each one knowing its place without asking.

I hadn't yet tagged him with a thousand-pounder, but he knew it was coming, his heavy legs getting even heavier, as if he were pulling the floor around in his shoes. The weight that had been his advantage had turned into sandbags. He was moving in slow motion, trying to call up one last great effort, because the truth had dawned on him, that I was going to wear him out.

Half the pigeons returned, wings outspread then folding in as they settled, checking for owls—always a concern in the dark. If an owl glided in, its wings would be perfectly silent and *zip,* you would be a midnight meal.

And just like that, he got my thousand-pounder straight in his face.

The next thing he knew, he was looking up at pigeons. They were circling below the many stars that had just been added to the galaxy he lived in. And then I was on top of him. "Who hired Blades to kill Finn Sweeney?"

He was not quite with the program yet, his eyes still swimming around. Only a few times in his life as a brawler had he been knocked down, so it took getting used to. I put my hands around his throat and repeated, "Who hired Blades?"

"Who's Blades?"

I lifted his head and smacked it back down against the concrete floor. "Don't fuck with me. Who hired him?"

"He never said."

"Fine, so now you die." I tightened my grip on his throat. "See the sky? That's going to be it. Kunkel's last look at the world."

He started to buck underneath me, but I was cutting off his wind. I'd had it done to me, and you don't know up from down. He pushed at the floor with his feet, but he was like a fish on land, flopping desperately, breath impossible to catch. And then I realized I was killing him, and stopped. Suddenly, I no longer cared. I was done with the dark powers. He could keep what he knew.

He lay there, chest heaving as he fought for air. I stood over him, moved again by his forlorn chance in this broken town. He'd been an ignoramus from childhood. Brighter boys had used him for protection but left him behind when strength wasn't required. Patrick Blades, party event facilitator, had taken him around like an exhibit—*I command this mountain of muscle.* But Blades was a lowlife, and Kunkel knew that a dogfight was the best Blades could manage. The rest was hot air.

I walked away, down the ramp. There are some fights you don't want in your scrapbook, and this was one of them. Whoever hired that little weasel Patrick Blades could remain in the shadows. By the time I reached the Hummer, I heard the ox coming down the ramp. His voice echoed in the concrete building. "It was her."

I turned. He was walking a little unsteadily, but his face didn't look bad, just swollen around the forehead where I'd nailed him. I didn't know what had moved him to give me what I wanted. Maybe because I'd given him his fair fight. He said, "She hired him." He tucked his shirt in, rearranged his belt. His chest heaved in and out as he continued working to get his wind back. "Sweeney's wife, she hired Blades." He said it without any special emphasis, which is what gave it a devastating ring.

He took out a cigarette, offered me one. After big men fight, there's a sullen agreement between them, like two bull elephants at a waterhole; they know they're the top tier, and everybody else is a pretender. "Blades wanted me as lookout." He puffed heavily on his cigarette, as if it was restoring his equilibrium. "I said fuck no. Beat somebody up, fine. But not murder."

The kaleidoscope turned in my head, all the bright little glass pieces falling into a new pattern. Veronica's angry voice, the reptilian coldness in her eyes. Daughter Bridget, with the same voice, the same eyes. Angelina saying, *Bridget is a mercenary bitch.* Reed telling me about Finn's affair with Ruby. And Bridget realizing she was going to be dumped for a teenager. Humiliated in public and kicked down the social ladder.

But kill Finn, and she becomes the widow everyone comforts. With a TV station, the house on Millionaire Row, and everything else in his will.

"The little bastard tried to pin it on me," said the ox. "But your pal, the magistrate, didn't buy it. He's all right, that guy."

"I told him you didn't do it."

"Really?" He exhaled smoke into the night air, watched it drift away, as if it had contained a message he couldn't understand. "How about that . . ."

"How about this?" I called Little Joe, put it on speakerphone. "Joe, I'm with a guy who'd like to work for you. If you're still looking for muscle, he's got it."

"Tomorrow morning, nine o'clock."

When I ended the call, I said, "Don't say too much when you get there. They're not looking for diplomas."

He looked at me, puzzled again by somebody giving a shit about him. I said, "Kunkel, you might find this hard to believe, but I know who you are." I was seeing him again on the bounding main, dagger in his teeth, boarding the ship loaded with gold, the one that sails through all our dreams.

44

I steered the Hummer into the big parking lot, got out, and walked through the elaborate garden where Finn had been deadheaded along with the petunias and marigolds.

My phone vibrated. I should have let it go to voice mail, but this call was coming from the dark powers, so I answered. "Veronica, I know you're having a rough time . . ."

"No, no, it's Bridget who's having a rough time. She needs you." She'd flipped from anger to harebrained inspiration.

I said, "She just needs time."

"This is your chance, Tommy. Step in, and she'll be yours."

"Like I said, I'm leaving town. Riding into the sunset."

"I know her so well. When she's hurting, her heart opens."

And I heard Uncle Silvio saying, *Bridget Breen has a hunk of coal for a heart.*

Veronica's voice was cloudy with cigarette smoke. "I know what I'm talking about, Tommy. Some other guy will sweep in while she's hurting, but it should be you. You'll protect her."

"She doesn't need protecting."

"That's where you're wrong. She's vulnerable right now. I don't want some fortune hunter getting her. Go and talk to her."

"I'm on the way to Las Vegas."

"For the love of God, Tommy, don't leave her alone. She might do herself in."

"She'll be fine, Veronica. It was nice seeing you again."

"Tommy—"

But I ended the call because Bridget was on the balcony, waving to me. I climbed the steps to the main door. Whimpering came from the other side. I opened the door and found Pigwiggen. But Pigwiggen had been dead for years. Finn had loved bullmastiffs, and here was a new edition. Bridget called down the stairs. "Don't let Hulk bully you."

"I know how to handle him." I put him in a wrestling grip, and he responded like Pigwiggen, shaking me around, enjoying his strength. It was the kind of match that could go to the floor, but I didn't have time. I let him go and headed toward the stairs, expecting him to follow. But he remained in the hallway, whimpering again.

"He's been like that for days," said Bridget, at the top of the stairs. "The caretaker put him in a kennel while I was gone. His feelings were hurt and now he's avoiding me."

I looked back down at the dog. A moment ago, he'd been lively enough, but now he was slinking away, revealing not hurt feelings but something else. Dogs are discerning beings and carefully choose those they'll be devoted to. He wanted no part of Bridget, but relying on her for shelter put him in a confusing position, and he padded unhappily away. I climbed the stairs, and at the top she held out her hands to me.

She'd conquered me once, and when a woman does that, she learns to read you; she anticipates your moods, senses the slightest change in your feelings. She may be ill informed about many things, but she's an expert on you.

Our eyes met, and she saw that I knew.

I said, "I'm leaving town. I got what I came for."

"And it's not me?"

I let go of her hands. "It'll always be you." A vase in the hallway held a spray of peacock feathers. Those bewitching eyes would keep their magical iridescence for years, and Bridget would keep hers, but she'd wonder why the dog was avoiding her.

"Tommy, Finn forced my hand. You don't know the whole story."

"I know enough of it. But I've no right to judge you. I killed Mike Muldoon showing off for you."

A faint smile crossed her face, admiration important to her, even now. "Is that what happened?" She wanted more.

"You were leaning against the bar. Every guy in MacBride's was checking you out, including Mike. He lost his head, and then he lost his life."

The smile disappeared. The scene had returned, of death on a barroom floor. "It was awful," she said. "I felt terribly sorry for you."

Somewhere in the house, a clock chimed. The dog was still whimpering to himself downstairs. Bridget stared at the parquet floor, as if tracing the intricate patterns of the inlaid wood. I waited. She looked up, and there were tears in her eyes. "He was going to leave me," she said, as if dumping Bridget Breen were a crime deserving capital punishment. "I lost my mind. I made a mistake. Like you did with Mike Muldoon."

Her only mistake was hiring a bargain-basement hit man. I said, "If you're worrying about me turning you in, forget it. I'm a Martini. We don't rat."

"It would've been kinder to let me think I'd gotten away with it."

"You *have* gotten away with it."

"But you know."

"And the dog knows. If I were you, I'd give him to somebody else, because he's never going to lick your hand."

"And you feel the same way." She didn't like me having a hold over her. She took my hands again, saw that I wasn't going to play, and let them go. "Some other time, I guess."

We walked down the stairs. When we reached the first floor, the dog was nowhere to be seen. She said, "I never liked dogs anyway. Except for you, my Saint Bernard."

So she did remember. "If I were you, I'd make up with Angelina."

"What do you mean? She and I never quarreled."

"Well, maybe you drifted apart."

"She told you that?"

"More or less. Anyway, she's a Martini. Hard as they come."

Bridget thought this over while the dog, somewhere far off in the house, was growling to himself, trying to figure out his situation.

She gave me a weak smile. "Having a killer for a friend won't bother Angelina—is that what you mean?"

"She's going to be running the new casino. It'll be exciting to know her."

"Please, don't go."

I took out my phone and played Finn's message. His breathing was labored and his throat constricted, but his dying words were clear enough. *Take care of Bridget.*

I put the phone away. "He didn't mean I should hold your hand."

The call had shaken her, her carefully groomed look coming apart around the eyes and mouth, but she quickly regained her coolness. "You always cleaned up after him."

"Not this time. This time, he'll have to handle it on his own."

"I've already scattered his ashes."

"And Mike Muldoon is six feet under. But he's always with me. So get used to it. Finn will always be around."

"I'm not like you, Tommy. I'm not a mystic."

I started walking toward the door. "Your mother called. She thinks we should get married."

"Is that a bad idea?" She slipped her arms around me, pulled me against her body, then stiffened. She opened my shirt and ran her hand over heat-resistant, strong synthetic fiber stiffened with resin. "What's this?"

"Never leave home without American Express and a Kevlar vest."

"You thought I'd shoot you?"

"It crossed my mind."

"Never, Tommy, never in a million years." Her eyes and body had softened, as if she were melting right through the Kevlar. She said, "It should have been you back in the day."

I lowered her arms, stepped away. "You'll find somebody better than me."

"No, I won't." There was certainty in her voice, but I didn't share it. As I left the house, I knew she would find a stand-in for Finn, rich and well connected. The dead might never forget, but the living find it pretty easy. A murderess would be running a TV station, hosting parties, making light conversation while burying Finn's memory ever deeper until it was less than ashes, until it was nothing at all. That was my Bridget, at whose feet I'd laid my boyish heart.

I stopped at the fountain in the garden. The spray went up, curved gently, tiny bubbles giving momentary glimpses of rainbow light. I spoke toward the little rainbows, asking them to carry my voice to the source of the light, in which I hoped my late friend now resided with his dog, Pigwiggen. "I couldn't kill her, Finn. Or send her to prison. You know that, right?"

I continued along the garden, telling myself I was done with Coalville, now and forever. But resolutions are like bubbles in a fountain: very pretty, and then they come apart. I might be done with Coalville, but it would never be done with me.

45

We're singing at midnight by candlelight, and I'm thinking of Finn, of all that we did and all that has been left undone.

Hear our lament
and calmly forgive our crimes.

The abbot's voice is deep, a sonorous rumble coming from his big frame. He welcomed me back without asking how my time outside the monastery had been spent. For him, the outside world is always the same—a test of faith. I'd returned; my faith had stood the test.

Tell us, Mary Magdalene, what did you see along the way . . .

I saw a man drive into the earth, where the flames received him.

God conquers hell and holds the circle of stars . . .

I saw a young woman throw off her addiction and drive to Sin City to start another life.

A circle of dim bulbs surrounds the head of the Virgin. Frequently, they don't work as power cuts out to the monastery. I've paid for repairs to the wiring, but this is rough country and service is unsteady. So as we leave the chapel, our way is lit by candles.

Who shall cause these little ones to stumble . . .

I saw the girl they call the devil child defy the world and make her way.

Which of you, being redeemed, would not love?

I tried love and watched her choose another.

The curse of the Martinis is stamped on my soul. That's why I came back to the monastery, to the only place on Earth where the curse is covered over, by prayer and meditation. The brothers who shuffle beside me over the worn tiles understand this. They've got their own curses to deal with, and the past chases them as it chases me. So our heads are hooded, our faces in shadow, to keep the curse from finding us. As I walk with them, I pray for Bridget. Even though my last look at her showed me the eyes of a killer, I remember instead the teenage girl on the football field, strutting in front of the band. If that's the way God wants me to remember her, I won't complain.

Each of the monks returns to his cell, to get a little sleep before the next call to prayer. My cell is small, like all the others; I just happen to be a bit large for the accommodations. But how much does a monk need? I gave the Hummer to the abbot, who uses it on the trips he takes to help women whose husbands have been killed or recruited by the cartel. When the cartel drivers in their armored SUVs see him in the Hummer, they salute him as one of their own. It amuses them to see him behind the wheel of that beast. But they fear him with an inexplicable fear. He has that effect, with his huge hands and the burn scar on his forehead. They fear me too. They know I've had interactions with their boss and that in some way, I'm connected.

But to what am I connected? I often ask myself that question. Is it to you, Holy Virgin whose eyes are stone? I pray at the foot of your statue for guidance and forgiveness, uncertain if you hear me. Or am I connected to your adversary, the Evil One of snares and pleasures? He, I know, is listening, for he gives me ample proof.

Do you fight it out between you for the worthless scrap of dreams that is my soul?